ANGER BANG

ANGER BANG

USA TODAY BESTSELLING AUTHOR

AVERY FLYNN

Entangled Publishing, LLC
644 Shrewsbury Commons Ave
STE 181
Shrewsbury, PA 17361
rights@entangledpublishing.com

Amara is an imprint of Entangled Publishing, LLC.

Edited by Liz Pelletier
Cover design by Elizabeth Turner Stokes
Dinosaur © Alena A./Shutterstock
Background © Evgeny Atamanenko/Shutterstock

Manufactured in the United States of America

First Edition May 2023

At Entangled, we want our readers to be well-informed. If you would like to know if this book contains any elements that might be of concern for you, please check the book's webpage for details.

https://entangledpublishing.com/books/anger-bang

Author's Note

When I saw the names Colter's Hell and Stinkingwater River as real places in Northwest Wyoming near Yellowstone National Park, there was no way I could ever resist the temptation of using a fictional version in a RomCom. Yes, there *really* is a Colter's Hell in Wyoming. However, it is not a tourist resort like it is in *Anger Bang*. Instead, the real Colter's Hell is an area of steam vents in the earth (known as fumaroles) as well as hot springs that cover one square mile at the mouth of the Shoshone Canyon, which the Shoshone River flows through. Back in mountain man John Colter's day, though, the Shoshone River was known as the Stinkingwater River. So while the eighties-themed reality TV wedding from hell in *Anger Bang* may take place in Colter's Hell along the Stinkingwater River, it is a very fictionalized version of the real-life place. Any extra stench, errors, or general silliness is my fault and probably written because it cracked me up.

Also, Lori and Jimbo are real, and you can actually go to see them at the Wyoming Dinosaur Center & Dig Sites in Thermopolis, Wyoming—which, truth be told, I moved closer to our fictional resort for story purposes. Yeah, I know. I'm like that. :)

Xoxo,
Avery

To Robin and Kim, who are the two best friends I definitely don't deserve but am lucky enough to have anyway. Y'all are completely messed up, have weird hobbies, and I'm honestly a little concerned about your obsession with printed planners (and I'm a Virgo!), but you are seriously my favorite people. Thank you for not letting me break up with you when my brain went haywire.

Chapter One

Feelings were things best folded into mental origami and stuffed into the back pocket of a pair of awful, turn-yourself-into-a-pretzel-to-get-them-off leather pants. And Thea Pope would know.

She'd bought a pair during a night spent online shopping while wine drunk on her couch in her Harbor City studio apartment and learned a valuable lesson: when one buys leather pants boozed up, one risks popping a hip out of place peeling them off when sober.

But why did her emotions need to stay shoved in the back of her closet, still in the back pocket of those fully-endorsed-by-Satan leather pants? Because Thea would never, ever, abso-fucki0ng-lutely EVER take them out and put them on again. Therefore, the devil pants would remain forever squashed up in a little ball on the floor of her closet, so she could pretend the pants—and, ergo, her feelings—didn't exist.

Issues?

She had none, because everything was fine. Totally fine. Without a doubt, perfectly fine—with a dollop of extra fine on top.

Fine.

This was exactly what she'd just told her therapist during their weekly session. Thea still felt grumbly that her best friend Nola had strong-armed Thea and their other best friend Astrid into signing up for private sessions, arguing that if they didn't all get "therapized" at the same time, they might grow apart.

But Thea didn't need therapy. She was fine. F.I.N.E. Fine.

"Are you trying to convince me you're fine, or yourself?" Dr. Kowecki asked, yanking Thea back to the here and now.

Thea glanced up at her therapist. Unlike Thea, Dr. Kowecki didn't fidget or fight to keep her gaze from melting back to the dark blue floral pattern of the Persian rug between the leather club chair where Dr. Kowecki sat and the leather couch where Thea—who was desperately trying to keep her cool exterior in place—sat clasping her hands tightly together in her lap. Who knew knuckles could turn *that* white?

"It's true," Thea said.

"And so the fact that you were passed over for the promotion at the museum is just 'fine'?"

Passed over for Perry, the old-money legacy with five years' less experience than her? She swallowed the automatic frustrated groan and just let that shit go. "I can't change it, so I'm choosing to move forward."

Dr. Kowecki lifted an eyebrow in question. "But you aren't upset that someone with less experience and fewer qualifying credentials than you got the job you applied for?"

"There's no point in getting upset." Or at least there was no point in showing it. She would be like a reed and let this epic bullshittery flow through her like the wind. "It's fine."

Dr. Kowecki slapped her notebook shut and, with jerky movements, snapped the cap back on her pen, then set both items down on the small table by her chair with an annoyed sigh. "That's become my most unfavorite word."

"Really?" Thea asked, her blood pressure skyrocketing as she grasped at any conversational topic that would put them back on an even keel, where she liked it. "Mine's bollocks. I had a roommate in college who thought cursing with British terms made her sound smarter." Thea discreetly wiped her suddenly sweaty palms on her jeans. "My roommate even started talking with a fake British accent. She was from Akron."

"Interesting but not the point." Dr. Kowecki took off her black-rimmed glasses and chewed on the end of the straight part as she let out a weary sigh.

Thea braced herself. She knew that sigh. It was the sigh of disappointment.

Thea had lots of experience with that sigh—starting with when she was twelve and lost the last bit of adorable-kid-sister look that her mom had parlayed into a minor success as a child actor in commercials. Of course, then Thea had become a gangly, zit-prone teen, and the casting calls—blessedly, for an attention-shy person like her—had stopped coming. Her mom had never forgiven her for that, but at least she'd focused all of her momager energy on Thea's sister. Jackie's acting career had gone—and was still going—very well for both of them. That meant that Thea had enough space to do what she really wanted—go to school for her BS and then her master's and then her PhD, so she could spend the rest of her life with bones. Dinosaur bones, that was.

Dr. Kowecki continued to gnaw on the end of her glasses—it was called the temple tip. Her therapist nibbled on it often enough during their sessions that Thea had looked up diagrams of eyeglasses to identify the technical term for that part.

"You've spent your whole life minimizing conflict to your own detriment. Don't you think it's time you stop?" Dr. Kowecki asked. "Isn't it the time in your life when you develop techniques to help you better deal with conflict rather than ignore it?"

That sounded...absolutely hellacious. And the last thing in the world Thea would ever want to do. "I'm fine with conflict."

There was that sigh again. "Tell me again about your sister's wedding?"

Thea bit back a groan. "It's a destination wedding in Wyoming."

One week of having to hang around Jackie's Hollywood friends while being followed by cameras for seven days solid, because the wedding and everything leading up to it was part of a reality TV special.

"And you're excited to be on TV again?"

Even the idea of being on camera had Thea's gag reflex working on an empty stomach. "No, but the museum gave me approval to work at a dinosaur fossil site nearby, so being at the wedding plus a dig outweighs that part."

Kinda.

Sorta.

Not really at all, but she was a reed, damn it, and this too would pass her like the wind. Plus, the opportunity to participate in the dig of a newly discovered deinonychus was beyond exciting. According to the museum gossip, the dinosaur wasn't just one full skeleton of the predatory, big-clawed feathered theropod, but *three*! This had led the local press to call it a velociraptor find, since the deinonychus was the inspiration for the pack-minded dinosaurs that were *Jurassic Park* fan favorites. Finding a complete skeleton was amazing, but uncovering three? Yeah, even homebody, never-asks-for-anything Thea would do whatever it took to witness this discovery.

So when the reality TV production team said they'd pay for her plane ticket out to Wyoming, she was able to sweeten her proposal to her higher-ups at the museum by explaining that, in exchange for letting her take a paid leave of absence to participate in the dig for two weeks after the wedding, they wouldn't have to cover any of her travel costs. It was the fastest—and only—dig approval she'd ever gotten.

She wasn't going to waste time being annoyed about the wedding or the fact that she'd have to be on camera again, at least the tiny amount that she planned to be. This was silver lining time, and she was going to get to spend time with the type of Late Cretaceous–period creature that first inspired John Ostrom to theorize that birds evolved from dinosaurs.

Life as a paleontologist didn't get better than that.

"Uh-huh," Dr. Kowecki said, sounding anything but in agreement and taking Thea out of her dino happy place. "And remind me again what the wedding is going to be like?"

Bile did a little swish-swish thing in Thea's stomach, a pool of dread with its own waves triggered not by the moon but by anything to do with her sister's reality TV wedding.

"It's themed," Thea said, starting with the details that were just ridiculous rather than panic-inducing. "The producers thought a retro eighties theme would be over-the-top enough for ratings and to get memeified for free publicity." Her stomach did the kind of loop-de-loop that she'd always thought only rollercoasters did. "The whole thing will be streaming practically live, *Big Brother* style."

"And you're excited about that?"

Thea straightened her shoulders and took a deep breath. "No, but my mom pointed out how important it was for my sister that I be there, so I can suck it up for seven days." She could. She would. She'd done it before, so it wasn't a big deal. "Anyway, it's not like the cameras will be focused on me when there are two celebrities at the altar."

Jackie had met Dex on set years ago in a dramedy set in a high school where all of the teenagers were played by actors in their late twenties. They'd dated, broken up, and reconnected a few months ago when they both got cast in the same show. Their shared agent had played matchmaker, and everything had evolved superfast after that until here Thea was, about to get on a plane out to Cody, Wyoming, for a weeklong destination wedding at someplace her sister must have messed up the name of in her texts. There was no way a place called Stinkingwater River existed in real life.

"You don't even hear yourself, do you?" Dr. Kowecki asked not unsympathetically.

Thea blinked in confusion. "What do you mean?"

"Every boundary crossing, every conflict, you just go fawn." The therapist put her glasses back on and locked her intense gaze on Thea. "Most people know the fight-or-flight trauma responses, but there are more. There is freeze, which is self-explanatory and why people find they have extreme difficulty making decisions and, therefore, isolate themselves."

She shook her head and sighed again, and Thea couldn't help it—her pulse ratcheted up to a billion. Whatever the heck fawn was, Dr. Kowecki clearly thought it was the worst of the lot.

As if confirming Thea's worst fears, her therapist continued, "Then there is fawn. Those are the people pleasers who have trouble setting boundaries and may lack a strong sense of identity. It's easier to go along—say, be on camera when just talking about it makes you start sweating like you just walked into a sauna wearing a full-length fur coat—than to deal with the problem at hand." Dr. Kowecki shot her an encouraging smile. "There is no right or wrong trauma response, and we experience them because we are wired by nature and nurture to do that. However, by acknowledging and being aware of your go-to trauma response, you can learn to better manage your stress levels and the triggers. In fact, I have an exercise I'd like you to try during your sister's wedding to better deal with stress and regain a sense of control over your life."

That sounded about as much fun as a destination wedding.

Thea opened her mouth to explain that she was fine and didn't need to do anything, but the look of don't-even-think-about-it on her therapist's face stopped the words before they could get out.

"When you experience a triggering event at the wedding," Dr. Kowecki said, "take a moment to realize what's happening to your body and then decide if another response—fight, flight, or freeze—may be better than a fawn response to get you what you need. This isn't about changing your body's response, but it *is* about learning the tools that will help you deal with conflict better."

Even the idea of it made Thea's palms clammy. "But everything's fine as it is."

It was a statement that would have sounded more convincing if Thea had managed to say it without sounding like she was apologizing.

Both of Dr. Kowecki's eyebrows went high enough to disappear under her short bangs. "But is it?" She paused for a second to let the question sink in. "Really?"

No. Not even close.

Sure, she'd never said the words out loud before, but would she have agreed to Nola's plan for their friend trio to all go to a therapist if she didn't subconsciously at least realize that her life was very much not fine?

The fact that just seeing her mom's name pop up on caller ID lately automatically had her reaching for a paper bag to hyperventilate in?

Not fine.

The way she'd just accepted her boss's decision not to promote her at the Harbor City Natural History Museum even though she was the most qualified candidate?

Not fine.

Agreeing to do the one thing she swore she'd never do and be on camera again after the absolute hell that was being a child actor?

Not fine.

Letting everyone walk all over her because it was easier to go along than to stand up for herself?

Not fine.

She knew that. And yet…here she was, in her therapist's office, trying not to freak the fuck out at the idea of trying something new.

"I've always been like this," Thea said, a bead of panic sweat slowly inching its way down the back of her neck as she battled the instinct to simply agree with Dr. Kowecki's plan just to avoid upsetting her. "I let things flow over me, like water over a duck's back. It's no big deal."

Rationalize? Her? Hell yeah.

"Thea, stuffing all of your feelings into a deep hole and pretending things are *fine* isn't the same as the acceptance you seem to think it is. Give this exercise a try. Open yourself up to the possibility of change. Really, isn't that the entire purpose of therapy? To grow and find your true voice?"

Yes.

Maybe.

Thea didn't know.

All she did know was that deep down, she really was beyond tired of being everyone's doormat. If this experiment could change that, then it had to be worth trying.

Chapter Two

Two days later, Thea was in Pepto-Bismol-pink hell and seriously rethinking her life choices.

She was drowning in lace, had flounces up to her literal neck, and was white-knuckling some kind of parasol thing that looked straight out of a 1980s high school prom hellscape.

"Don't forget your hat," her mom called out.

Thea closed her eyes and muffled her groan as much as she could. Of course there was also a hat. It was big and round, with layers of pink organza, and wide enough to cover both of her shoulders in shade.

This was when she should run—Dr. Kowecki would agree that flight was a legit response to all of this, right? But changing old habits was easier in theory back in Harbor City than it was when she was face to face with her mom.

Yeah, the real reason why they said you couldn't go back home again was because you automatically turned back into your preteen self around your family. And twelve-year-old Thea had been all about controlling the chaos by going along to get along.

Come to think of it, thirty-one-year-old Thea was, too.

All right. She really *wasn't* fine.

Still, did she yell about how ridiculous all of this was? Did she lift up her hoop skirt and make a run for it? Did she go ice maiden so her mom would reconsider that maybe all of this was a bit much?

No.

No.

Aaaaaaand no.

Instead, she turned around and headed back to the ultra-glam wedding party RV, where she took the hat without rolling her eyes because that's who she was in this family, the pushover go-along-to-get-along introverted nerd sister. "Thanks, Mom."

Bridesmaid dresses were often atrocious—this was an accepted part of being in a wedding—but Thea's sister had taken the cliché and blown it up to an argentinosaurus size. God knew the dress felt like it weighed the same two hundred thousand pounds as the one-hundred-and-thirty-foot-long sauropod. Of course, that dinosaur was in southwest Argentina, and Thea was in Colter's Hell, Wyoming.

Talk about truth in advertising. The name said it all.

As she marched toward the mouth of the Stinkingwater River Canyon, she couldn't mistake the hint of rotten eggs hanging in the air from the hot spring's natural sulfurous hot water vents. This was what happened when reality show producers had several million dollars riding on the cable TV celebrity wedding of the year and needed to dial up the drama by making everyone as miserable as possible to make bank on their investment.

"Thea, honey," her mom said as she came to stand beside her. "I know this is a bit much. But your sister, well, your sister is gonna do things her way, and you've always been happiest making things work for other people. It's your superpower!"

Yeah, making it work for other people sure didn't feel like one.

"Jackie just has her heart set on making this the perfect eighties-themed destination wedding like the TV people wanted, and I promised to do whatever I could to support her." Mom let out a blissful sigh and pressed her hand to her heart. "She is the star, after all."

Two air kisses later, followed by a motherly tsk-tsk as she looked at the way the waist seams in the bridesmaid's dress held on for dear life if Thea inhaled a full breath, because sample size she most definitely was not, and her mom walked back to the RV. Thea knew what her mom was thinking. If Thea worked out more. If she'd been more outgoing. If she'd go see that plastic surgeon *everyone* used to refresh and enhance. If she'd only do those things, then she wouldn't be working in a museum with a bunch of dusty old bones but could instead be among the sparkling stars like her sister Jackie.

She knew that's what her mom was thinking because she'd told her directly to her face enough times that Thea had it memorized.

It was the story of Thea's life.

Jackie, as the former child star of two kid-channel TV shows, was the gravitational vortex for their family since their mom decided her kids were going to be famous and uprooted them to Hollywood. And through pure determination and some questionable deals, Mom had made it happen for Jackie.

Introverted, sarcastic, dinosaur-obsessed kids like Thea didn't do so well in showbiz. So Thea had opted for college, graduate school, and a degree in paleontology. All while Jackie had moved on to being a twenty-eight-year-old playing a high school senior on The CW and getting married to her former costar in what maybe, possibly, could be a publicity stunt gone horribly wrong.

Even now, minutes before the pre-wedding festivities were set to begin with a to-be-filmed dress fitting, the head producer was in the RV Thea had just left, poking at every one of Jackie's insecurities while simultaneously priming her woe-is-me, why-doesn't-everyone-adore-the-bride sense of entitlement.

Thea had tried to get the producer to stop, but Jackie had shot her a villain-of-the-week glare. Then she'd followed up with a lecture about how Thea didn't understand how things worked in Hollywood, and that she just needed to mind her own business.

Standing outside in the hellfire-and-brimstone stench of the Stinkingwater River was better than having to hear more of that, so Thea had left. Sure, it was a record-setting ninety-three degrees and the parasol-hat combo did next to nothing against the powerful rays of the Wyoming in August sun, but she'd followed her therapist's advice and had chosen flight!

Of course, now sweat was starting to trickle down the back of her neck, and the idea of just keeping her mouth shut and doing what she was told in the air conditioning was sounding like a much better plan of action. What she wouldn't give to be back in Harbor City.

Looking around to make sure no one was watching, she took her contractually forbidden cell phone out of the pocket built into her monstrosity of a dress and hit up her two favorite people in the whole world.

She held up her phone so the camera could get as much of her dress as possible in the frame.

"Oh my God," Nola said as soon as her face popped up on the screen from her corner office in a high-rise in Harbor City's financial district. "What are you wearing?"

Astrid continued to apply her makeup (tips at the bar went way up when she did the smoky eye) and asked, "Have you met any hot cowboys yet?"

Some of the tension eased out of Thea's shoulders. "My bridesmaid's dress and no."

"Boo on both counts," Astrid said and then stuck out her tongue. "What's the status on the groomsmen?"

"I'm not here to get laid," she said, rolling her eyes. "Nola, help me out here."

Astrid pointed her contour brush at her phone and jumped in before their friend could say anything. "That is totally not what I was told being a bridesmaid was about. Of course you're there to bang the hottest groomsman. There are wedding rules."

"The entire week is being *filmed*," Thea reminded her friends.

Nola grinned. "There are worse things than the country watching some hot guy chase you around a wedding."

"No, there aren't," Thea deadpanned, and both her friends laughed, as expected.

Smoothing her blonde hair back—as if a single strand would have the audacity to slip free of her severe bun—Nola set her expression into serious-contract-attorney-that-puts-up-with-no-shit mode. "You hanging in there with all of the family stuff?"

Thea squared her shoulders and forced her lips into a smile. "I'm—"

"Fine," her two best friends said at the same time.

Wow. Maybe she really did say that too much.

"How about a ski instructor?" Astrid asked as if she and Nola hadn't just called Thea out. "You're close to the Rockies, right?"

Nola rolled her eyes. "It's August, Astrid."

She stopped mid-blot of her second coat of deep red lipstick and let out a dramatic gasp. "Don't you rain on my boner parade, Nola."

"You two are stone-cold messes," Thea said with all love and no censure.

Astrid shrugged. "And you're right there with us."

"True." And it was. They may not be the likeliest of besties, but their little misfit trio had been together through a million tragedies and celebrations. They were one another's rocks—even when they were half a country apart. "Love you guys."

"We love you, too!" Nola and Astrid said together.

They said their goodbyes, and Thea made the short walk back to the RV, while giving herself a mental pep talk about how fine everything was. Going with the flow just worked. It was fine.

Old habits really were a bitch to break.

She was hesitating outside of the RV when a large, man-shaped shadow fell over her. Startled, she did a little jump-turn thing while letting out a high-pitched squeak.

What she saw next didn't make her panicked pulse slow down, though; it sped up. No man should look that good in a tan tux with a powder blue ruffled tuxedo shirt.

He was tall enough that she had to take a step back to get a look at his face, but it was worth it. He had tropical paradise blue eyes, a square jaw covered in salt-and-pepper scruff that managed to look accidental and deliberate at the same time, and a nose with a bump that told tales about it being broken at least once but probably more. It was enough to make her breath catch. Then, one side of his mouth went up in a crooked smile, and her pink panties embroidered with *Always The Bridesmaid*—thank you, Jackie—went up in flames.

"If you don't laugh at what I'm wearing, I'll share my flask." He unscrewed the top and held it out. "You look like you need it."

"It's that obvious?" she asked as she accepted the offering, a sizzle of awareness zinging up her arm when their fingers brushed.

He chuckled, a deep rumbly sound. "Only to anyone with eyes."

Bracing for whatever was about to burn all the way down her throat to her empty belly, she took a swig from the flask. Lemon. Lime. Bubbles. The shock of soda when she'd been expecting whiskey or gin or even straight-up lighter fluid sent the liquid down the wrong pipe as she spluttered and gasped for air.

"That," she said, using the back of her finger to dab at her watery eyes, "was *not* what I expected."

He gave her an intense look, as if he needed to check for himself that she was okay, then gave her a lazy smile. "The best things in life rarely are."

"Sorta like this wedding?" The words—which were the very opposite of reality, considering the air around them reeked of rotten eggs—tumbled out of her.

"This," he said, leaning over and lowering his voice, "is *exactly* the nightmare I expected."

Eyes wide with shock at someone actually saying it out loud, she stared up at him, and a laugh—her real one that was loud, nasally, and gave off more than a little hint of woodpecker—burst out. "It *is*."

She slapped her hand over her mouth and stifled the last of her chuckles while they shared a knowing glance.

"With the exception of getting to meet you, of course," he said, watching her as she started to take another drink from his flask. "You have to be the one person in the world who could make that outfit look good."

Shocked at his words and the shiver of anticipation they sent up her spine, she did a shit job of using her depth perception and bonked the lip of the flask against her teeth.

Wow.

Watch out for Thea Pope, world. She's setting a land-dork flirting failure record and putting her dentist's kids through college at this rate.

"You're kidding, right?" He had to be.

He shook his head and winked at her. "Not in the least."

Was he flirting with her? No. People didn't do that. They flirted with Jackie. They ignored Thea, which was more than fine by her. Dinosaur bones, she got. People? They left her at a total loss.

In her head, she said thank you with an air of confidence and mystery before flirting right back. In real life, she made some kind of gurgling, grunting sound and took another drink from the flask—at least this time she didn't make a total fool of herself by forgetting how to swallow or breaking a tooth.

Instead, she just took the drink and then stood there about as useful as the itty-bitty arms on a T. rex while the man looked at her with an amused grin. Wow. Her minor in communications with an emphasis on public speaking (a hell only made worthwhile by the hope that she'd someday make a discovery so important that she'd have to present at academic conferences) was really coming in handy.

Yep. It was just her, the hot guy who carried a flask full of Sprite, the sulfur stench of the fumaroles and hot springs dotting the landscape, and the silence of a shy paleontologist who couldn't string two words together.

Fan-fucking-tastic.

Just when the moment was on the verge of morphing from awkward to downright pitiful, the RV door flew open, slamming against the outside of the RV with a metallic thump. Jackie stood in the doorway, her hands on her Disney-princess-levels-of-poof wedding dress.

"*You* are not supposed to be here," she said, looking directly at the guy. "It's bad luck. Plus, you were supposed to shave off that stupid scruff before filming started."

Unlike nearly everyone else who'd ever been told to do something by Jackie, though, he didn't cower or immediately agree. Instead, he threw back his head and laughed. Loudly. Right into the cloudless blue sky. Then, without a single word, he turned and started walking toward the groom's RV.

Mouth agape, Thea held out his flask. "You forgot this."

He looked back over his shoulder and gave her a slow smile and wink. "Keep it."

Oh my.

Her panties were barely even a memory at this point.

Jackie swiped the flask from Thea and downed a long drink. "Oh my God," she spluttered after the first swallow, "it's Sprite. Who keeps soda in a flask? Oh. My. God. He's such a weirdo. Come on, it's time!"

The dress fitting.

Yeah.

That's what Thea was here for, not meeting a hot guy way out of her league who looked like a sexy badass even in a dorky early-eighties tux and drank straight Sprite in a hip flask.

Chapter Three

Kade St. James didn't believe in astrology, tarot cards, religion, or doing what he was told just because that's the way things were done. He did, however, believe in his gut.

And what his instincts were telling him was that if even the bride's friends were in total misery having to be here at the wedding from hell, then there was no hope that any of this was going to work out as planned.

So instead of giving in to the temptation to sweet talk that awkwardly sexy bridesmaid into ditching Colter's Hell for a weekend in the mountains away from the TV cameras, the bridezilla, and the all-around ridiculousness of this wedding, he was going to talk sense into his brother. Kade would do just about anything for Dex—including wearing the ugliest fucking tuxedo in the entire world—but even brotherly love had its limits.

"You do realize this is the dumbest fucking shit you have ever pulled me into, right?" Kade said as he strode into the RV that production had declared the groom's.

"Love you, too, bruh," Dex said as he scrolled through social media on his phone, not bothering to look up.

Kade glared at his younger brother as he lay sprawled out on the couch in the RV the production team had outfitted with enough alcohol to make a frat house jealous. Never mind the fact that neither he nor his brother ever touched the stuff. There was something about growing up an alcoholic's kid that changed your perspective on all things booze-related.

"Dex, be serious." Kade grabbed a wad of cocktail napkins that said *Jackie and Dex Forever*, scrunched them into a ball, and flung them at his brother's head, scoring a direct hit. "You cannot go through with this. That woman cannot be someone you want to spend the rest of your life with."

His brother's only response was to flip him off.

Yeah, they'd had this conversation already at least a million times, but too damn bad, because they were gonna have it again. This was Kade's last opportunity to twist his baby brother's head back on straight before he made the biggest mistake of his life.

Living in Hollywood had turned Dex smooth-brained if he thought marriage was a solution for anything. As they both knew from watching the disaster that was their parents' relationship, marriage was toxic sludge for the soul. And that was before he even factored in the bride. Jackie had already ordered him to shave, to forego riding his motorcycle before the wedding, and to get a fucking haircut. He'd told her hell no. Obviously. There was no way that woman wasn't marrying his brother for a publicity stunt, and Dex deserved way better.

"You cannot go through with this," Kade said as he got a Sprite out of the mini-fridge and popped the can open. "Marriage is already a nightmare of epic proportions without shackling yourself to *that* woman."

"Jackie is just stressed," Dex said with a shrug. "We both have a lot riding on this wedding making big ratings numbers. And you know this is the best move for me. No one can pay for the kind of word-of-mouth publicity *Hero X* will get from all of this, and God knows the cast fucking needs it so it picks up a distributor with deep pockets."

And that was reason six hundred and twenty-eight why Kade refused to let any of his true crime books be turned into movies. There was no way he'd commit to all of the bullshit Dex had to do just to get his own movie, *Hero X*, off the ground—not that the Hollywood machine would ever do things the right way anyway. It would be all flash and blood and jump scares about the crimes instead of delving into why people did what they did and the impact it had on the victims.

Kade rubbed his palm against the back of his neck as he shook his head. "And I thought I was a cynic about marriage."

"You are, along with everything else." Dex shot him a shit-eating grin. "Hell, if it wasn't for that mutt you call a guard dog, I'd think you were the ultimate asshole."

He opened his mouth to stick up for Patton's skillset, but what in the hell could he say? The French bulldog–corgi mix was all bark and no bite—also barely any tail, but that was to be expected.

"I may be the ultimate asshole, but I'm an honest asshole at least," Kade grumbled as he stared out the window at the mountains in the distance. "I don't pretend that love is anything other than a temporary hormonal imbalance and that if you put blind faith in someone else the only outcome is bad shit."

"And this is what happens when you spend your life writing true crime books," Dex said, motioning toward him with his can of soda. "You think everyone is up to something shitty."

"Only because they are—a fact of life that you seem to have spent almost three decades denying."

It was true and had been for their entire lives. Every move they'd made growing up, going from embassy to embassy, Dex had been sure that this was the one where their mom would change. She'd wake up before one in the afternoon. She'd ask about what happened at school. She'd basically give a damn about anything beyond what was in her glass.

Meanwhile, Kade had figured out by move number

six that it was never going to happen and had adjusted his expectations accordingly.

Oh, it may take time for the truth to out itself—not everyone was as upfront about only being in it for themselves as Jackie, which (truth be told) he kind of admired about her—but it always did eventually. That's why he didn't pretty things up, he didn't bullshit, he didn't pretend to save other people's feelings.

And if that made him an asshole? So fucking be it.

Dex had never realized the truth about people, let alone their own mom—not even when she'd finally left. He'd always held out hope that she'd come back and everything would be perfect, while Kade had wondered why it had taken fourteen years for the inevitable to finally occur.

"I've been a realist since birth," Kade said. "The question is why you of all people have finally seen the light."

Dex shrugged and went back to staring at his phone. "Things change."

Kade waited for his brother to say more. He *always* said more. The kid was born talking and had never stopped—well, minus the two weeks after their mom left.

"You're going to do this."

It wasn't a question. Kade knew his brother too well for that, and Dex knew it, which was why he didn't bother answering. Instead, he tossed his phone onto the couch cushion and focused all of his attention on Kade.

"Even more, I need you to do me a solid," Dex said. "Actually, I need you to do two of them."

Now *that* made Kade's oh-fuck alert go off. "I've already agreed to be your best man for this farce. What more could you possibly need?"

Dex got up and grabbed a bottle of Dr Pepper out of the fridge. He twisted the cap off and downed half of the twenty ounces in one long gulp, then took a short break before going back to it. Kade knew better than to expect answers until the bottle was empty. His brother took his Dr Pepper very seriously, which was why his agent made sure to include a clause in all his contracts demanding his on-set fridge include sodas flown in from Waco, where it was invented.

"First," Dex said after he got the last sip of soda, "be nice to Jackie. She might come off as a pain right now, but she thinks this wedding is the only way to save her career, and it has her a little on edge."

"A little on edge?" Kade repeated back. "The woman is demanding I shave my beard, cover my tats with makeup, and learn TikTok dances for the reception."

"It's unhinged, yes, but Jackie knows what she's doing," Dex said. "She's been in the business for almost twenty years. The transition to adult roles is kicking her ass, but she's gonna get there. I don't doubt her for a minute."

Kade scoffed. "Spoken exactly like someone with Stockholm Syndrome."

"Fuck you." Dex flipped him off again, then let out a harsh breath and seemed to steel himself. "The second is Mom is gonna be here tomorrow."

The record-setting heat of August turned frigid in less than a heartbeat, and Kade would have sworn in court that the whole world stopped moving in the point three seconds it took for him to process his brother's words. The woman who'd left their family in *a foreign city* was here? The woman who'd never even bothered to send a Christmas card for five years after she'd hit the road? The woman who hadn't even shown up for their dad's funeral? The woman who now reached out to Kade every three months like she had a calendar reminder set that said "make amends with eldest child" that he religiously ignored? *She* was here?

And there's only one reason why Elenore St. James would be here.

Dex had invited her.

The little shithead.

He turned on his brother, an icy rage burning him from the inside out. "No. Fucking. Way."

Dex lifted his hands, palms outward, and took a very smart two steps backward. "I know you've been hesitant about reconnecting, but—"

"Hesitant?" The word roared out of Kade like a curse. "Try no fucking way, not even if the world was about to end and all I had to do to save it was say five words to that woman."

"Grow the fuck up," Dex hollered back. "She did what she thought was best for us."

"She left the country—*she left us*—and never looked back."

Kade had overheard his dad talking on the phone once, knew it was with their mother right after she'd left. Sure, Kade had only heard one side of the conversation, but it was kind of hard to misunderstand things like "just talk to them," "give them a chance to say goodbye," and "help them understand why." But Elenore St. James had apparently wanted a clean cut, and he'd sworn that night that he'd give his mother exactly what she wanted. That didn't change just because she'd sobered up ten years ago and had spent the past decade trying to make amends.

Amends were for the people who actually gave a fuck.

Kade sure as hell didn't.

"There's more to the story, Kade, and it's past time you pulled your head out of your ass and listened to her long enough to find that out," Dex said. "If you just give her five minutes to—"

Kade cut his brother off. "Not gonna happen. Ever."

He and Dex glared at each other, neither even thinking about backing down. They never did. They'd spent the past few years arguing about their mom, with Dex wanting Kade to give her a second chance. Yeah, it wasn't going to happen. Kade would do just about anything for his younger brother—except talk to their mother.

Not now.

Not ever.

Dex let out a tired sigh as he flopped back down onto the couch. "Kade—"

"I'll be your best man," he said, cutting him off. "I'll bite my tongue around the bride. I won't even try to talk sense into you about this absolutely fucked-up reality TV wedding that's going to leave you real-life married. What I won't do, though, is talk to the woman who gave birth to us. You got that?"

Dex mumbled a string of curses under his breath but nodded. Kade opened the RV door, needing to get out into the wide-open spaces of Wyoming to shake off the itch of unease scratching against every part of him.

"But what if not talking to her is a mistake?" Dex asked.

Kade barely paused halfway out the door. "It's not."

Then he walked away. That was the one lesson his mom had taught him that he'd never forget.

Chapter Four

Someone in production was deep in their eighties nostalgia at the first night's live-streamed wedding party cocktail hour, and Thea didn't think it was possible to be more sick of a decade she hadn't even been alive for.

Fine, her mood was sour after spending the entirety of the bridesmaid dress fitting being told that she could double up on Spanx or asked if she could suck in her gut and hold her breath each time the camera was on her.

So much for Hollywood being all about body positivity. Where were her apple-shaped sisters with solid, muscular legs to hang out with in solidarity? No doubt they were waiting outside of casting offices being told they just weren't right for the part. Right about now she was more than ready to band together with them and burn the whole system down.

Wow. All of that Mountain Dew she'd guzzled fifteen minutes ago after tossing the hoop skirt across the room when she'd finally gotten to change out of the bridesmaid dress must have just kicked in. Her fellow scientists may have proven that there was no such thing as a sugar rush, but she sure felt like she was dancing on the thin string of an adrenaline-spiked high-wire. It was like her whole body was telling her it was go time.

Except she wasn't a go time kind of woman. She was a melt-into-the-background-and-avoid-the-cameras-at-all-costs kind of woman. Too bad she stuck out like a sore thumb in her flowery cotton skirt and white tank top, with her hair pulled back into a simple ponytail. She'd thought tonight's event at the resort's barn was a relaxed meet-and-greet type of first night get-together.

Yeah. Not even close.

Somehow she'd missed the memo that the entire week leading up to the wedding was eighties cosplay, each evening being a party-like-it's-1982 event. The barn had been decorated like the original *Footloose* prom and everyone was in their Madonna, Springsteen, or Prince and the Revolution best. Seriously, how did the others manage to get their hair that high? One of the bridesmaids had bangs that stood half a foot straight up from her forehead.

Thankfully, the producer, a perpetually stressed out–looking woman named Justine Cummings, was ignoring Thea's obvious misstep for bigger game—Jackie, who'd gone AWOL.

Sorta.

As far as the TV crew knew, the bride had absconded. In reality, though, Jackie was hiding behind a humongous bronze statue of mountain man John Colter after he'd left the Lewis and Clark Expedition. The artist had created a haggard, snarly, fuck-you-and-your-horse statue, so basically Colter looked exactly like someone who'd have a hell named after him.

"Are you sure they're not heading this way?" Jackie asked, her voice barely louder than the A Flock of Seagulls song "I Ran (So Far Away)" blasting out of the speakers surrounding the dance floor.

Thea scanned the crowd, her gaze stopping on the flask-carrying mystery man. He was in a black T-shirt and jeans that were worn but definitely not acid-washed (thank you, Baby Jesus). At least she wasn't the only one who missed the eighties cosplay memo.

"Hello, earth to Thea," Jackie said, her tone taking on the Valley Girl sound that was totally eighties. "Can I do this or not?"

"Yeah, you're good," she said without bothering to peel her attention away from Mr. Cool Drink of Sprite.

"Thank fuck," Jackie muttered before taking a shot.

It wasn't that the alcohol wasn't flowing around them, but her sister was taking shots of tequila when a vodka company had sponsored the wedding. Justine had threatened everyone with a painful death via being drowned in the Stinkingwater River if they even accidentally got any non-branded alcohol on camera during the live streams. Of course, Jackie hated vodka, and the rules weren't ever really meant for the family princess.

What kind of alcohol Jackie was tossing back was the last thing occupying Thea's mind, though. She couldn't look away from her mystery guy over by the bar, but she must have made a sound—please God not a moan—because Jackie peeked around the statue.

"Who are you even looking at?" her sister asked.

Thea squeezed her eyes shut. Fuckity, fuck, fuck. Why did she have to be such an open book?

"The guy from this afternoon," she said before she could think of something other than the truth.

Improv had never been her thing.

"Ugh. Dex's brother, Kade, is the worst." Jackie poured a third shot. "I do not understand why Dex picked him to be his best man. He's unpleasant. Says no to everything. And thinks he can just act on his own instead of realizing this is an ensemble project, where we all have to work together seamlessly or our careers will crash and burn."

So *that's* who he was. She'd heard bits and pieces about the brother during the fitting this afternoon. According to Jackie and her pair of fellow actress bridesmaids, Kade was boring, always reading, hot but not hot enough to get away with being that annoying, and—worst of all—not involved in the showbiz industry at all.

"It makes complete sense that he's the best man. They are *brothers*," Thea said, her breath catching when he turned and caught her staring.

Heat beat her cheeks as she jerked her attention to the floor littered with glittering confetti and neon-green and hot-pink tissue paper flowers that had fallen from the hastily-put-up decorations.

"Well, he's still an asshole with an asshole name," Jackie said, her words slurring together just the slightest bit. "I mean, his name is Kade St. James. What the hell kind of dumb name is that?"

"He didn't name himself." God knew she wouldn't have picked Thea, which conjured up a whole mysterious-and-tough image that did not conform to the reality of her boring thick dark bangs, thicker glasses, and waaaaay thicker thighs.

"Well, he's thirty-four, so he's had plenty of time to change it. Thank God Dex has barely spoken to him since I told him yesterday how rude Kade is to me all the time. I mean, he actually complained about a beautiful destination wedding. This is a once-in-a-lifetime experience in rural Wyoming here. I was all like, it's just part of the process, buddy. Stop being selfish and deal with it."

"And he didn't take that well?" What a shocker.

"You wouldn't believe it," Jackie said, totally missing the sarcasm in Thea's tone. "He rolled his eyes at me. Can you believe it? So. Rude. I told Dex, but he said it was too late to swap Kade out for one of his cuter and nicer friends. Then it wouldn't be such a total embarrassment for me if one of my bridesmaids banged the best man—yes, I caught them mid fuck-me stare when we got here. Why they are even checking Kade out, I have no idea. I mean, he's just the worst. Plus, now I'm stuck with him in all of my wedding pictures."

"Won't he be a part of your life forever when you're married?" Thea turned and faced her sister, accepting the small mirror Jackie shoved into her hands to hold up for her sister before she reapplied her lipstick.

"Sure, but that doesn't mean he has to be the best man." Jackie smacked her lips together, added a second coat of red, and then winked at her reflection. "I mean, look at us. You're not my maid of honor, and you're my only sister. I wouldn't even have had you in the bridal party at all, but the producers insisted."

Thea stood there, her stomach twisting as humiliation burned her from the inside out.

She tried to process what in the fuck her sister had just told her, but her lungs were too tight. Her glasses must have suddenly become the wrong prescription, because things had gone blurry. And no matter how much she replayed Jackie's statement in her head, she could not get it to make sense.

Her sister, though, didn't notice Thea's shock. She just took her compact mirror back and dropped it into the borrowed designer clutch she was carrying.

Then, a Prince song started playing. All of the bridesmaids squealed with excitement—no doubt because the song had part of a social media dance craze that had even made it to Thea's dinosaur side of things. The DJ called the bride and the bridesmaids to the center of the dance floor to show their moves. And Jackie took off without a glance back at Thea.

The song was blaring over the speakers, but Thea stayed frozen to the spot, watching her sister and the other bridesmaids managing to all be half a beat off while doing the synchronized dance moves as the cameras caught every second of it.

She just kept hearing Jackie's words over and over again in her head.

The producers insisted.

If there had been a chair anywhere near, Thea would have crumbled into it. Sure, she and Jackie had their issues, but they were sisters. That was a sacred bond—one that lasted through thick and thin, through good times and bad, through sickness and in health. But it wasn't enough for Jackie to want Thea to be a part of one of the biggest days in her life?

Oh, that hurt. Badly. It was the kind of jagged pain that caught her off guard and hit a secret sensitive spot so vulnerable she hadn't even known it was there.

Desperate for a way out of the reception before the shock had worn off and she did something horrible, like break into tears where the cameras could spot her, Thea's gaze landed on Kade, the man Jackie was dead set on none of her bridesmaids fucking.

And that was the very moment when a lightbulb blazed to life. Fuck flight. She was going to channel all of this embarrassment and hurt into a fight response—and she was going to fight dirty.

She was going to have sex with the one man here that her sister hated the most.

Tonight.

Probably on top of that hideous bridesmaid dress still strewn across her bed.

And she'd maybe even let him spank her with that damn pink parasol—or better yet, maybe feisty Thea would spank him! It was going to be a glorious anger bang with a guy she'd probably rarely if ever see again after the wedding and who seemed like the kind to deliver on multiple orgasms—which she'd be able to remind her sister of for the next *forever.*

She'd tell Jackie just how damn good his brother's rough hand felt against the inside of her thighs. And the thing he'd do with his tongue? All of that, she'd tell her sister all of that every Thanksgiving in graphic detail as her sister passed the sausage-and-cornbread stuffing.

There would be details. So. *Many*. Details.

Remember how you said you didn't want any of your bridesmaids to fuck Kade?

Remember how you didn't even want me as a bridesmaid?

And yet I was and I did. Oops!

Petty?

Yes.

A win-win for her?

Fuck yes.

Okay, maybe having multiple orgasms in a single night of revenge sex was pushing it, but at least one good toe-curling, forget-your-own-name climax that would have her seeing T. rexes in confetti-covered party dresses was definitely what she needed. Was that really asking too much compensation for this wedding-week hell?

Maybe, but fuck it. She was doing it anyway.

Sometimes, revenge came with orgasms. That was the beauty of it.

Fucking Kade St. James—Jackie's most hated guest—was the perfect way for Thea to get back at her sister.

Crossing her fingers behind her back, she sent up a quick prayer to the patron saint of revenge orgasms and made her way over to Mr. Tall, Hot, and Completely Hated By Her Sister. She reached up—way up—and tapped him on the shoulder before she could lose her nerve.

Kade turned around and smiled. The way his grin was higher on one side than the other sent a wave of desire through her warm enough that she started fanning herself with a crushed tissue flower before she realized what she was doing.

He discombobulated her. It was her only excuse for what happened next. If she would have been herself—a grown-ass woman in her early-thirties, a respected paleontologist, a human who could name every one of the bones in the one-hundred-and-twenty-two-foot-long titanosaur at the American Museum of Natural History—the question would never have tumbled out of her mouth quite like it did.

"So, you want to get out of here and have a no-strings-attached, hate-the-bridezilla fuck?" she asked—right as the extra-loud eighties synth-pop music stopped playing.

There were four whole beats of silence—and then every camera in the room that was live streaming the party turned and focused on Thea.

Chapter Five

Kade had never been caught speechless in his life. Yeah, he wasn't exactly known for being super talkative, but that wasn't because he didn't have the words. He just usually didn't like anyone enough to say them.

Right now, though? He didn't have a fucking clue.

But the nerdy-hot bridesmaid with the wide-rimmed glasses and the sexy, gap-toothed smile was turning eighteen shades of red while everyone in the barn watched with eyes the size of salad plates.

He could see the gears working as she tried to figure out her next move, since he highly doubted that telling the entire world she wanted to hate-fuck him had been her plan—yes, there was no way the people watching the live stream at home missed her invitation. Production had the whole barn mic'd up to hell and back.

Then, the whispers started from the wedding party.

The remotely controlled camera on the bar whirred as it no doubt zoomed in on the bridesmaid's face.

She swallowed and pressed her lips together, beads of sweat dampening the strands of hair that had worked their way free of her ponytail.

He would have sworn he saw panicked tears in her eyes, but she blinked them away before he could confirm. That's when her chin trembled. It wasn't a lot, just a couple of twitches, but there was no missing it. And if he caught it, so would everyone else watching live at home and in person. Her gaze veered over to the camera on the bar, then widened as realization hit. Her attention immediately skittered back to him and then dropped to the floor as she let out a quiet, miserable groan.

Oh hell.

He could *not* let this woman cry in front of the whole world when it was obvious, even if he'd been looking down from the space station, that she did not do public tears.

Fuck.

There was only one option—not that it was a bad option or even one he wouldn't have chosen otherwise. The woman wasn't boring or stuck up or self-absorbed. Nah. The bridesmaid who didn't belong was hot, ballsy, and funny. However, he couldn't just toss her over a shoulder and walk out of there or even just say yes and walk out with her. He had to sell it. He had to be a fucking actor.

Christ on a cracker.

That wasn't his job. That was all Dex. And yet…

"Babe," he said, feeling like a total fool as he put a rough growl in his tone. "I thought I was going to have to keep begging you to give me a chance. You're all I've been thinking about since we met."

She jerked her head up, something a lot like grateful hope in her eyes.

"Let's get out of here," he said, holding out his hand to her.

The right corner of her mouth kicked up in a half smile, and she took his hand. He lifted their enjoined hands and kissed the back of her knuckles before they walked out of the barn as the jackass of a DJ put on Madonna's "Like a Virgin."

The rotten-egg smell of the fumaroles that sent puffs of hot gas into the air every evening hit as soon as they walked through the side door leading out to a huge paved garden area with seating everywhere. He grabbed one of the wicker chairs on the patio and shoved it under the door handle.

"I don't know what to say now," she said, looking down at their hands still clasped together.

"Well, we don't have time to think about it," he said as he looked around, scoping the area for camera folks, "because we've got to move fast if we're gonna get out of here before the camera guys figure out they can go out the barn's front door to get to us."

"We're ditching them?" Her shoulders hitched up closer to her ears as her gaze darted from the door to him and back again. The woman looked guilty as hell. "The contract and release production made me sign said I'd cooperate with the camera crew."

Yeah, so had his. Fuck them.

They'd have to prove he was ditching them, and for all they knew he was just going for a walk. With the woman who just asked him if he wanted to go fuck just to piss off the bride? No one was ever going to believe he was going for a nice, quiet walk, but that wasn't the point.

What was the point? That no one who wasn't after their fifteen minutes or reaching for the next rung on their acting career ladder would stick around to make sure the camera crew caught up with them.

Was that what she was doing? Had he read her wrong in there? Maybe all of her awkward shyness was put on? Was this a case of production setting up all of this for the drama so she had to find a reason to keep him here?

He couldn't explain why, but the idea of this being fake pissed him off. Was this her audition piece to break into TV? Was *he* just her publicity stunt?

"Is that what you want?" Kade asked, his tone harsh. "To have them catch us? How sensational do you want it? Do you want me to pick you up, press you against the wall, wrap those long legs of yours around my hips, and grind against you so viewers can imagine exactly what you're gonna get when I fuck you tonight?"

Her eyes went wide behind her glasses, and her perfect pink mouth formed an *O* of surprise. Yeah, if she was an actress she was a really good one, because she managed to get shocked, turned on, and what the fuck something else to cross her face in quick succession. Of course, all of that was followed by a bullseye-red flush of embarrassment on both cheeks so bright that no one could fake it.

"Oh God," she said as she covered her face. "Everyone at the museum is going to have seen me. I am never getting a promotion now."

Museum? Promotion?

"Shit." *Maybe dial back the asshole, St. James.* "Okay, that just sort of came out. I'm not gonna do that."

She dropped her hands and looked up at him. Did she look disappointed? Fuck, his *dick* was disappointed.

"You wanna get out of here?" he asked, doing his best to not sound like some kind of aggressive gym bro with three times the daily recommended dose of pre-workout in his system. "I want to get you out of here. But we gotta go now. Are you good with that?"

She bit down on her bottom lip and nodded.

"Come on." He tightened his grip on her hand, and they took off at a quick clip, heading straight for his RV, which this resort had instead of cabins or hotel rooms for the guests.

You think that's the right call, brainiac?

Yeah, his RV was the second place production would look once they realized they missed them at the barn. Hell, they probably already had a crew stationed behind a boulder like uninvited voyeurs.

He made a left at the narrow gravel path. It took them past the resort's staff quarters, through a wrought-iron kissing gate, and after a silent walk over the rocky terrain out to a scenic overlook of the canyon that was upwind from the river. There were a few lounge chairs set up back from the overlook near a firepit. While he got a fire going using the nearby supplies to take the bite out of the mountain-chilly evening, even in summer, the bridesmaid sat down on one of the chaises.

She still hadn't said anything since the barn. Instead, she just kept sneaking looks at him as he lit the kindling set between the logs.

This was where Dex would have started telling stories to put her at ease. Kade didn't have that ability. Sure, he was a writer, but the kind of real-life crimes he wrote about wouldn't put anyone at ease, let alone a woman he'd only met today as they sat in the middle of nowhere.

So, have you ever heard of the Hatchet Man of Harbor City?

That wasn't creepy at all.

So instead of freaking her the fuck out, he sat down on the lounge chair facing her across the crackling fire. "I'm Kade St. James."

"I've heard," she said. "I'm Thea Pope."

His gut sank. "Pope as in the bride Jackie Pope?"

She nodded.

Fucking great.

"This is all some sibling rivalry gone to extremes?" he asked.

She shrugged and then held her hands out so they were closer to the fire. "Not quite."

He laid back on the cushioned lounge chair to work out what he'd just stepped in, but the explosion of stars in the sky shut down his brain for a moment.

Out of the corner of his eye, he saw her shoot him a questioning glance before following his lead and looking up.

She let out a little gasp. "Wow."

Then she relaxed back on her chair and they sat there quiet for a few minutes, admiring the Milky Way. Nothing like seeing flecks of light from stars a bazillion miles away that were probably already dead to twist a person's head on straight and make them wonder about the answers to life's big questions—and the smaller ones.

He glanced over at Thea. "So what did your sister do to get you so mad you want to fuck me to get back at her?"

"The list is too long to go into it." She let out a long sigh and turned on her side to face him. "But the final straw was she apparently didn't even want me here. It's her *wedding*. And I'm her *only* sibling. She let slip the only reason I'm here is because the production team made her ask me to be a bridesmaid."

And he'd thought Jackie was bitchy before. "Ouch."

"Exactly," she grumbled. "Before I came out here, my therapist gave me an assignment where I'm supposed to try out the other stress trigger reactions, even though they don't come naturally like fawning."

"Fawning?" he asked.

"Basically, going along to get along and avoid conflict. There are four—sometimes more, depending on who you talk to—stress responses: fawn, flight, fight, and freeze."

Interesting. He'd heard of fight or flight—what true-crime writer or reader hadn't?—but fawn and freeze were new to him. Not that that bit of knowledge was at the top of his things-to-think-about list at the moment. Instead, he couldn't stop watching Thea's mouth. The woman had fantastic lips, full and ripe for kissing.

"So which response is seeing if I want to go fuck?" he asked before he thought better of it.

Her gaze flicked over to the fire, but not before he caught the heat in it. "Fight."

He took a stab at the why and asked, "Because your sister has hated me since the day Dex introduced us?"

She nodded.

Kade got that. Desperate times and all that.

She sat up and pivoted to face him, even as she kept her gaze averted. "I know it doesn't make a ton of sense but—"

"Actually, it does," he said, all of the pieces coming together like the plot of a book. "And I'm more than happy to be your fuck boy for the night—or let people think I am. Lady's choice."

She chuckled. It was a soft sound that made his dick hard. Hell, it hadn't been that long since he'd banged a fellow author, who was about as into relationships as he was (not at all), but for some reason being around Thea had him keyed up. She was sexy, in that girl-next-door way, in her tank top and skirt with her long, dark hair brushing against her freckled shoulders. The temptation to slip that strap lower and find out if she had freckles anywhere else had him fisting his hands to stop himself before he forgot that this was just going to be for show.

Thea toyed with the fringe on the pillow she held in her lap, peeking up at him as she paused to nervously gnaw at her bottom lip. "Does that mean you might actually want to hook up for real, or was all that in the barn only pretend?"

Chapter Six

Who *was* she right now?

Thea had no idea.

She was a paleontologist, a woman who had two friends and felt that was more than enough, and she scheduled her self-care (AKA masturbation) sessions for Wednesday nights and Sunday mornings. She rarely talked to strangers. She didn't initiate conversations. She never pushed for the things she actually wanted.

And yet here she was, in all of her dorky glory, asking a man she'd just met earlier that day to have sex with her.

Sex she'd brag about to her sister.

Revenge sex, just like she'd imagined.

Of course, it wasn't going to happen. He was just giving her some pity hope.

Guys like Kade St. James never gave her a second glance. Men like him, with their sandpapery low voices that made her heart speed up. Men like him, who looked like they'd been in more than a few bar brawls and had won them all, weren't interested in finding out more about a mousy bookworm like her. Men who exuded so much sex appeal it was hard to look them straight in the face without breaking into giggles.

Kade was the ultimate of *that* kind of guy.

From the tip of his nose that had obviously been broken a time or three to his strong, calloused hands to the way he looked at the world as if he was daring it to fuck with him, the man was the textbook definition of would never be interested in a pushover, nose in a book, wallflower like her.

What had she been thinking in approaching him?

Her heartbeat sped up and her palms got damp as she tried to swallow past the embarrassed panicky feeling making her throat tight.

Seriously, maybe there was something more than pungent gas coming out of the fumaroles back at the barn—she wouldn't put it past the producers to spike nature for the sake of ratings. Airborne aphrodisiacs at a weeklong destination wedding seemed like the perfect bit of chaos that would keep the audience glued to the live stream twenty-four seven.

"I'm sorry about that," she said as she stared down at the tips of his scuffed boots. Why was she looking at the brown leather work boots rather than Kade? Because actually looking at his face was beyond her capabilities at the moment. Yeah, she wasn't particularly proud of herself, either. "I shouldn't have put you on the spot back there. It wasn't fair to you. I mean, *look* at you. Then look at me—" She shut her mouth hard enough that her teeth clanked together. Too bad she did so too late and now all of what was swirling around in her brain was outside of her mouth. She exhaled a groan of misery. "I should go."

She stood up and whirled around to the path they'd taken to get here, intent on getting away from Kade and the site of her latest humiliation as quickly as possible.

That counted as flight, right? There, she'd gotten a twofer of fight and flight on the same night. Her therapist would be so proud. Meanwhile, her heart was hammering against her ribs, her palms were all sweaty, and she had enough adrenaline rushing through her system to power a small city.

"Thea."

It wasn't an order for her to stop, and yet she did, his gruff tone making her bite down on her lip as electric anticipation fluttered in her stomach.

"Turn around and look at me"—he paused for half a breath—"please."

This was when she should be putting one foot in front of the other.

Right.

Left.

Right.

Left.

Right to the safety of her glammed-up RV. She might even—translation: definitely would—break into the welcome basket of alcohol and hope that in the morning she wouldn't remember any of tonight's awkward humiliations.

Yeah, good luck with that, Theadora Eloise Pope.

Fine, she'd go raid Jackie's booze stash, too. Maybe even her mom's. Seriously. It was gonna take a crate of sponsored vodka to make her forget tonight.

Instead of doing any of that, though, she let herself get tugged around by some invisible string so she was facing Kade.

He was standing now and had shoved his hands into the pockets of his jeans as the breeze coming down off the mountains ruffled his dark hair. She'd needed the heat from the fire a few minutes ago, but when one side of Kade's mouth moved three whole fractions of an inch higher on one side in what was probably his version of an encouraging smile, getting any warmer was the last thing on her mind.

"Tell me your plan," he said.

Plan?

She had a plan?

Well, usually yes. That was kinda her thing. Schedules and planners and ten-point agendas were her happy place. But now? She was flying by the seat of her pants, and she had no fucking clue what was supposed to happen next.

Unsettling? Try clammy-palms-and-heart-palpitations petrifying.

He let out a little scoff of a chuckle, and the corner of his upturned mouth went up a little bit higher. "Were you proposing a friends-with-benefits situation?"

"I was, but we aren't friends," she said, the words coming out before she could stop them. "So acquaintances with benefits for the night."

Thea snapped her jaw shut faster than a mousetrap.

Yeah, little too late with that one.

Kade cocked his head to the side and shot her an indulgent, crooked smile. "Does that mean we *can't* be friends?"

Was he flirting?

With her?

Did he not understand she was already a sure thing? None of it made sense. When she tried to unravel the reason why the guy who looked like he knew exactly how to use only his thumb to grievously injure a man was sounding as if he was totally into being temporary friends with benefits, all she got was a brain full of white noise.

Well, that was a lie.

She had white noise and fantasies of him wearing only that cocky smile she'd seen outside of Jackie's trailer when he'd told her to keep his flask. The image sent a shiver of dirty delight through her, and she let out a shaky breath.

This was a bad idea.

This was absolutely tempting.

This was a my-sister-is-in-a-bridezilla-induced-temporary-insanity situation.

She wasn't gonna do this.

Or was she?

She shouldn't.

Then why in the hell did you propose a one-and-done anyway?

Because she was so damn tired of everyone just expecting her to smile nicely and accept whatever they offered. Because she wanted to stop being a welcome mat. Because she wanted to be the kind of woman who saw what she wanted and went for it. Because she wanted to win just this once so she'd know what it felt like. She'd wanted all of those things for her entire life and had never even gotten close. Well, that stopped now. Thea Pope was going to make her dream come true.

Maybe.

If she could get up the courage.

Four steps.

That's all that was between them. Her gaze went from his mouth to his broad shoulders, to the way his T-shirt did nothing to hide the fact that he was as solid as a brick house, to the way his jeans hung to his hips and—

Was that the outline of a very nicely proportional thick dick pressing against the denim?

Sure, it *could* be a trick of the flickering lights from the firepit or her imagination or wishful thinking.

Or it could be real and that meant he was thinking all of the naked, sweaty, orgasmic things she was, which meant maybe he kinda liked her, too, and then—

Thea shook her head, scattering the cacophony of her thoughts and grasping tight on the only way she could imagine this working. *Yeah, maybe you should have thought about the logistics before you asked in front of the entire world if he wanted to get an anger bang out of their systems.*

That was true, but that didn't mean it was too late. She could make this happen. She had to make this happen. All they needed to do that were three things: parameters, rules, and clear expectations.

And by *they*, she meant herself, because this way lay danger. She could feel it like a dark current under the desire rushing through her.

In another century, Kade would have been the rakish smuggler getting women from one end of the coast to the other to toss good sense and their reputations aside along with their skirts. Totally her fictional catnip. In real life? Even the idea of speaking to someone like Kade made her break out in a cold sweat.

Oh. My. God. Thea. Pull it together.

She let out a steadying breath. Fight. Flight. Fawn. Freeze. She had an option, if she was brave enough to take it.

And she really wanted to be.

"No personal information," she said, barely recognizing her voice as she took an appreciative glance at his substantial inseam before moving down toward Kade's scuffed boots. "No connecting," she continued, wishing like hell she could squash the nervous squeak in her tone. "Just for fun tonight."

Wow. That sounds so sexy. How could he ever resist, Thea?

"With orgasms?" he asked, not bothering to hide the laughter in his voice.

Heat that made the face of the sun seem downright arctic blasted up from her toes, and she looked back up at him. "Preferably."

For a second, he didn't say anything. He just stared at her like he was skeptically weighing his options as the fire crackled and somewhere in the distance a coyote howled. Finally, he let out a weary sigh and shot her a look that veered waaaaay too close to pity for Thea not to flinch.

"No offense, but..." He paused, obviously giving her a chance to brace herself for what was coming next. "This doesn't exactly seem like it's your usual MO. Are you sure this is the kind of thing you're into? You seem more like a roses-and-rosé kind of woman, maybe strip Scrabble on a wild night."

Strip.

Scrabble.

Thea had no idea why, but the fact that it *did* sound so much like her version of a too-freaky-for-words good time scraped against the inside of her heart—because it might be who she seemed like, but it wasn't who she *wanted* to be.

She didn't want to be the center of attention like her sister. She didn't want to be a Machiavellian momager like her mother, always looking for the next big move. But that didn't mean she wanted to be overlooked, underestimated, and dismissed for the rest of her life.

She wanted to be seen, respected, and valued. And that realization sparked a fire inside her, and suddenly she wasn't staring at Kade's boots anymore.

"Why?" she asked, taking two steps toward him, her whole body vibrating with a million tiny jolts of badassery she didn't even know were inside her that had totally surprisingly flickered to life. "Is it because I don't look like I'm ready for my close-up like the rest of the bridesmaids?"

He raised an eyebrow in question. "More like because I never knew someone could blush so much that it was visible in the dark."

"I'm not blushing," she said, desperate to hold onto that sizzling, powerful feeling inside her that had already started to ebb. "I'm overheated from the fire."

"Really?" Dubious didn't begin to describe the doubtful look on his face. "Look, you seem like a nice, sweet woman, but—"

And at that moment, all of the buzzy lines of electric need and want and determination to really go after it and put herself first for once crashed together, and she was surprised the air didn't smell like a summer thunderstorm.

What he was doing right now was what always happened to her. People always thought she was sweet and nice and not to be taken seriously because she had always let them.

Not any more.

Theadora Eloise Pope was going to be the woman she'd always secretly wanted to be—starting right now.

"I am not sweet, and I am not nice," she declared—okay, she was, but that didn't mean she had to be everyone's favorite pushover for the rest of her life.

She cleared the space between them in half a breath, her heart hammering against her ribs as adrenaline and desire raced through her body. Standing toe to toe with him, she looked up at Kade, taking in his crooked nose, square jaw, and the unconvinced look in his eyes, and did the last thing anyone who knew her would expect.

She kissed him.

Chapter Seven

Every single thought in Kade's head went poof the instant Thea's lips crushed against his, except for one: she sure as hell didn't kiss like a woman who'd spent most of their conversation staring at his boots.

The asshole that he was, he'd figured any kiss with her would be hesitant at best and an awkward clash of teeth at worst. He hadn't been so wrong since he bet Americans' true-crime obsession would be satiated when all the Netflix documentaries started streaming.

Thea Pope kissed like a woman determined to prove the world wrong.

Her fingers were in his hair, holding tight as if to keep him in place. Oh yeah, she didn't need to worry about him going anywhere. He may have fooled himself into thinking she was too quiet and shy to really mean what she said about having an acquaintances-with-benefits thing, but he knew better now. He'd have to be stone-cold dead to miss that fact when her soft lips were glued to his like they were sharing oxygen on their way up from the depths of the ocean.

Thea was all in—and so was he.

The realization severed whatever this-probably-isn't-a-good-idea ties had been holding him frozen in place. He deepened the kiss as he dropped his hands to her hips, pulling her tight to him. Fuck, she felt good, with her lush body pressed against his so close he could feel the hard, pointed tips of her nipples against his chest. She let out a soft moan and slid her hands down between them, setting off a line of crackling fire that went all the way to his hard cock.

Damn. It was always the quiet ones.

He should have known.

Don't get him wrong—the kiss, her touch, was hot as fucking hell at high noon during the dog days of summer, but there was more than a little something to be said for taking their time.

"Whoa," he murmured as he grabbed her southbound hands before they got to the top button of his jeans. "Is there a reason for the rush?"

She looked up at him, her eyes dark with lust and her lips kiss-swollen. "Is there a reason to go slow?"

"The fact that you just asked me tells me yes." He grinned at her. Oh, she was about to find out *all* the answer to that.

Annoyance flickered in her suddenly narrow-eyed gaze, and she stiffened in his arms. "Look, I'm not some tender virgin paleontologist. I have sex. I have toys. I masturbate in the shower with the shower handset on pulse."

The image of every one of her curves slick and soapy as she cupped her tits with one hand and directed the pulsating water toward her clit with the other came to him fully formed before he could take his next breath. Nothing he'd ever seen before or imagined had been so damn hot. Fucking A. He was burning up, and it took everything he had not to just go along with her plan for speed—but that wasn't going to happen. He wouldn't let it. A man who'd rush with a woman like Thea was a special kind of fool.

"There's more to great orgasms than just repetition," he said as he whirled her around so her sweet cushy ass nestled up against his cock.

The moment they made contact, he had to close his eyes against the rush of lust that blasted through him. Fuck. He let out a harsh breath and mentally grabbed hold of his wavering sense of control, steadying it again before he lost it.

The iron grip he always kept on himself was what made sex the perfect release—in no small part because of the mix of desire and denial that reinforced the rigid walls that compartmentalized his life. Work here. Play there. Family and friends over there.

Order had to be retained.

Always.

And no weeklong fuck fest with the bride's awkward, hot sister was going to change that—and it would be for the whole time they were here, whether she realized it yet or not. It was time to show her exactly how this was going to go.

He gave the area around them a quick scan for cameras and lurking production crew as he skimmed his palms over her hips and down the outside of her flowy skirt. Not spotting any—which was unlikely anyway, given how far past the staff-only barrier they were—he began bunching her skirt up, little by little, inching it upward as her breathing grew shaky. Meanwhile, he was having trouble remembering to breathe at all. There was just something about Thea that wound him up tighter than a metal spring.

Fighting against every overwhelming urge he had to just yank her skirt up or simply slip his hand underneath the hem, he continued achingly, slowly as he pictured her wet pussy swollen with desire. She may argue that she wasn't sweet, but he was willing to bet the advance on his next book contract that she tasted like honeyed heaven, and he couldn't wait to be proven right.

"Thea," he said against the sensitive spot behind her earlobe that smelled of fresh juicy peaches, cotton sheets straight out of the dryer, and unexpected trouble.

"Yes?" she said, the single word sounding more like a sigh than a response.

"You're a scientist, right?" Yeah, he'd been listening when she gave him that what-for.

She nodded.

"So what I'm proposing is an experiment," he said, stilling his hands even though it was the last thing he wanted to do. "We do things my way." He dropped a quick kiss behind her ear. "Take our time."

"Out here?" she asked, sounding more than a little interested.

He kissed his way down the side of her throat. "Yes, out here."

He could feel the war raging inside her as lust battled with the risk of getting caught by another wedding guest, by the cameras, by someone from the resort. This was when he should step back and give her space to make up her mind. Normally he would have, but there was something about being with Thea out here in the middle of nowhere with only the stars for company as the fire crackled behind them that took him somewhere he didn't normally go, someplace a little less controlled than usual.

So as she battled her better angels, he started raising her skirt again at a torturously deliberate pace until the cool mountain breeze that never seemed to stop blowing brushed against her now exposed panties. Resisting every single instinct yelling for him to do otherwise, he stopped moving, breathing, and even fucking thinking. The rest of everything and everyone else tied to this ridiculous wedding from hell disappeared. There were just the two of them on the edge. And just when he was about to get lost in the heat and the want and the anticipation of it all, she let out a needy, desperate groan. Not answering that sound with a touch, a kiss, a reason for her to make it again was a punch to the gut, but he stayed the course.

"If you'll let me," he said, holding tight to the material

of her skirt bunched in his hands, "I'll show you exactly how good it can feel to draw all of this out, to give yourself time to anticipate, to need, to be desperate for what comes next."

She pushed her hips back, grinding her ass hard against his dick. "Kade."

"That's not a yes."

He moved his right hand from her skirt to the inside of her smooth thigh, just resting it there and letting her feel the heat of his touch as she imagined what he'd do next. Giving her time to think up the possibilities, he skated along the line of too much and not enough.

She moved to turn in his arms, to face him, but he slid his left arm across her waist, holding her in place. Her skirt dropped down, covering his hand on her thigh.

"Uh-uh-uh," he said. "You said nothing personal, only acquaintances. You already kissed me once. Any more and that would start to feel very personal."

"I can kiss without it being more," she said, sounding almost sure of herself.

"Maybe I can't."

She stilled against him, and he held his breath, waiting to see what she'd do next. One. Two. Three heavy heartbeats. Then she took one arm and covered his arm around her waist before lowering her other hand and slipping it to the side of her skirt to cover his on her thigh.

Thea peeked over her shoulder at him. "Yes."

Thank. Christ.

"Spread your legs, Thea."

She did, her body relaxing against his as she rested the back of her head against the pocket of his shoulder. Yeah, that wasn't going to do. Not at all. He glided his hand up her inner thigh, getting within an inch of her damp heat and then sliding away before repeating the move again and again as she tensed with need in his arms. Instead of giving her what she obviously wanted, though, he took his time, relishing the feel of her against him and the way she rubbed her ass against his hard dick as he teased her.

Was he an asshole for toying with her like this? Yeah, he was, but she'd thank him for it—not right away, but eventually.

Thea groaned with frustration when he came within a hairsbreadth of the damp center of her panties yet again.

"Enough." She used her hand on top of his to urge him higher, to try to get him to touch her, to sink his fingers inside her.

"Now now, Thea," he said, holding firmly away from her sweet pussy. "We are in the middle of an experiment."

She closed her eyes and let out a frustrated sigh. "You're horrible."

"Yes." He dipped his head down close to her ear. "But you're not nice, either. You said so yourself."

"This experiment can work both ways, you know," she said, sounding as if she almost just might mean it. "I could torture you with slowness, too."

The laugh burst out before he could stop it. She narrowed her eyes over her shoulder at him but didn't move away. Yeah, she knew the truth of the situation, too.

"No lies between acquaintances with benefits," he said. "We both know you're too impatient for that." He traced a circle on her inner thigh with his fingertip. "You're hungry for that orgasm." She squirmed against him, rocking back against his aching cock. "You want to have it hard and fast and now, but you're going to have to wait." He stilled his finger. "I'm gonna make you savor everything that comes before, during, and after. I'm gonna leave you wrung out and sated."

"Big promises," she said, her voice low and breathy.

He chuckled. So much for the woman who turned tomato red when discussing their mutually beneficial arrangement and spent way too much time staring at his boots as they talked. It seemed there was a little spice to all of Thea Pope's sweetness. She hid it well, but there was more to her than she let most people see. Fuck, she probably didn't even realize he'd gotten a peek, but it was hard to shield things when all you could think about was coming.

He glided his fingertips an inch or so higher on her inner thigh before stopping again. "But you want me to deliver on those big promises, don't you, Thea?"

She let out a needy moan as she encircled his wrist and then tried to pull his hand up toward her hot core. She didn't get far. Hell, he didn't let her nudge him an inch.

"You can have that. I'll give it to you," he said, his voice rough as a wave of lust rushed through him. "I'll push my way under those wet panties of yours. They are wet, aren't they?"

He waited for her to nod in agreement before he went on. "I'm going to circle that clit of yours so softly you are gonna want to kill me, but don't worry, the pressure will increase with each rotation until it's just right. And the only thing you'll be able to feel or think about is my fingertips. You're going to be so slippery, so soft. I just know it. I won't be able to resist sinking my fingers inside you, plunging them in deep, and filling you up."

Fuck, he could picture her, feel her, smell her sweetness so vividly that he was ready to abandon his plan and sink balls deep into her right now. It took him a couple of deep breaths, but he got himself back on track before he gave into temptation.

"Don't worry, though. I'm going to rub the heel of my palm against that hard clit of yours. Eventually, I'm going to finger-fuck you just right, just the way you want, and you're going to come all over my hand so hard you're going to feel it in these cute ears of yours." He nipped her earlobe. "So now that you know exactly how big my promise is. Tell me, Thea, are you ready for me to deliver?"

Chapter Eight

Thea's legs were trembling, and she'd lost any sense of time or place or who she was. All she knew was that Kade St. James was pure evil.

Was she ready for him to deliver? As if anyone could on those kinds of sinful promises. But still, she couldn't help but hope like hell that he really would.

"Yes," she said.

In the next breath, she was in the air, one of Kade's arms around the small of her back and the other behind her knees as he carried her in a fireman's hold over to one of the lounge chairs by the firepit. Her body was trying to regain her equilibrium, but her brain had speeded ahead into speculation mode.

Was he a firefighter? That would explain the smooth-skinned burn scar she'd felt on the back of his strong hand when she'd tried to move it up her thigh earlier.

Not that it mattered.

Not that she wanted to know.

Not that she could stop thinking about it, him, them, or this ridiculous plan of hers.

Her mind spun, racing toward the possible outcomes of this one rash decision. There were so many. Her mom's disappointed reaction. Her sister's fury. The fallout that would come from her boss at the museum when he found out about the live stream—and he would find out. All of the negative results built one on top of another in her mind like a fast-paced game of Tetris, and she couldn't keep up. Her rushed breathing and the way her heart started beating faster and faster had her feeling like she was going to jump out of her skin.

"Thea," Kade said, pulling her out of the overthinking hell she'd put herself in as they sat down on the lounge chair with her on his lap, his arms loosely holding her in place. "Are you okay?"

"I'm fine."

There it was, that word again. Somewhere, she was sure Dr. Kowecki shivered as if a ghost had walked over her grave.

"You don't seem fine." He looked down at her, his eyes narrowing. "You look like you're about to sprint to Mars."

"I'm. Fine."

He scooped her up off his lap and plopped her onto the lounge chair's pale blue cushion as far as she could get from him as he sat on the end.

"Nope." He picked up her foot and pulled off the Keds she'd been wearing, taking her foot in his warm, strong hands. "You're not."

She would have argued, but that's when his thumb pressed against the top of her arch and she couldn't stop the moan of pleasure that came out instead of her protestations.

"What are you doing?"

"Taking my time."

A what-the-fuck-is-going-on giggle escaped. "This is all part of slow orgasms one-oh-one?"

"Something like that."

Her eyes fluttered shut along with her mouth as he rubbed her foot, the pressure—hard in some places and a feather-soft touch in others—unwinding all of the tension that had balled up inside her as her brain went wild with one thought after another. By the time he tugged off her other shoe, she was beyond pliant. She was goo—straight-up, blissed-out goo. Oh, her brain was still trying to do its thing, throwing out intrusive thoughts like poisoned darts, but they fizzled into the ether before hitting their mark.

"I shouldn't like this so much," she said.

"Why not?"

"Because I'm being lazy, just taking."

"And you think that makes you selfish?"

How she managed the energy to nod, she had no idea, but she did just the slightest bit.

"Maybe watching is what really turns me on," he said, his voice low and growly. "Maybe seeing you get all hot and then all melty and then turning up the heat again is what makes my cock so fucking hard."

Suddenly, the heat coming from the small, contained blaze in the pit felt like a firestorm. The images this man could paint in her head—it really wasn't fair. He had tapped into some level of lust she hadn't realized was there but damn did it feel good.

"Is that really what turns you on?" she asked before she could stop herself, because she was desperate to know the answer.

"Partly." He switched to her other foot and went to work easing all of the tension she hadn't even realized was balled up in the arch of her foot and the base of her toes and along the side of her heel.

God. She was immobile at this point. It was just one wave of warm, melty unwinding yes after another. All of this from a man she knew next to nothing about beyond that her sister hated him. Never mind the usual background deep dives she did on other guys before even agreeing to coffee. Yeah, she had a special spreadsheet for that.

She tilted her chin down, moving her gaze from the million stars to the rough-hewn face of Kade St. James. "Are you a firefighter?"

"No personal information, remember?" he said, shooting her a teasing grin before turning his attention back to her foot to give it one last long, hard stroke. "Okay, Thea Pope, are you still just fine?"

"No. I'm so much better." Fine may never be in her vocabulary again.

His hand moved up from her foot to her calf in a leisurely tease of motion. "Should I stop?"

Even the idea of that had her ready to scream in frustration. "No."

"Are you sure?"

Her gaze locked on those bright-blue eyes of his, and she knew in an instant that even the slightest bit of hesitation would end this whole interlude.

"Yeah. I'm sure."

He let go of her and stood up, then sat back down straddling the chair so he was facing her, spread her legs, and then draped them across him so her calves rested on his muscular thighs. He didn't look at her at first, just stared at her legs as he glided his fingertips over her skin as if he was as tossed into the craziness of the moment as she was.

His gaze traveled up over her skirt still covering her thighs. He stopped for a moment on the strip of bare belly because her white T-shirt had worked its way up her abdomen. It took everything she had not to cover that inch-wide path with her arm before he noticed how the skin was puckered and squished by the band of her skirt. Before she could, though, he reached up and tugged down on the side zipper, not enough to undo her skirt completely but enough that the waistband stopped pinching her tender flesh. He brushed the pad of his thumb over the red mark, then leaned forward and dropped a barely-there kiss on the spot.

He lifted his head, a fierce look on his face. Then, before

she had a chance to translate that look, he moved with a swiftness that showed just how much control he had when he was delivering his slow, hot torture. He grabbed the hem of her skirt and shoved it up to her waist, leaving her bare from there down except for her *Always The Bridesmaid* panties.

Looking up at her, his jaw tight and his eyes dark with lust, he gave her that cocky one-sided grin of his. "That's the last bit of fast for a while."

"Meanie."

"You'll be calling me more than that before I'm done with you," he said. "Now close your eyes."

It was like when he told her to turn around earlier. She didn't have to listen to him, she didn't have to do what he said, but here she was, letting her eyelids shut as a shiver of anticipation shot through her.

His touch was the best kind of torment as he took a lazy path up her legs. He stopped to trace a circle on the sensitive skin on the inside of her knees before moving up and gliding his fingertips over her thighs. At first, it was just the outside, but then he crossed over to the front and dipped down to skim a soft touch over the small watercolor Pterodactylus tattooed above her right knee.

"What dinosaur is this?" he asked as he traced the lines.

"None. It's a flying reptile."

"So this didn't evolve into a bird?"

She shook her head. "Nope."

He traced the rest of the flock flying up her thigh before disappearing around her hip. "You're full of surprises, aren't you?"

Then he followed the line of her panties from her hip to the center of the now desperately damp cotton. She lifted her hips up off the chaise, desperate for him to touch her.

"So impatient."

"Please, Kade." Beg? Her? She was ready to do that and

so much more if he would just touch her where she wanted.

He glided the back of a knuckle over the center of her panties. It wasn't all that she wanted, but it was more than he was giving her before. She gripped the iron arms of the lounge chair, her hold tight enough that the beveled edge ate into the palm of her hand. Still, he moved so slow, drawing out the anticipation of each touch until all she could focus on was the hope that this time, he'd give her exactly what she wanted.

"Kade," she half groaned, half whined when he gave her clit the briefest caress before moving on.

"God, you have the prettiest mouth," he said, making it sound like a promise he'd cross a desert on foot to fulfill. "I cannot wait to see those pink lips wrapped around my cock later."

Even more amped-up desire slammed into her, rough and hard and sudden. Fuck. Just when she thought she couldn't be more on edge, that mental image flashed into her mind and she nearly came just from the idea of it. And that's when he finally tugged the center of her panties aside and touched her bare flesh for the first time.

He let out a harsh breath. "Look at how fucking gorgeous you are. So wet. So pretty. So ready for me."

He pushed two fingers inside her, stroking the bundle of nerves just along the entrance while he made leisurely circles around her swollen clit, moving at such a deliberate pace that she couldn't breathe, couldn't think, couldn't do anything but beg him for more.

"I cannot wait to hook your legs up on my shoulders so I can feast on you. Fuck, Thea. I'm going to lick that sweet pussy of yours until your thighs are shaking and you're cursing me to hurry up and make you come."

She was going to explode into a million pieces. That was all there was to it. Between the intensity of feeling his fingers filling her up as he stroked her clit and the pictures he was building in her head with those promises, she wasn't sure if she was coming or going, alive or dying, about to see heaven or sinking into hell. She was all of it and none of it all at the same time.

"Kade," she said, fighting to get his name out because forming coherent thought seemed beyond her. "Please."

"It's okay. I got you."

And he did. It wasn't that the speed changed so much as the pressure increased as he circled her clit and plunged inside her, hitting every sensitive spot over and over again as the bliss built inside her, until it refused to be denied and she came, her orgasm sweeping through her like a giant rogue wave, demolishing every thought and every feeling except the pleasure.

She was still trying to remember who and where she was beyond one very happy woman when Kade dropped her skirt back into place and stood up, moving very fast for a man so devoted to being slow.

"That's it?" she asked, blinking as she tried to process the change when her brain was just so much satisfied white noise.

"Not by a long shot," he said, looking around as if he, too, had forgotten where they were, "but the experiment is to take our time. Remember?"

Every part of her screamed no. She was primed, perched on the edge, and more than ready to have a toe-curling, make-the-whole-world-go-blank orgasm right the fuck now. But it was fine. Just fine. Totally fine.

The fuck it is, the voice in her head snapped. *You know how an experiment works, and this isn't it. So stand up for yourself and ask for what you want.*

Thea swallowed past the nerves and forced herself to look up at Kade. He was sucking her juices off his fingers, and *holy shit* add the look absolute ecstasy on his face to her list of kinks.

"You've forgotten the other part of an experiment," she said as she sat up, not sure where she'd found this confidence. Great orgasms did that to a woman, she supposed. "We're testing a hypothesis, right?"

He nodded, watching her like a man who was making plans—deliciously dirty plans. "Yeah."

Letting out a steadying breath, Thea looked him straight on. "So that means we need a control group."

One of his eyebrows went up, but he stepped closer, not stopping until he was standing between her spread legs. "And that would be?"

"The option where we go fast." She raised her hand and let her fingers brush against the top button of his jeans.

"It's been a long time since I've taken any science classes, but that doesn't seem all there is to it."

She popped open the button and lowered his zipper. "Wyoming reality wedding from hell rules."

He chuckled, a low rumbly easy sound that belied the dark intensity in his eyes. "We'd be finding out for science."

She fought to concentrate enough to answer, since lust was making forming words so damn hard. "Exactly."

He cupped the side of her face, his thumb tracing the line of her mouth, dipping inside. Desire, hot and liquid, spread through her as if she hadn't just climaxed a few minutes ago, as if she hadn't come in years. He grabbed her wrist, pulling her hand away from his parted jeans and the hard dick she was so close to freeing.

"So we go fast, huh?"

She nodded. Doing more was an impossibility. She wanted it too bad. Her whole body, every nerve, every sensitive spot, every inch of her all focused on him as he pulled his wallet out of his pocket. While he fished out a condom, she laid back on the wide lounge chair, determined to memorize every moment of this.

"Spread your legs," he said, nearly growling out the order. When she complied, he let out a short hiss of breath. "Lift your skirt."

Again, she complied without hesitation, some part of her knowing that this was exactly what she needed and definitely what she wanted. When he shoved his jeans down and freed his hard dick, her breath caught. Kade St. James had every reason to be cocky. Thick and long, it was mouthwatering.

He rolled on the condom, his intense gaze focused on her wet panties. "Take them off."

Thea didn't have to be asked twice. She wasn't just entranced—she was obsessed. She lifted her hips and slid them down her legs before spreading them wide again. The sound he made was the stuff dirty fucking fantasies were made of, and she shivered in the best way possible. He nudged off his boots and got rid of his jeans and boxers like a man who'd never heard the words meander, dawdle, or hesitate.

Then, his hot gaze moved up her body as he grabbed her ankles and pulled her flat on the chaise before getting between them and sinking into her inch by glorious, thick inch. Yeah, she'd had every intention of going fast, but there was too much of him for that. He was forced to take his time, but once he was inside her, filling her completely, all bets were off.

Keeping her eyes closed so she could concentrate on the feeling of being split like this, she lifted and undulated her hips, fucking him from below him and taking him deeper before easing back and letting him almost slip out. Over and over again she took him in, tilting her body so her clit rubbed against him as he met her every move.

"Fuck yes," Kade groaned, his hands grasping her hips and pushing himself deeper inside her. "Take all of that."

Yes, thank you, she very much would. Again. And again. And again. Until she was right on the edge of coming again, her core tightening in anticipation before an electric bolt shot through her as she climaxed hard.

Kade's grip tightened, and he plunged into her once, twice, three more times before burying himself as deep as possible and coming.

Ten minutes, an hour, six lifetimes later, Kade pulled out and stood up while Thea slowly came back to herself. Reality rushed back in like an avalanche. How in the hell could she have totally forgotten about the fact that there were other people on the planet, let alone that a good percentage of the ones closest to them were armed with cameras live streaming every moment of the wedding? The very last thing she needed was to have the production team find her with her skirt up after coming so hard her toes curled—again. Yeah, her boss at the museum would really love that.

"It's okay. We're still alone," Kade said as he tossed the condom in a nearby trash can and then helped her up. "Let's get you back to your RV."

They got dressed and made it back down the stony path to the guest section of the resort, making sure to keep to the dark part of the walkway when they passed the barn, which was still lit up with music and laughter pouring out of the open windows. Keeping an eye out for stray cameras, they wound around to the back of the RVs where the bridal party was staying.

Her legs still shaky from the orgasms and the fact that she really just did that, Thea walked up the three metal steps to her RV and opened the door. Before walking inside, though, she turned, suddenly nervous about what she was supposed to do next. Did she kiss him? Give a cavalier "see ya, hot stuff"? Run inside without saying anything?

Thea had no clue. Announcing she was up for a hate fuck

in front of a room full of cameras and then getting fingered while still fully dressed and laying on a lounge chair before having toe-curling sex wasn't exactly her usual Saturday night, let alone a Monday night, which it actually was.

Thank God for small favors, though, because she didn't have to figure out what happened next. Kade made short work of the two steps behind her, wrapped her ponytail around one fist, and pulled her head to the side before proceeding to kiss the sensitive spot where her shoulder and neck met, sending a lightning burst of desire through her. Then, almost as fast as he started, he stopped and looked down at her with such an intense desire in his eyes that she was surprised she didn't combust.

"Unless I read things wrong, you had fun. I sure as hell had fun. I think we should continue the experiment. Who knows, it may take until the wedding at the end of the week to figure out if slow and intense or fast and dirty is better."

"You're saying we have an obligation to science?"

"Exactly." He tucked a hair behind her ear. "So what do you say?"

She didn't even have to think about it. "Yes."

"See you tomorrow, Thea Pope," he said with a wink, and then walked down the steps and started down the dimly lit path toward the groomsmen's RVs.

Did she watch him until he disappeared into the night? Hell yeah. That was an ass a person didn't look away from. Then she walked inside the RV, flopped down on the bed, and shoved the frothy pink bridesmaid dress off the comforter and to the floor. Oh, she'd no doubt hear about how she'd stolen the spotlight (even if unintentionally) from her sister tomorrow, but tonight she'd bask in the unbearable anticipation of what was going to happen next.

Continue the experiment.

Yeah, that was definitely happening. She couldn't wait.

Chapter Nine

The next morning, Thea woke up to an insistent and uninterrupted banging on her RV's door.

"Open up, Thea!" Jackie hollered.

With a dose of what-the-fuck adrenaline rushing through her veins, she yanked a hoodie over her sleep tank and sprinted out of the tiny bedroom as all of the possible disasters that would have her sister pissed off that much ran through her head. As she rushed through the narrow living room, she cut a glance at the clock above the large window above the built-in couch. Seven in the morning? Oh God, this had to be bad. Jackie only ever rolled out of bed before ten if she was forced because she had to be on set.

Thea flung open the door to find Jackie standing there in oversize sunglasses, neon-pink leggings with a matching sports bra, a pissed-off expression that had etched deep lines between her eyes, and a full face of no-makeup makeup.

"Was this your whole goal?" Jackie snarled as she turned her phone around so the screen was facing Thea. "Really? During my wedding, you'd do this?"

"I thought we weren't supposed to have phones," Thea said, her panic jumbling up her brain.

"Yeah, I told them that wasn't happening," Jackie said with a huff. "And things like this are why."

Thea blinked a few times and wiped the sleep out of the corner of her eye as she peered at the screen. It was a post from Moxie Gossip:

FORMER CHILD STAR EARLY FAN FAVORITE IN WYOMING
WEDDING WACKINESS

She flinched back with secondhand offense. Yes, she was still pissed off at Jackie, but they were sisters, and that meant something. Jackie had hustled and fought for the past five years to move past being pigeonholed. Not to mention she was still working on a regular basis. She wasn't a former anything.

"You've done a lot since your child acting days, and they're a bunch of assholes for calling you that."

Jackie whipped off her sunglasses and shoved them into her hair. "They aren't talking about me, Thea. They are talking about *you*." She turned her phone around to face her and swiped across the screen before flipping it back around. "Look, you're all over the socials. Twitter fucking loves you. You're a trending sound on TikTok. And on Instagram, they're posting where-to-buy-it videos of your outfit. You. Are. Every. Where."

"What?" Thea twisted the hem of her oversize hoodie, more than ready to turtle up inside it. "No. That can't be right."

Jackie sucked her teeth and narrowed her eyes. "Oh, I'm a liar now?"

"That's not what I mean, I just—" She stopped herself in the middle of what would have been her usual placating speech to calm her sister down and get everything back onto an even keel.

She inhaled a deep breath and checked herself. Her heart was going a million miles an hour. Her palms were sweaty. She did *not* have mom's spaghetti all over her shirt, but that old anthem from Eminem was stuck in her head anyway because she was having those kinds of nerves. She let the song roll in her head for a bit, the steady beat keeping her from spinning out with the overthinker's urge to find each and every problem and a possible solution. She didn't need all of that. She had options. Fawn wasn't it. Freeze wasn't getting her anywhere. Flight? Yeah, in the middle of nowhere Wyoming with her sister (who was a lot stronger than she looked, thanks to multiple hardcore workout sessions a week) between Thea and freedom? Wasn't going to happen. That left fight. But did that mean battling, or could it just be standing up for herself?

She let out the breath she'd been holding and leveled a steady gaze at her sister.

"That's not fair, and you know it," she said, keeping her voice as steady as possible despite how much she was shaking on the inside. "I'm the last person to ever want any kind of headlines."

Okay, it was just a baby step to not wearing a metaphorical neon sign that said WALK ALL OVER ME, but it was enough forward momentum to have her lungs so tight it was like she'd just sprinted up a flight of stairs. In a horror movie. With a headless ghoul hot on her heels.

Jackie opened her mouth, no doubt with a burning hot retort that was going to leave Thea a pile of ashes. But instead of slinging flaming hot sarcasm, her sister just closed her mouth and let out a frustrated sigh.

"I know," Jackie said almost apologetically, her shoulders sinking. "I gotta go talk to Mom. We have a lot riding on this, and she'll know a way to recenter things."

Without waiting for any kind of response, her sister turned and started toward their mom's RV while Thea told herself that all of this would blow over. Everyone was having a good laugh at the dorky paleontologist who obviously didn't fit in making a fool of herself. All she needed to do was stay away from the cameras for a while. Then, the producers would go back to focusing on Jackie and Dex as the happy couple, and Thea could remain in the background like she always wanted and where she needed to be to stay off her boss's radar at the museum so he didn't yank her permission to go on the dig after the wedding.

Easy fix.

She was about to go back inside her RV to hunker down for the day when Jackie stopped mid-stride and turned back to face Thea. Her sister lifted her hand to her forehead to block out the sun as if she didn't still have her ginormous sunglasses on her head.

"Don't even think of flaking out on the hike this morning," she said, smacking her gum with gusto. "All of the bridesmaids have to go, and if you don't show up the only question anyone will have is where you are."

Thea bit back a groan. The hike. So much for hiding out from the cameras. "I'll be there."

Jackie stared at her as she blew a humongous bubble and then slid her sunglasses down into place before walking away.

This was just perfect. Flight was pretty damn tempting right about now. But Thea had made a commitment to be a part of this wedding, and she was going to keep it, even if her sister never wanted her there in the first place.

What F-word stress response was petty stubbornness? Fuck-you-ity? Yeah, that's what she'd be going with today.

An hour later, she was in the eighties-theme-compliant neon-green workout gear that matched all of the other bridesmaids. Unlike Jackie in her blindingly bright neon leggings and sports bra, though, she and the grumbling bridesmaids were in high-cut leotards over shiny leggings with a cropped sweatshirt that hung off one shoulder. They looked like Jackie's backup singers in a demented new wave cover band.

Forget fuck-you-ity—flight seemed the much better

choice right now. Before she could figure out how to fake an illness, however, the air shifted as someone moved to stand next to her. A big someone who came up so close to her that her hip was right up against his.

"If you go anywhere and leave me alone with these jokers wearing *this*," Kade said, his gravelly voice sending a shiver of anticipation through her, "I will find a way to get my revenge—one you'll love and hate at the same time."

She pivoted so she could take in what he was wearing that had annoyed him so much.

A better woman would have kept the grin off her face. Thea was not that woman.

Kade was wearing a tight white tank and a pair of bright-yellow short shorts with white piping around the edges that showcased his hard, muscular thighs to perfection. That was the first thing she noticed about his shorts. Then her brain processed the fit. They were tight, hugging his ass and leaving absolutely nothing to the imagination about what he was packing in his jockeys—there was no way he could wear anything else without it showing so the only other option possible was free-balling, which in those shorts was just asking for a wardrobe malfunction.

Was it wrong to be both hopeful and afraid at the same time? Because she totally was. Yeah, she was a bad person. She could live with that.

"You are wearing underwear, aren't you?" she asked, blurting out the question before she could stop herself.

He raised an eyebrow, his gaze dropping to her mouth a half second before he reached out and tucked a stray hair from her side ponytail behind her ear, gliding his fingertips ever so slowly down the side of her neck. "Of all the things you could say right now, that's what you gave the go-ahead to?"

Her lungs tightened as she tried to remember what in

the fuck they were talking about when her whole body was tingling with awareness. Kade. Wedding. Eighties workout clothes. That was it!

"They're tiny shorts," she managed to get out, her gaze dropping to the baseball cap he held in his free hand.

"Don't remind me," he grumbled. "They make me look like an asshole. I think your sister took her revenge for the fact that she despised me on sight by ordering my clothes a size smaller than needed."

"No way. That would only get you more camera time," Thea said, knowing that would be the last thing her sister would ever want to share. "I know I'd have a hard time looking away if I was watching at home."

He hooked a finger under her chin and tipped her face so she had to look him in the eye. "And here?"

Oh, God. The man could be wearing a burlap bag and she wouldn't be able to avert her eyes.

Do not say that out loud, Thea! Try to maintain a little bit of dignity here.

Luckily for Thea, a group of crew members picked that moment to show up, saving her from herself.

"All right, people, we gotta take some group shots for the socials, and then it's lights, camera, action," said Justine, the producer, looking way too comfortable in her hiking boots, T-shirt, and loose-fitting khakis. Her attention landed on Kade and Thea. "You two, in the center."

Everyone stopped and turned to look at Thea and Kade. They were not friendly, happy looks. Thea's gut dropped. Kade intertwined his fingers with hers and squeezed her hand.

Thea looked around, swallowing past the lump of oh-fuck clogging her throat. "Shouldn't that be Jackie and Dex?"

"They'll be in the chairs right in front of you," Justine said, not looking up from her phone. "We let the live stream viewers pick the photo arrangement. They wanted you two in the middle."

"Let's just do it and get it over with," Kade said as he put on his baseball cap, a grim expression on his face.

"Going along to get along?" she asked. "Don't tell me you're a fan of the fawn response."

He flashed that crooked grin of his at her and wrapped an arm around her waist, pulling her against his side. "Figure the sooner we're done, the sooner we can get back to our experiment. Are we trying fast or slow today? We really should have made a schedule."

The flush of desire he invoked was almost enough to negate the sea of acid swishing in her stomach from a mix of guilt and embarrassment as they walked over to their spot behind Jackie and Dex. If she'd been in court, she would have testified that everyone around them could take one look at her and know exactly what she was thinking, what she'd done last night, and how much she was looking forward to doing even more. Dr. Kowecki would no doubt tell her that she was overthinking things, and she wouldn't be wrong. They were surrounded by people intent on being the center of attention. The last thing the group of actors was probably thinking about as they turned it on for the cameras was Thea.

Still, she couldn't seem to shut off her brain, even with all of the images Kade had inspired last night that had led to a very sleepless, hot-and-bothered kind of night. What if someone noticed?

"Careful there, Dr. Dino," Kade murmured, his palm settling on the small of her back, making her skin sizzle with desire. "I wouldn't want to have to kiss that shocked look right off your face in front of everyone."

Oh God, she wanted that and she didn't—she just didn't know a damn thing anymore.

Pulling herself together, she whispered back, "No more

kissing, remember?"

His hand slid lower until he was cupping her ass. "I'll make up for it in orgasms."

Whatever she was going to say to that—what could she?—was silenced by the on-set photographer, who started telling everyone to give him happy, give him thrilled, give him the best time of their lives.

"And since you were curious," Kade said, leaning down so his lips brushed the sensitive shell of her ear while the photographer clicked away at his shutter. "I went commando."

Chapter Ten

Never in his life had Kade ever worried about flashing his nuts. Then again, he'd never worn anything this fucking short in his entire life. Chafing was a serious concern. It would have been a damn tragedy if the mandatory wedding fun hike had been an actual one. Instead, it was a made-for-Instagram quick trip up a well-worn trail to Black Bear Brewery.

The bridesmaids had been ordered to hang together toward the front, leaving Kade to spend the half-hour walk watching Thea from behind. It was not a hardship.

The woman had a great ass.

But he also clocked the cameras zoomed in on his reaction to her. Fuckers.

For him, this was all about figuring out whether he wanted to draw out her next orgasm like a slow build that finally broke like a summer storm or if he should make it hard and out of nowhere, because both would be fun as hell and the perfect way to spend a week that otherwise was a slice of pure evil.

For the production crew, however, the hike and the attention on Thea and him were all about the live-stream ratings and that sweet sweet ad money. Kade was about ready to drop the "Do I not entertain you" line when his internal oh-shit alert went off.

He was scanning the woods for a bear or another attacker and nearly missed it when Dex veered around the bridesmaids, bypassed his bride, and—under the watchful lens of the live-streaming camera—hustled over to a dark-haired woman standing on the brewery's pine front porch and threw his arms around her in a massive bear hug before picking her up and swinging her around.

Kade stopped dead in his tracks, his whole body going numb.

Even after fifteen years, Elenore St. James still looked almost the same as she did the last time he'd seen her. The same dark hair that matched his and Dex's, now mixed with some gray. The same blue eyes that, when focused on a person, made them feel like they were the only soul in the world who mattered. But her smile when she turned it on him at that moment? It was the same—exactly the same hesitant, hopeful smile he remembered. It was the one that would widen and fill the person she was smiling at with enough sunshine that they'd forget there had ever been gray days—unless, of course, that person was Kade.

He knew better.

He knew his mother's smile lied.

"Oh my God, this leotard is giving me the absolute biggest wedgie," Thea said as she hooked her arm through his and tore his attention away from the cute little mother-son reunion that made him want to puke.

And that's when the fact that there was a camera focused right on him registered. Oh yeah, there were two cameras getting every second of Dex and their mom, but Justine had one cameraperson zeroed in on him. No doubt she'd done her research on every member of the wedding party to wring as much drama as possible out of this wedding. Years of honing her skills as a reality TV producer had to have given her the ability to smell blood in the water. She knew which vein to cut to get the results she wanted.

But here was Thea, like a quickly applied Band-Aid to

stop the flow. How in the hell she'd known, he had no clue, but he wasn't about to fight the life raft she was offering.

"You have got to come over here so we can be the first ones to take the self-guided brewery tour." She tugged him away from the front of the brewery and over to the side of the log-cabin-like building where the other bridesmaids and groomsmen were gathering around a surly lumberjack-looking guy holding a tray of beer flights.

"Are they still following?" Thea asked, her voice barely a whisper.

Kade checked over his left shoulder and spotted the cameraperson sort of standing behind a tree. "Yeah."

"Well then, let's just start that tour." She all but dragged him through the door into what looked like a supersized garage filled with tanks, each decorated with an oversize sticker showing a bear in attack mode. No one else was in there—no doubt they were all dealing with the rest of the bridal party outside.

Thea peeked behind them once the door swung shut and let out a relieved sigh. "Mom let it slip that the brewery wouldn't let them film inside. You doing okay? Who was that? You looked like you were staring down the grill of a Mack truck."

"My mother," he ground out from between clenched teeth. "And as long as I don't have to come that close to her again for the rest of this week, I'll be just fine."

Seemingly unperturbed by his snarl, she crossed her arms and gave him a mock glare as she leaned against the wall. "Are you trying to steal my word?"

Her word? For a second, he wasn't sure what she meant, and then he remembered that she'd said it last night. Watching her unwind from her versions of "fine" had him up most of last night with his hand wrapped around his cock. It hadn't been enough. He took a step closer to her, leaving barely any space between them. The urge to touch her had his entire body hard with want and need. Lust, hot and demanding, rushed through him. Yeah, he wanted to go slow to really give Thea what she obviously needed, but it just might kill him from lack of blood to the brain.

"I'll take that word," he said, his voice low and raw with want, "if it means you can't say it ever again."

She bit down on her lower lip and looked up at him through her thick glasses. "You sound like my therapist."

He leaned closer, his hands pressed firmly against the wall on either side of her, letting her feel him without ever touching her at all. "That is definitely not what I was going for."

Color bloomed in her cheeks as he dipped his head down and she parted her lips, wetting them with the tip of her pink tongue. Fuck, this woman's mouth. It was hypnotic, and for the first time since he was a teen, he just wanted to kiss. He wanted to cover her mouth with his, tease her with his tongue, deepen the kiss, and keep going forever until they were both breathless and lost in each other. Not that his dick wasn't so hard his balls hurt in anticipation of doing a helluva lot more than just making out.

He was so close. Only a few inches and he'd be breaking their no-kissing rule. He didn't think Thea would object. Hell, she looked like she was ready to grab his shirt and yank him the rest of the way down.

He shouldn't.

But damn did he want to.

"Thea!" Jackie hollered. "There you are!"

Kade didn't jump back from Thea, but he straightened, putting a few inches of sunshine between them that felt like miles.

Jackie's gaze went from her sister to Kade to his undeniable hard-on pressed against the ridiculously small shorts. She made a gagging face.

"Oh my God. Really?" She rolled her eyes. "We are all waiting on you for the bridal shower. All of the bridesmaids, Mom, and my future mother-in-law have to be there. Come on, Thea, I gave you the schedule."

Jackie flounced out of the brewery, letting the door smack shut behind her, obviously expecting Thea to follow.

"Do you ever just want to tell her to fuck off?" he asked.

"All the time," Thea said, but then her expression softened. "But there's more to Jackie than just this bridezilla persona."

He shook his head, not seeing even a hint of that being true. "That's what Dex says, too, but I sure as hell haven't seen it."

Thea cocked her head to the side. "He's not wrong, and if she's actually shown him her soft underbelly, then maybe there's more to this wedding than a PR stunt."

He flinched. "God, I hope not. No offense to your sister, but getting married is about the worst thing a person can do. Do you know how many spouses kill each other every year?"

And that was on top of all the regular fights and problems—some of which he was lucky enough to witness before his mom left and after her abandonment with stepmoms one, two, three, and (until Dad passed away) four.

"Wow," she said, blinking in surprise. "You could have just gone with divorce rates, but murder ratchets things up a notch or twelve thousand."

Way to go, dumb-ass. Do you want to take her through the background information you learned for your last book that was too gruesome to publish while you're at it?

He grimaced. "Sorry."

She chuckled. "No worries. I better go, though." She ducked under his arm and headed for the door. "Are you sure you'll be okay?"

"I'll live." By himself. All alone. Him against the world. Just the way he fucking liked it.

That wouldn't pass the lie detector, buddy boy-O.

He shoved that know-it-all, unreliable narrator to the back of his head and stuffed a pillow over its mouth as he walked Thea to the door and the wedding hellscape that waited beyond it.

"So what's next for the groomsmen?" she asked as he opened the door.

He winced. "Horseback riding."

Her gaze did a slow dive from his face down to his thighs before she looked back up at him, one eyebrow cocked. "In those shorts?"

When his only response was a growl, she simply laughed and then braced her shoulders and walked out to face down a bridezilla.

• • •

Many, many—too many to fucking count—hours and two sore balls later, Kade lay sprawled out on the bed in his RV. He didn't have the energy to do much, but he did have enough to make himself two promises. One, he was never getting on a horse ever again—especially one named Nutbuster. Two, he was never going to let Dex lead a trail ride again. They'd ended up on the wrong side of the river on accident, but Kade had spotted camera men hiding behind a knot of huge tumbleweeds so he hadn't believed it.

Anything for the drama with these people.

But now Kade was happy as a writer on deadline in a cabin in the mountains with no distractions sitting by himself in his palace on wheels. Of course, that didn't mean he wasn't still thinking of Thea.

And he wasn't just stuck on how her ass looked in that

leotard or how her face had looked when he'd told her he was free-balling it before the pictures.

He couldn't stop thinking about the fact that she'd come to his rescue with his mom. No one did that. Dex would say that was because the only beings Kade didn't growl at were him and the dog, but his brother exaggerated. Kade usually just ignored everyone else. But Thea? Yeah, she was un-ignorable.

If she hadn't announced her wedgie condition in front of the cameras, God knew what would have happened. He didn't want a reunion with his mom at all, let alone while the cameras were catching everything.

He should thank Thea. It was just good manners.

Or excuses to talk to the sexy paleontologist.

After letting out a sigh of surrender, he picked up his phone, grabbed the call sheet with everyone's contact information on it, and punched in Thea's number.

KADE: *Did you know your kidney is worth around $160K on the black market?*

He hit send and then immediately wished he could recall the text.

Opening with that? What the fuck, man. What is wrong with you?

Oh, and to her, it was just coming from a random, strange number.

Wow. Way to go, shithead.

KADE: *This is Kade by the way.*

THEA: *Should I be worried? About my kidneys?*

He let out the breath he hadn't realized he was holding. She responded, and it wasn't with a "fuck you, weirdo." That was a good sign. Right?

KADE: *I'll protect you. Did you know people with DUI convictions in Ohio have to use yellow license plates?*

He hit send before he could stop himself.

Seriously, my dude, what is your major malfunction?

And why was his pulse going ninety miles an hour while his stomach felt like he was going over Niagara Falls in a wooden barrel? He was a grown man, not some teenage fool. He talked to women all the time without ever mentioning murder—okay, fine, there wasn't really a whole lot of talking going on with the women he hung out with, but that wasn't the point. Something about this wedding had broken his brain.

The three dots indicating she was texting back appeared and disappeared before a message finally showed up.

THEA: *Are you trying to flirt with me?*

KADE: *Depends.*

There you go. No mention of even a misdemeanor.

Baby steps, asshole. Baby steps.

KADE: *Is it working?*

THEA: *Maybe.*

He sat there grinning at his phone like a fool and then high-fived the air. Yes, he was immediately embarrassed by himself.

KADE: *Then yes.*

THEA: *Did you know that there have been more dinosaur fossils found in North America than on any other continent?*

He settled back in his bed, picturing Thea on her bed, with her glasses and an oversize T-shirt on. From an ex? No, he didn't like that.

KADE: *Did you know the elbow is the strongest point on your body, which is why you should use it if someone ever grabs you from behind?*

Maybe she was wearing a tank top—the kind that was so thin it was more of a tease than a cover-up—and those ridiculous bridesmaid panties from last night. One strap of her top would have slipped down off her shoulder, so she would have just given in and let it hang there. Yeah, he liked that. He liked that a lot.

THEA: *Good to know when it comes to keeping both my kidneys. Did you know that the Dreadnoughtus schrani is the biggest dinosaur ever?*

That sounded fake, but that was the thing about real life—it was often filled with more bullshit than fiction. That was part of the reason why he'd stayed on the nonfiction side of crime writing.

KADE: *Did you know managers commit more criminal offenses than hourly employees?*

THEA: *Did you know there are about 700 known species of extinct dinosaurs?*

KADE: *Wait, does that mean there are species of non-extinct dinosaurs? Are you telling me Jurassic Park is real?*

THEA: *If I answered that, I'd have to turn you into one of your crime stats. What's up with that, by the way? Are you some kind of investigator or attorney or something?*

He had to force himself not to respond with the truth. There was a reason why he didn't have chats with women he hooked up with. That's how people moved from the fuck-buddy section of his life to the something-more section. He didn't do that shit. He liked his life compartmentalized, with the lines well-drawn in permanent marker.

KADE: *No personal stuff, remember?*

THEA: *Exception to the rule because I already let it slip that I'm a paleontologist.*

She does have a point.
Shut up, brain.
And you want to tell her anyway.
Do not.
Then why are you typing?

KADE: *I write true crime.*

For a few minutes, his phone remained obnoxiously quiet. No incoming text vibrations. No rings. No nothing. He wasn't pissed. The conversation didn't matter anyway. And another thing—

His phone buzzed and his whole mood lightened in half a heartbeat.

Sucker.
Fuck off, brain.

THEA: *Holy shit. I just looked you up. Nice author photo.*

KADE: *Googling me is a rules violation.*

THEA: *So what are you going to do about it? ;)*

She just added in an emoji? And not even a full one but the weird kind where it was just punctuation? Like a boomer? And he was smiling?

Fuck me running. You are so screwed.

For once, he didn't have an argument to make with that annoying voice of reason.

KADE: *You'll find out tomorrow.*

THEA: *Don't remind me about morning yoga.*

KADE: *Better get your Zs, then.*

THEA: *I'm already all snuggled in.*

KADE: *Oh yeah? You're in your PJs?*

Too much? Not enough? He had no fucking clue, but his heart rate stayed jacked up while he waited for the fuck-you response that she was probably in the middle of composing.

THEA: *Like you earlier today, I'm commando. Night, Kade.*

Kade stared at his phone, hoping against reality that she'd send photographic proof of that, but he knew better.

He tossed his phone down onto the bed and then closed his eyes and pictured how she looked the other night with her legs spread, the way she'd bit down on her bottom lip as she came all over his fingers. Fuck. He grabbed his cock and started to stroke it when his phone buzzed next to him. Thea's name flashed on the screen, along with an alert of an incoming photo. Still holding his dick, he picked it up and swiped up to reveal a picture of Thea's bare leg curled around a twisted white sheet. He swiped and revealed a second picture showing a sheet draped across her naked hip with her hand wrapped around the material as if she was about to pull it back. Mouth dry and cock hard from anticipation, he swiped again, more than ready to see the next photo in the progression.

Instead of Thea, though, it was an animated T. rex covered in confetti, dancing to that old Rick Astley song. She'd Rickrolled him. Despite his and his cock's legit disappointment, he busted out laughing.

Oh, she'd pay for that tomorrow. Yoga was about to get a lot more interesting.

Chapter Eleven

The next morning, Thea thanked the synth-pop gods that she wasn't being forced to wear yoga gear from four decades ago. Instead, she walked out of her RV under the midmorning blue sky in her softest dinosaur-covered leggings and T-shirt decorated with a cartoon of a T. rex trying (and failing) to carry all of its grocery bags from the car to its house in one trip. Poor short-armed dino.

At least Kade would be there, she reminded herself as she started down the path from her RV to the designated yoga space. That would make being up this early with a bunch of people who did daily yoga a little more fun.

Her breath caught, and she stumbled over her own two feet, sending her off the asphalt path.

Wait. Why would Kade being there make a difference?

It shouldn't. It didn't. She just hadn't had coffee yet to bring her brain online. That was all.

After all, she didn't even *know* the guy. The whole point of their little agreement was that they were in a mutually beneficial situation—not a relationship, not even a possibility of that. They were simply participating in an experiment for the week.

Kade was a nice enough guy for a hookup, and that's all this was—nothing more.

Yeah, too bad the extra little spring in your step tells a different tale.

She sucked in a deep breath, counted to ten, and let it go as she shoved that little truth bomb back into the deepest, darkest corner of her brain, where it belonged.

She didn't know anything about Kade St. James. She didn't *want* to know anything about him beyond if his dick would feel just as good the second time. Period.

Come-to-Jesus conversation with herself completed, Thea got back on the path and followed the sound of people who were way too cheery before their caffeine fully kicked in.

The scent of lavender and rose oil hit her nostrils as soon as she made the final turn.

All of the bridesmaids and groomsmen were basking in the sun's yellow rays as they stretched on their mats. Unlike her dino yoga pants (which for the record were neither scientifically nor historically accurate but still made her giggle), everyone else was in modern-day custom workout gear emblazoned with the name of a chain of L.A.-based yoga studios that were color-coordinated with their personalized mats.

Thea looked down at her outfit that was coordinated by theme but definitely not color and the nondescript black yoga mat she'd grabbed from a production assistant. As if she didn't stand out already, this was just going to make it even worse. Great. Just great.

Jackie was off to the side, only a few steps from Thea, taking a long drink from her sparkly water bottle adorned with the word *Bride* in Swarovski crystals and the logo of a caffeinated water company, looking at Dex doing sun salutations next to his mom, who was meditating.

There was a camerawoman fussing with her equipment nearby, but she wasn't filming yet.

That was a good thing, because the look on Jackie's face as she watched Dex was of such raw yearning that Thea almost looked away, embarrassed at catching someone in such a private moment. Then, the camerawoman said something to Jackie, and her sister transformed instantly. All softness disappeared, replaced with a kind of excitable positivity that all but screamed I-am-the-happiest-woman-in-the-world. It looked 100 percent genuine, and at the same time it broke Thea's heart.

That's when Jackie spotted her, and her gaze narrowed. "Nice outfit."

Thrown off by the reaction, Thea lifted her rolled-up mat. "Dinosaurs love yoga! What doggie dinosaur loves yoga but can't do it? The T. rex. Hard to do downward dog with itty-bitty arms. Get it? Rex? Like the dog name?"

Was funny one of the *F* trauma responses? It had to be. What else explained the people who laughed at wakes and that horrible, grade-F dad joke she'd just attempted? Fuck it. She was counting it.

Jackie nailed her with a you-are-so-weird look before turning back on her smile and focusing on the camera, while Thea tried to ignore the way her whole body had tightened like she was expecting a blow.

That's what she got for thinking there was anything vulnerable about her sister. Jackie was a force of nature. Always had been. Always would be.

Thea blinked away the tears that had come out of nowhere. Jackie's attitude shouldn't bother her anymore. She'd been like this since all of the talk about the wedding started.

And then there was her. The dorky fawn-at-all-costs sister who wasn't even supposed to be at the wedding, according to the bride.

"Psst, Thea."

She whirled around at the sound of the voice she'd been hearing in her very vivid and steamy dreams all last night. Kade stood off to the side next to a motorcycle, its chrome gleaming so brightly in the morning light it's a wonder she didn't see it like a beacon before now.

He held out a canary-yellow motorcycle helmet and gave her a crooked grin that could melt panties three counties away. "Wanna ditch yoga?"

The simple answer was yes, but life wasn't always so simple—at least not hers. "Where would we go?"

"It's a surprise," he said with a cocky grin.

She laughed, and some of that less-than feeling ebbed into the background. "That sounds like I should worry about my kidneys."

"It'll be worth it for a peek at Lori and Jimbo."

Now he had her attention. All of it. "No way."

"Yes."

She let out an excited squeal that got the attention of the rest of the bridal party, but to hell with them. There was a Hesperornithoides and a Supersaurus to go see.

"I'll take that as a yes," Kade said, not even sparing the other people a glance.

She nodded, expecting him to hand her the helmet, but instead he gave her a pair of thick, dark motorcycle leggings that she slipped on over her yoga pants. They matched the motorcycle jacket he handed her next.

Slipping the jacket on, she gave him a questioning look. "You just keep extra gear with you at all times?"

He shrugged his broad shoulders. "Something like that."

She should ask more questions, but there was not one but two dinosaurs to go see, and there would be time to ask why he had all of this later. "How did you know about Jimbo and Lori?"

"Had to do something when I couldn't sleep last night," he said, handing her the yellow helmet.

"So you googled nearby dinosaurs?" That seemed more than a little completely unlikely.

"Yep," he said before putting on his helmet and getting on the bike, then revving the engine.

That got the attention of everyone at sunrise yoga. The camerawoman swung her lens around to them.

"Don't even think about it, Thea," Jackie said, her annoyed tone cutting through the motorcycle's engine. "We have to do the sisterly bonding activity for the live stream right after yoga. It's sponsored. Agreements were made. Money changed hands!"

Thea was already starting to hand her helmet back to Kade. Old habits and all that. But she stopped herself right in time. A SponCon sisterly bonding activity? Jackie hadn't even wanted Thea at the wedding, but she'd sold the time they would spend together? Oh, fuck that.

Everyone else just watched them with their mouths agog while Jackie marched ever closer. Thea would have sworn on a Bible that her heart could be heard hammering against her ribs over the motorcycle's badass engine.

Kade didn't say anything. He just watched, his expression totally inscrutable behind the dark visor of the helmet he'd slid on. But she got the message anyway. She had to make her choice.

Fawn.

Freeze.

Fight.

Flight.

Excitement bubbling inside her chest, she made her choice by pulling on her own helmet. She swung her leg over the motorcycle and sat down behind Kade, praying her ass would fit because that would kind of ruin the effect of the whole running-away-with-a-bad-boy-on-a-motorcycle thing. Yeah, she was a retired child actor with no intention of ever going back, but that didn't mean she didn't love a little bit of drama now and then.

Miraculously, her ass fit perfectly on the seat, but there really wasn't very much space left between them. One deep breath and her boobs would be pressed up against his back. Where was she going to put her hands? Sure, she *knew* where she was supposed to put her hands, but knowing and doing were two different things when it came to touching Kade St. James. The man was dangerous.

"Thea!" Jackie yelled, almost to them now. "It's a contractual obligation!"

Thea froze, stuck between what she wanted and how she'd normally behave in this situation. However, in the end, the final choice was made for her when the motorcycle started moving. She dropped her hands to Kade's hips and held on, hoping she wouldn't go flying like her heart was at that moment—especially when she saw the look of grudging admiration on Jackie's face half a second before the camera swung back to her sister and she settled her expression into one of absolute disapproval.

Thea laughed and slid her arms around Kade's waist, letting herself relax against his back as they hit the highway and left the resort in their dust.

Dr. Kowecki was right—this really did feel good. Check that. This felt amazing, like she just might be finding the Thea who would never be a doormat again.

Chapter Twelve

What Kade experienced every time he walked into a bookstore and that first whiff of book hit him straight in the face, Thea looked like she was going through as she stared at Lori, which at three feet long was the smallest dinosaur to have ever been discovered in the state of Wyoming. He knew that because it said so on the explanatory card at the fossil's base that he'd now read at least eight times while Thea *ooh*ed and *aah*ed and took in every millimeter of the fossil.

"Isn't she gorgeous?" Thea asked with a happy sigh. "So the theory is, because she had these long, thin arms and gangly legs with a pretty short tail, Lori here wasn't a runner but instead probably lurked in the undergrowth before going in for the attack."

He took a closer look at the mean-ass claws on the dinosaur's hands and feet that would slice and dice whatever it was planning on having for dinner. "Looks like Lori could have been an amazing horror movie villain."

"Well, the Hesperornithoides miessleri is a close relative of the velociraptor," Thea said, putting on what he'd come to realize was her professor voice.

That she'd go into paleontologist mode while surrounded by fossils didn't surprise him. What he hadn't expected was that he'd find it so hot to see her in her element. He'd kept asking questions long after his brain had reached the point of being overwhelmed with information just so he could hear her talk. She was smart, had a unique ability to break things down and avoid using jargon that intimidated or confused things. This wasn't about ego for her; it was about pure, unadulterated love. Translation: hearing Thea Pope talk about dinosaurs was sexy as fuck.

"Velociraptor?" he asked. "Like from *Jurassic Park*?"

"The very one." She nodded and tucked a long strand of dark hair that had escaped her ponytail behind an ear.

The woman loved her ponytails—she always had her hair pulled back into one. He was becoming a fan himself. He'd spent way too much time last night fantasizing about wrapping it around his hand and tugging as he fucked her.

"So you just accidentally found this place?" Thea did a slow circle as she held out her arms to encompass the nearly sixty mounted dinosaur skeletons, her perma-grin on full display.

"It kept popping up on all those ads on news sites I was reading."

Thea turned her full attention to him, which was saying something, since they were surrounded by dinosaur bones and more educational dioramas than it was probably legal to have in one place. "Were you researching your next book?"

"Just acting like a doom-scrolling junkie."

What he didn't mention was he was getting served nothing but dinosaur ads since googling *her*—and reading *all* of her research papers online and articles until the wee hours of the morning. The ads were what had given him the idea to take Thea on a motorcycle ride, which had led to here, which had led to a big-ass dinosaur museum with a woman whose smile was so big it was making him grin. His facial muscles were going to be sore from the overuse after years of only smirking at the most.

Thea looked up at him, cocking her head to the side, her expression serious. "My therapist would say you need to find an outlet for all that stress your doom-scrolling is no doubt giving you." She paused a beat, and her world's-happiest-woman grin came back. "Of course, I would say that just means you need more dinosaurs in your life."

Or maybe more dinosaur lovers.

Whoa, asshole. Dial back the not-gonna-happen. You can't even kiss her. This is just a weeklong fuckfest. Nothing else—not that you do that other sort of thing.

Maybe not, but as he watched that perfect, high round ass of hers as she walked over to another display, he couldn't stop thinking about her, either.

A half hour later, they'd moved on to admiring Jimbo the Supersaurus and the display of a massive Tyrannosaurus rex rushing a badass-looking triceratops when he overheard the mom of three kids (one grade-schooler in a dinosaur costume and two obviously bored middle schoolers) tell her wife, "That woman from that one show that we binged last month is in the gift shop with a camera crew."

His gut sank. He didn't need to sneak a peek himself to know who the mom had to be talking about.

They'd made it longer undiscovered than he thought they would, but damn, he really would have liked a little more time, if only—

The sight of the door behind the triceratops with "Staff Only" written on it snagged his attention. He didn't think. He didn't wonder if this was the right move. He just knew he had to do it.

"Come on." He slid his arm around Thea's back and started fast walking around the mammoth—no pun intended—display toward the door. "We gotta go."

"But I was looking at that. Did you know that the triceratops' horn isn't a horn at all but is made out of the same soft protein that makes up human fingernails?"

"I did not." He glanced over his shoulder toward the

gift shop, the exit of which was crowded with autograph seekers. The middle schoolers had ditched their mom and were busy in frenzied selfie mode, no doubt with Jackie in the background of every shot. "But I did know your sister is here with a camera crew."

Thea let out a tired sigh, and her steps slowed for half a second before she sparked back up when she spotted their intended destination. "The closet?"

"It's good for at least another couple of minutes before they drag us back to Stinkingwater."

And he'd take every minute he could get.

That doesn't strike you as odd?

The answer to that was a solid yes, since, as a writer, he spent most of his time alone having imaginary conversations with people who weren't in the room with him. (Yeah, fiction writers didn't have the market cornered on writer weirdness.) But with Thea, it was different.

With one last look toward the gift shop, he opened the closet door.

Thea hustled inside, and he followed, shutting the door behind them.

There was a little window high up on the wall that brought in enough light to show they were in a small supply closet. The walls were lined with shelves stacked with toilet paper, cleaning supplies, and plastic T. rexes. There was barely room for him and Thea in here, but it was better than being out there.

"You, Kade St. James," Thea said, giggling like a kid who'd just gotten away with sneaking out of the house for the first time, "are a bad influence."

He shifted so that he was facing her as she stood with her back against a shelf full of brown folded paper towels. She looked up at him through her dark lashes. The closet was small, but it was big enough for them to have a few inches of space between them.

Of course, that was the last thing that was going to happen. He moved closer and dropped his hands to her hips, hooking his fingers in the loops of the motorcycle pants over her leggings, tugging her forward until she was pressed up against him.

"A bad influence is exactly what you need in your life," he said as he dipped his head down, hovering right above that tempting mouth of hers.

She let out a shaky breath and reached between them, grasping the hem of his T-shirt and lifting it. "Too late. I already know your secret."

"What's that?" He lowered his mouth, coming within millimeters of her lush lips before changing course and kissing along her jaw before making his way to that spot by her ear that made her shiver.

"You're a secret softie. You probably even have a dog that the shelter said was unadoptable, too."

That was a direct shot. He took a half step back and looked at her, trying to figure out how she knew. Had Dex told her?

Thea's eyes went wide behind her very-serious-paleontologist dark-rimmed glasses. "Oh. My. God. You do! What's the puppy's name?"

He groaned. "Patton."

"And what kind?"

Smug Thea was quite something to observe. This was a woman who, despite all evidence to the contrary in how she acted around other people, loved being right.

"French bulldog–corgi mix," he grudgingly admitted.

"And what did the shelter say when you adopted him?"

She was enjoying this way too much. He wanted to hate that. He couldn't.

"That he'd been returned three times for being an

asshole."

She let out a moan that sounded way too close to an awwwwwwww for him. "So you found a kindred soul."

"You don't know me." At least she definitely shouldn't know him. They'd spent what, two and a half days together?

"Really?" She teased the skin above his jeans' waistband with her fingertips. "Sounds to me like you don't really know yourself. God, I sound just like my therapist. I'm gonna get Nola and Astrid for this."

"Is that your therapist?"

She shook her head. "Astrid and Nola are my best friends, and Nola got both of us to start seeing her therapist. Separately, of course."

"What? Was she after the referral discounts, or pulling some kind of con?" He hadn't heard of a therapy-related Ponzi scheme, but that didn't mean it hadn't happened.

"You know"—her thumb brushed the button of his jeans—"they say cynics are often the biggest closet optimists."

"Well, I'm in a closet right now, but that's the only thing you got right there."

She shrugged. "So you say."

He encircled her wrists with his hand and lifted her arms above her head, pinning them to one of the shelves. "Wanna know what else I have to say?"

She bit down on her bottom lip and nodded.

He slipped his free hand under her ridiculous T. rex T-shirt and pushed it up over her tits. Her hard nipples pressed against the thin material of her cotton sports bra. Watching her face, he pinched her nipple through the soft material, rolling and tugging it as her eyes darkened with desire.

"Before this week is out," he said, switching his attentions to her other nipple, "you're going to beg me to break that dumb rule of yours and kiss you until you finally find something you like more than dinosaurs."

"Impossible."

"Why, because you think that no-kissing rule is important?" He dropped a line of kisses against her silky skin above the line of her sports bra, his cock so hard it ached.

She arched her back and tilted her chin, giving him more of her to kiss. "No, because the only thing I like more than dinosaurs are, God help me, Astrid, Nola, and my family."

That gave him pause, and he looked up. "Even your sister?"

Before she could answer, the closet door swung open to reveal a very pissed-off Jackie with a very happy cameraperson behind her already hitting the zoom.

Sidestepping in front of Thea to block her from view, he turned and glared at the cameraperson, who wisely took a step back. The bride-to-be, however, didn't even flinch.

"Can you two even try to keep your pants zipped for five fucking seconds?" she sputtered. "I mean really, you are surrounded by a bunch of gross old bones. What kind of sickos are you?"

"The kind," Thea shot back as she squeezed past him in the narrow closet while shimmying her shirt down, "who is desperately trying to avoid you."

Kade had no clue who was more shocked at her fiery response, him or Jackie, whose eyes had rounded to the size of dinner plates. Judging by the now-huge grin on the cameraperson's face, though, there was at least one person absolutely thrilled with the way things were going.

He, however, didn't give a shit at the moment about any of that.

"Whatever," Jackie said with a huff, recovering before Kade did. "You two may be getting all the love on social because of your obvious play for attention at the party, but that doesn't mean you can go diva. We are all here for *my* wedding, and it's time you two act like it."

"You mean yours and Dex's wedding," Kade said.

He was dead set against this whole fiasco, but that didn't mean that his brother was just some kind of prop for a Jackie Pope production.

Jackie turned her attention to him, her eyes narrowing into slits. "And your mom is looking for you. She says she has something to tell you."

Yeah, that wasn't going to happen. His mom had nothing to say that he wanted to hear. He crossed his arms and made a noncommittal grunt before he let the truth slip out in front of all of America that was watching the live stream.

Thea slipped her hand into his and gave him a squeeze. "We were on our way back anyway. Promise, pumpkin."

Jackie's pissed-off expression slipped for a second, revealing sisterly concern for all of half a second as she looked between them, and then the bridezilla returned. "Well, make sure you do. We cannot miss our little bonding time"—she slapped her hand over the mic clipped to her shirt—"unless you feel like paying the fifty-thousand-dollar penalty for failing to meet the sponsorship obligations."

Then she slammed the closet door shut in their faces, much to the cameraperson's audible disappointment.

"I guess we better get back," he grumbled.

Thea lifted herself on her tiptoes and gave him a quick kiss on the cheek. "Maybe we can take the long way to the resort."

Now that, he could make happen. If they got lucky, they'd run out of gas in the middle of nowhere and have to spend the night together—alone—under the stars.

Chapter Thirteen

Much to Kade's disappointment, though, they did not run out of gas. Even worse? Jackie and her mom were waiting for them—along with Dex and their mom—in front of his RV. Mom looked so much like she had when he was a kid that for a second, he couldn't stop the hope that filled his chest like helium, and he started to smile. That lasted all of two seconds before reality came at him like a dart, popping that hope like a kid's birthday balloon.

"Fuck me," he grumbled, settling his face into its usual snarl.

"You wanna turn around and go back to that closet?" Thea asked, the pity in her voice coming through loud and clear on the Bluetooth headphones in his helmet.

"Without a doubt," he said.

Be alone with her in a space so small there was no way *not* to touch her? That sounded like his version of heaven.

But it was too late, and they both knew it.

He parked the motorcycle next to the RV, and they took their time walking over to where their families were waiting. That's when he spotted the producer and the camera operator off to the side, as unobtrusive as they could be while still being able to catch every moment of this unrelenting hell. Just fucking great.

Grimacing, Kade stopped and pivoted his body so he was looking his brother dead in the eyes without seeing his mom, even though she was right next to him.

Dex glared at him, obviously seeing what he was doing. Yeah, it was immature and stupid, but it was better than losing his shit in front of the cameras.

"Mom and I were going to grab lunch and wanted you to come," Dex said, breaking the silence.

"No," Kade replied without hesitation.

He didn't see his mom deflate, but he would have sworn on a stack of Bibles that he could feel it as if there was still a part of him that was tied to her that he would never be able to completely destroy.

Dex cursed under his breath and shook his head in disgust. "That's it?"

Kade shrugged, leaning full into his assholery. "No is a full sentence."

How many years had he spent wishing for this kind of moment when his mom just wanted to hang out with him and Dex? Too many to even count. But he'd grown up. He'd learned. He'd finally understood. There was absolutely no reason to go back and do all of that again. Second chances were for people who still gave a shit. Kade didn't.

His mom took a step forward, her hands clasped tightly in front of her, her eyes pleading. "I know you're angry with me still, Kade honey, but if we could just talk, I'm sure we could figure out a way forward."

The urge to give in, to say yes, to do exactly what he would have done if she had come back when he was fourteen was like receiving a sharp kick to the kidneys, nearly knocking him sideways. But he stopped himself before he could give anything away.

Instead, he finally turned his full attention to his mom and made his voice as flat and cold as North Dakota in January. "Oh, you want to have a little mother-son chat, just me, you, Dex, and everyone watching at home?" He jerked his chin toward the cameraman standing off to the side. "That sounds downright cozy."

"I just want a chance to reconnect," his mom said, reaching out to him.

He flinched back and shoved his hands into the pockets of his jeans. Thea shifted next to him, inching just a bit closer, as if she was trying to block him from the cameras. That wasn't going to happen, but he appreciated the effort.

"Yeah, the time for that was when I still gave a fuck," he said without heat but with plenty of condemnation. "It's twenty years too late for that."

"There's no need to be a complete asshole, Kade," Dex said, taking a half step forward.

"Yeah," he said, his voice hard, "actually, there is."

Kade looked at his brother, the person he loved more than any other human in the world. He'd protected him from the worst of their mom's drunk days. He'd distracted him when their dad got pissed off from all their questions about where Mom had gone and when she'd be back. He'd shown up to this absolute clusterfuck of a wedding. But this? This was too much.

"It's okay," Mom said, lowering her hands and curling them around her middle like a shield. "When you're ready, I'll be here."

The irony of that statement wasn't lost on him. The woman who abandoned him, who didn't return an email or a text after she left was going to be here for him? It took everything he had not to start laughing, especially when his mom did what she did best—she left, walking down the path that lead to the river.

Dex shot him a look of pure disgust. "You know, giving people a second chance every once in a while won't kill you."

"She doesn't deserve it," Kade said.

"How the fuck would you know?" his brother all but

hollered, his frustration hitting peak levels. "You've never even given her a chance to explain."

Kade didn't say anything. There weren't any words left.

There was an awkward silence—well, awkward for everyone but the camera crew, who kept rolling no matter the circumstances. He got it. They had their job to do, and he'd signed up for this ridiculous fucking disaster of epic proportions.

"That was uncomfortable for everyone," Jackie said, stepping around Dex so she was directly in front of the camera before turning to address Thea. "But now that you're back from your diva fit, you can take care of our special activity all on your own."

Thea let out a tired sigh. "Doesn't me doing it by myself negate the whole sisterly bonding part of the activity?"

"You should have thought of that before you took off with *him*," Jackie said, big red splotches appearing at the base of her throat as her voice got scratchy with suppressed emotion. "I thought I could always count on you, but I guess things have changed."

Her entire body tense, Thea seemed to shrink right before him. Before he realized what he was doing, he took her hand in his.

"You know I'll always be there for you. What do you need me to do?" she asked her sister.

"You have to glue all of the faux flowers provided by our lovely sponsor Flowers In A Minute on to the wedding heart. It's going to be behind Dex and me when we say our vows." Jackie pointed to a massive plain white foam heart that was so big it was sitting on a flatbed trailer so it could be driven to where it needed to be for the ceremony. "After the ceremony, they're going to be selling replicas on the website for other brides to complete with their bridesmaids. You know, the ones who show up for the bride when they're supposed to."

"Jackie." Thea's voice went up a notch as she gaped at the heart. "That thing has to be ten feet wide."

"Now, Thea," their mom said, flapping her hands in the air as if she could fan her oldest daughter into chilling the fuck out. "It's your sister's big day, and we need to come together to make it happen. You've always been there for us when we need you. We can depend on you for this little favor, can't we? Especially when you and Jackie were supposed to do it together, but then you went off with Kade and messed up the schedule?"

Thea's shoulders started to droop as her defiant glare melted and her gaze sank to the trio of tumbleweeds caught up under his RV, but she didn't say anything. She didn't meekly agree. She didn't throw her hands up and fight. She didn't walk away. She froze.

Clenching his jaw tight enough he was surprised he didn't crack a molar as he kept reminding himself that this wasn't his fight, he cut a glance over to the spot where his mom had been standing with Dex. Now it was just his brother leaning against the RV's door, glaring at Kade as if he was the one who'd abandoned them. He'd never done that. He never would. He didn't leave people he cared about behind. He didn't leave them to deal with obnoxious brides on their own. He didn't leave them to build ten-foot-wide flower hearts just because they were the ones who always took care of that shit.

Kade would never be that person.

Never.

"I'll help," he said, the words coming out before he even realized he was going to speak.

Thea glanced over at him, her chin trembling just the slightest bit. "You don't have to do that. *I'll* do it." She turned to her mom and Jackie, her voice gaining strength. "But only on one condition."

"Oh really? You have conditions now?" Jackie asked,

sounding slightly less snotty than usual.

What a pain in the ass. She needed to just agree to whatever Thea said.

Letting out a shaky breath, Thea firmed her stance as if she was expecting a blow but still refused to back down. "You stop expecting that I'll do whatever you want whenever you want me to. I expect to be asked." She turned to only her sister. "*Nicely*, if you can manage it."

Thea's mom snorted in disbelief. "My goodness, you act as if—"

"Mom," Jackie said, cutting off their mom. "Shut up."

"What is going on with my children?" their mom asked with a huff. "So disrespectful."

The sisters stared at each other, exchanging some kind of silent communication that only sisters had while he watched, helpless to protect Thea from whatever was coming next. He fucking hated that.

"It's a deal," Jackie finally said.

Shoulders straight and her chin held high, Thea gave her sister a quick nod. "Thank you."

Then she slipped her hand free of his and started toward the giant-ass foam heart and four billion fake flowers in piles around it. Kade stayed behind, glaring at Jackie, who simply raised her eyebrows and gave him a look that seemed to say, "What are you going to do about it, loser?"

What *was* he going to do about it? The one thing he could do right now. Go stab a foam heart with hard plastic stems so the woman he couldn't stop thinking about didn't have to do it by herself. There was a metaphor in there somewhere, but his writer brain was still too pissed off to make it.

"What are you doing?" Thea asked when he caught up with her.

He shortened his stride to stay in step with her. "Helping you."

"Why?" She stopped and pivoted so they were face to face before looking up at him, her face scrunched in confusion. "That's not part of our experiment."

He grabbed a rose and jabbed it into the foam, unable to shake his irritation about his mom being here and Jackie being her usual bitchy self. "Neither is you agreeing to help me avoid seeing or talking about my mother for the rest of the week, but I'm hoping you're open to an addendum."

"Only if you agree to do the same for me." Thea handed him a new rose.

He took it, their fingers brushing and sending a jolt of awareness that shot right to his dick and shifting his mood. "Done."

"Well, then." She tapped the tip of her faux rose to his as if they were clinking champagne glasses. "Here's to our experiment."

Yes. Their experiment. Fuck acquaintances for the span of this wedding from hell, trying to figure out if faster or slower was better. That was all there was between them. Except that wasn't what it was beginning to feel like. At least not for him, even though that's all she was to him or could be—all anyone could be. That's what made this whole thing make sense. Thea Pope fit perfectly into the just-for-fun compartment in his very organized, very everything-and-everyone-had-its place world.

He always planned his books in spiral-bound notebooks.

He always wrote on a laptop in his living room with Patton snoring at his feet.

He never dated the same woman more than three times and didn't have relationships.

He wasn't built for those things. There was just something inside him that was missing.

There wasn't space for anything more than random hookups, and he liked it that way.

So why are you helping Thea?

He didn't have an answer for that one, so he pushed the question away and focused on the woman in front of him. No hardship there.

"Not part of our experiment?" he said, trailing the back of his knuckles along her jawline. "That's only because you've never realized that DIY decor is a kind of slow-fucking foreplay all its own."

Her eyes darkened with desire despite the giggle that escaped. "What am I going to do with you?"

He dipped his head down and whispered close to her ear, "You have four and a half more days to do whatever you want to me."

A blush pinked her cheeks. "There are so many possibilities."

The woman was right on that one, and they were going to try out all of them.

Chapter Fourteen

So much for the possibilities, because Kade seemed determined to stay just outside of arm's reach—at least when it came to her touching him. He, on the other hand, seemed to be always touching her.

His palm on the small of her back to help steady her as she stretched to jab a flower in an open spot near the top of the foam heart.

The brush of his fingers against hers when he handed her a bunch of neon-pink faux roses. He was always there, every time she turned around, so close she nearly ran into him over and over.

She'd never been more aware of someone in her life.

It was like a constant buzzing vibrating through her. She could smell the soap he'd used that morning in the shower each time she inhaled. When she was supposed to be picking out a new bunch of fake flowers to add to the foam heart, her gaze strayed to Kade. For a few moments, she got lost looking at him. The line of his jaw. The way his broad shoulders stretched his T-shirt. How his crooked smile curved upward in the opposite direction of the crook in his nose and balanced everything out. He wasn't model perfect. He looked like he'd rather stab someone in the eye than spend three hours in the gym, but he also had that thick, hard body of someone who would survive the zombie apocalypse with the help of his trusty shovel that he'd name Beauregard.

A stronger woman than Thea would have gotten mesmerized watching how the muscles in his forearms looked as he picked up the stepladder and moved it over so she could fill the next section of the heart with flowers. She'd never had a hope of not falling under his spell as the low thrum of desire, warm and insistent, made her entire body feel like tinder just waiting for a spark.

Even right now, as she stood on the top step of the ladder when she of the shitty balance should be paying attention to her stance, all she could focus on was the fact that he was right behind her. Oh, she couldn't see him. But he was there. She'd bet the bank that if she slipped and fell back, he'd catch her.

It was unsettling and enticing all at the same time, because it wasn't just how he looked that had her on the edge—it was the fact that she liked *him*.

There was no way this was going to end well for her, but she couldn't seem to make herself walk away—not when all she wanted was to walk *toward* him.

So why aren't you?

That was the question.

"You know," he said, grinning up at her. "If you keep staring at me like that, I might start to worry that I'm growing another head or something."

Embarrassment at getting caught staring heated her cheeks. "I was just wondering something."

"What's that?" he asked.

What would it take to get you to take me to my RV and fuck me boneless right now?

Desperate much? Do not say that out loud.

"Do you—" She hesitated, trying to come up with something—anything—to say other than that. "Do you have any Band-Aids in your RV?" Um. Okay, that was lame as hell, but it was out there.

His jaw tightened. "Are you hurt?"

She was not. She nodded anyway. "Paper cut."

He looked around. She wasn't near even so much as a single sheet of paper anywhere near here. After a few moments, the *V* lines of confusion between his eyes smoothed out, and he leveled a sexy smirk at her. "That sounds awful."

"Yeah," she agreed. "The worst."

He took her hand as if to look for the nonexistent cut and glided his thumb across her uninjured palm, sending a wave of tingly awareness through her. She held her breath, biting down on her bottom lip to stop from moaning or begging or making some other embarrassing sound that would tell him exactly how much she wanted him right now. Not that there was any way for him to miss that. Her sports bra and thin T-shirt weren't exactly made for full, hard nips coverage. Then there was the fact that her breathing had gone all hinky, her voice had turned husky, and she was practically melty with want.

Oh yeah, but don't make any noise. That would give the game away.

His thumb went from the palm of her hand to the inside of her wrist, setting off sparks of desire that made her core clench. She kept her shit together, though, right up until he lifted her hand to his mouth and kissed her palm.

"We better get you some first aid." He winked at her and then glanced over at the nearby camerawoman documenting their faux flower DIY before turning his focus back to Thea and dropping his volume to a whisper. "Give me a minute. I got a plan. Meet me at my RV."

He took a few steps away and pulled out his phone.

"Oh fuck," he said, loud enough that there was no way the camerawoman could miss it. "It's Dex. Shit's about to go down. I gotta go, I'm sorry."

"Go ahead," Thea said, playing along.

He dropped a kiss on her forehead and took off around the corner of the barn where the welcome party had been held. She kept on sticking the plastic stems into the heart while listening out for the camerawoman. It took a minute or two, but eventually, curiosity must have gotten the better of the woman, because Thea could hear footsteps moving away. Peeking over her shoulder, she caught sight of the woman quick-footing it toward the barn where Dex was.

And that, she surmised, was her cue. She shoved the last handful of eye-piercingly bright fake roses into the heart and took off toward where all the groomsmen's RVs were. She hurried, taking cover where she could behind sheds and the resort's pickups and random bushes to avoid getting spotted by the production crew wandering around catching candid moments of the wedding party. By the time she got to the RV with Kade's name written on a whiteboard on the door, nervous sweat was beading at the nape of her neck and her heart was hammering against her ribs. She sprinted up the three metal steps leading to the door and lifted her hand to knock, but before she made contact, it flew open. Kade yanked her inside and slammed the door shut behind her.

In the next heartbeat, she was off the ground, pressed up against the door with Kade's large hands cradling her ass as she wrapped her legs around his hips.

"I thought you'd never get here," he said, squeezing her ass like he'd been thinking about doing just that for hours.

Needing to touch him, she steadied herself by holding his shoulders, thrilling at the contact. "Does that mean you have a Band-Aid for me?"

"Babe, I *am* your Band-Aid." He pulled her against him so there wasn't an inch of space between them, his heat seeping into her as she rubbed herself against him. "By the time I'm done, you'll feel better than you ever have."

Understanding what she needed, he pushed up against

her, his hard cock pressing into her aching softness, pinning her lower half to the door.

"Daaaaaaaaamn," she groaned, not giving a shit anymore about showing just how turned on she was because his dick was hitting just the right spot, not moving her hips so she could rub herself against him, the center of her yoga pants embarrassingly wet already.

"Oh," he said, rocking against her. "You like that."

She nodded, then let her head fall against the door, the back of her skull hitting with a thunk she barely felt.

"Babe," he said, one hand moving to the hem of her T-shirt and slipping underneath. "Be careful. I like how that brain of yours works."

She would have used said brain to come up with some kind of witty comeback, some teasing banter, some flirty chitchat, but the feel of his fingers on the bare skin of her stomach chased every single thought in her head away. All she could do was arch into his touch while grinding against him, so hungry for contact that nothing else mattered.

Kade nipped the spot where her shoulder met her neck, sucking and kissing on the spot as his hand traveled upward. Slowly. Millimeter by frustrating millimeter. By the time he finally cupped her breast, it was like she'd waited years. Her eyes squeezed closed, and she let out a soft gasp of satisfaction as he drew his thumb over her hard nipple, teasing the sensitive point until she thought she was going to lose her mind.

"Fuck, you're hot," he said against her neck as he made his way up to her ear. "No more interruptions today. I don't care if the entire production team breaks into the RV, I'm going to bury myself inside you and fuck you until you come all over my cock."

"Yes," she whispered, barely able to hear her voice over the rush of desire.

"What was that?" He grazed his teeth over her earlobe. "I want to hear you."

"Yes," she groaned louder this time.

Then instead of immediately doing what he promised, what she was dying for, the talented bastard chuckled as he moved his hand to her other nipple, so he could tease and pluck and toy with it, too. All the while that mouth of his, which she wanted everywhere all at the same time, went from her ear to her jaw to the edge of her lips already parted and ready for his kiss.

Self-preservation, though, saved her at just the last moment.

"Not there," she said, turning her face to the side despite her desperation to feel his lips on hers.

She couldn't explain how she knew, but she just knew that if she did, she wouldn't be able to find her way back when she got home—alone—to Harbor City. Kissing Kade St. James would mark her, change her. It would make all of this seem real, and she *had* to remember that it wasn't. It was just an experiment and a way to get back at her sister. It didn't mean anything. It was just for fun.

But a kiss? That was something else.

He paused and let out a harsh breath and rested his forehead against the doorframe. Then, he lifted his head and looked straight at her, his eyes dark with desire and an intensity she wasn't used to being the focus of.

"Fine," he said, the word coming out like a low, rumbly dare. "But I'm going to kiss every other square inch of you but that sweet mouth." He lowered her so her feet touched the ground. "Take off your clothes." He reached behind his neck and pulled his T-shirt off over his head, tossing it to the side. "All of them."

She would. She had every intention of doing exactly what he said, but she couldn't. Kade's chest wasn't just a wall of hard muscle that made her mouth go dry. It was his canvas. A weathered owl, its wings outstretched so that the tips went from one shoulder to the other, was tattooed across his chest. It looked almost like it had been drawn on him with charcoal, complete with shading and layers. She wanted to stroke at each feather with her finger. She wanted to trace the lines with her tongue. She wanted to touch and taste him until he was as drugged with desire as she was.

She wanted.

She needed.

She had to have.

"Thea," he said, snapping her attention back to his face. "Get naked. Because if I have to take your clothes off, I can't guarantee they'll be in working condition after I'm done."

She stared at him, too turned on to fucking move.

"Babe," he said, his rough voice practically a warning growl. "Now."

Chapter Fifteen

Thank fucking God, she reached for the hem of her T-shirt and in one smooth motion pulled it off. Her bra went next, and Kade offered up a silent thank-you to the fates, the universe, and all the gods for that as he fisted his hands to keep from reaching out.

He wasn't just skating along the edge of his control—he was barely holding on. Fuck the bullshit experiment they were playing at. He had to have her.

The smart money bet was that he would make it about another five seconds before he fell straight off—happily—into oblivion. And when she looked at him like that? As if she was about to lose her damn mind along with him? He wasn't sure there was anything better.

She was soft and sweet enough to eat—something it felt like he'd waited forever to do.

The instant her fingers went to the waistband of her leggings, he held his breath. When she shimmied the stretchy material down over her full hips, his knees almost buckled. By the time she kicked them off and stood there without a single stitch on, he let out his breath in a harsh muttered curse of appreciation as he looked her up and down. Then he looked some more, memorizing the curve of her tits, the way her pale pink nipples puckered, the small watercolor Pterodactylus tattooed above her right knee, and the span of her strong thighs that drew his attention up to her pussy.

He'd waited as long as he could. Fast it was.

Closing the distance between them in two strides, he cupped the back of her head with one hand and tilted her face up. Her lush mouth was only inches from his, so tempting, so fucking perfect. But instead, he brushed his thumb across her bottom lip, not hard but rough enough to push it sideways before dipping his thumb inside. Keeping eye contact, she sucked on it, swirling her tongue around the end and giving him a million dirty ideas.

"Fuck, Thea."

She shot him a sassy smirk. "Please and thank you."

He slipped her glasses off and put them on the built-in desk by the door. "You're a real smart-ass when you want to be."

"Only around you," she said, her voice breathy.

He glided his finger down the length of her neck, relishing her shiver of pleasure in response. "So I'm the lucky one, huh?"

"I won't argue with that."

He barked out a laugh. "Me either."

Then he scooped her up and tossed her over his shoulder, smacking her juicy ass for good measure.

She let out a squawk and then laughed. "You'll pay for that."

"I don't doubt it."

He tossed her down onto the bed, careful enough that the pillows barely moved. Before she had a chance to recover, though, he had one of her ankles in each hand and pulled her down to the end of the bed so her ass was right on the edge. He sank to his knees and spread her legs, keeping his hands on her thighs. Then he feasted, licking, sucking, and teasing her folds swollen with desire and so damn wet for him.

She fisted the sheets as he ate her up, begging him to speed up and slow down and do that again and please oh God please yes. He followed every direction, circling her clit with his tongue, sucking on it and pressing his thumb against it in a pulsing beat as he slid two fingers inside her. She tightened around him as he twisted them and rubbed that spot right inside her entrance that made her groan and issue incoherent pleas—for what, he had no idea but he did his best to give her anyway. He continued to tease and tempt and take her closer and closer until she cried out his name. She came hard enough that her thighs clamped down on his head, holding him in place as if there was anywhere else in the world he wanted to be. He sucked her clit one last time as her legs went slack and then moved up to the bed, leaning over her as she caught her breath.

His mouth still slick with her, he kissed his way up her body over her soft belly and up to her round tits. God, this woman. He could spend the rest of the week in bed with her, just kissing and licking and touching every bit of her. The sounds she made when he rolled her hard nipple between his forefinger and thumb made his cock fucking ache. He continued to touch her everywhere he could, the curve of her hip, the line of her shoulders, the dip of her waist, the soft roundness of her belly. He couldn't get enough, but he forced himself to stand up and step back from the bed.

He pulled his wallet out of his pants and took out a condom. "Just say the word and we're done now."

Still on her back, she propped herself up on her elbows, looking him straight on. "More, please."

"Thank fuck." He tossed his wallet onto the bedside table and made quick work of his shoes and jeans.

Condom in hand, he paused, looking at the perfection that was Thea Pope naked and spread out on his bed. Her legs were splayed, her inner thighs rubbed red from the scratch of his short beard, and she had the languid look of a woman who was still coming down from her orgasm. He wrapped his free hand around his hard cock and gave it a few strokes as he looked his fill, as if that was possible. Then his gaze caught hers and she smiled at him, slow and satisfied.

It was the kind of sight that stayed with a man, and he had no doubt that when he closed his eyes a week, a year, a lifetime from now, he'd be able to picture her just like this.

"Kade," she said as she glided her fingertips from the base of her throat to the valley between her tits. "Stop looking and fuck me."

She said it with just enough teasing sass that he couldn't help but smile. Other people might look at her and see the shy paleontologist, but he knew there was so much more to her than that.

"Yes, ma'am," he said with a wink as he tore open the wrapper and then rolled the condom on.

His whole body was one live wire when he sat down on the edge of the bed. He had every intention of wrapping Thea's legs around him and burying himself inside of her, but she had other plans. She pushed him back until his head hit the pillow and then straddled him. Planting her hands on his shoulders, she positioned herself above his straining cock and stayed there.

"Is this you deciding to try out the slow hypothesis?" he asked, grabbing a hold of her hips.

One of her eyebrows went up. "When it is, believe me, you'll know."

Then, finally, she lowered herself down onto him as he drove upward until he was buried inside her warmth. His balls tightened, and he nearly lost it right then. He stilled, clenching his jaw, and pulled back from that edge. That's when she got the revenge she'd promised him that first night, squeezing his cock with her inner muscles while he stayed frozen.

"Thea," he said, half protesting for her to stop and half

pleading for her to keep going.

"Told you I'd get you back for teasing me so much out by the campfire." She planted her hands on his chest and rocked her hips forward. "We're not going slow anymore."

He could have argued. He probably should have flipped her onto her back and regained control of the pace, drawing out each thrust until she was beside herself with want. That's what he wanted, to imprint on her so that every time after him part of her would always remember this moment with him.

But as the classic song went, you couldn't always get what you wanted but you could get what you needed—and he needed Thea Pope.

He gripped her fleshy hips, holding her tight enough that she looked down at him.

"That's right," he said, urging her on. "Look at me while you ride that cock. I wanna watch your face when you come again."

She let out a mewl of pleasure and picked up her pace, grinding down so her clit rubbed against him with every downward stroke. Then she was going up again, riding him hard and fast, rubbing against him as she chased her orgasm just as he tried to hold his off.

"So pretty." He watched her tits move, swaying with the rocking motion before his gaze traveled up to her face as she bit down on her lip in concentration. "So goddamn beautiful."

She arched her back and moved her hands from his chest to his thighs, holding him hard enough that he could feel her round nails biting into his skin as she took him deeper. It was so much and not enough—he wasn't sure it ever would be. He held on for dear life as she fucked him, taking him higher and higher as his balls tightened. Fuck. There was no way he could last much longer—something that she no doubt knew as she got her revenge for that ass slap and drawing things out the other night, because now she had him ready to beg for her to keep going and to please, whatever she did, not to slow down.

"You wanna go fast?" he asked.

Her eyes fluttered shut as she started riding him harder, her hips bucking against him. "Yes."

"Then I'm gonna give you that." He'd give her whatever she wanted.

He flipped their positions so she was on her back underneath him. Her legs tightened around his hips as she lifted herself to keep fucking him from underneath. He met her halfway, coming into her like a man finally finding himself home again after a lifetime away.

Over and over, he thrust forward, sinking balls deep and pulling back before crashing forward again until her core clenched as she came. And as he watched the bliss crash over her, something broke loose inside him and nearly made him lose it right then.

He couldn't name it, couldn't even begin to identify it, but he knew without even a whiff of doubt that everything was different now. It worked that way with the books he wrote—there was always a moment when things just clicked and everything that seemed like a chaotic mess before fell into place. Looking into Thea's eyes as his climax fought its way to the surface and he sank one last time into her, he knew his life was never going to be the same. Being with her had changed everything. It had changed him. After that, it was just the best kind of fucking oblivion as the entire world rushed out on a wave of intense pleasure that only left him and Thea.

When the world came back into focus, he was bracing himself on his forearms so he wouldn't crush her. It took a minute for him to catch his breath as he came fully back to earth. Then, he rolled over so he lay beside her. She didn't say anything but shifted her hand so it was close enough that she could wind her little finger around his as they stared at the ceiling.

Finally, he forced himself up so he could get rid of the condom. When he got back in bed, she was already snuggled in, waiting for him with a sleepy smile.

It only took a minute for his eyelids to grow heavy and his breathing to even out, but he wasn't ready yet to give in to sleep. Like the fool he was, he wanted one more chapter before he crashed out.

"Tell me something," he said, taking her hand and winding his fingers between hers.

She let her head fall to the side so her cheek was against his shoulder. "About what?"

"You."

He felt her smile against his skin. "What do you want to know?"

"Everything." The truth came out before he—a man who made his living picking just the right words—realized what he was going to say.

"My favorite color is green. I think vanilla is loads better than chocolate. I can't dance." She snuggled closer, fitting herself up against him. "Your turn."

"I'm a diehard Ice Knights fan. I do my best writing after my second cup of coffee and before my fourth. I think glass elevators are the worst invention in the world."

"Kade?" she said after a moment.

"Yeah?"

"I think we're becoming friends."

Oh, we're going to be so much more than that.

The words were on the tip of his tongue, but he couldn't say them. Not yet. First he needed to plot out his plan to get Thea to see this as more than a fling, more than an experiment. That meant not spilling his plot twist early. So instead, he lifted her hand and brushed a kiss across her knuckles before turning onto his side and tucking her against him so they fit together perfectly. He dropped his arm around her waist, cupped her breast, and held her tight as he tried to plot his way into making this something more than a wedding fling.

But still less than a relationship, right, because you don't do those—ever? He didn't know how to respond to his nagging inner voice, so he closed his eyes and just ignored it. For now, at least.

Chapter Sixteen

Over the next few days, Thea kept finding herself again and again in Kade's RV. Needless to say, her ability to ditch her sister, her mom, and the entire camera crew had reached elite levels. It also helped that Kade's RV was backed up to the area blocked off for resort staff only, where the reality TV show's cameras weren't allowed.

Somehow her clothes, every bone in her body, and her ability to stay away from him for longer than thirty minutes at a time had evaporated. She'd tried to explain it to herself as the thrill of sneaking around and the petty fun at getting back at her sister by banging the best man Jackie abhorred all over the resort. Of course, she knew she was lying, but she'd deal with the reality of the situation after the wedding when they all went back home.

For now, she was living in the unplanned moment, newly baptized into the church of spontaneity, and as long as she kept her head straight, everything would work out just fine.

She silently reminded herself of that as she traced a lazy line over the owl tattoo spanning Kade's chest while they lay in his bed. The sheets were tangled around their legs as they lay naked, with her draped over him. Technically, they were supposed to be playing racquetball with the rest of the wedding party—the bridesmaids accessorizing with bright-blue leg warmers and the grooms with blue and white–striped headbands. They'd made their appearance, and once all of the cameras were focused on Jackie and Dex as they took the court in matching parachute pants and Members Only jackets while the Go-Go's played over the loudspeakers, she and Kade had snuck off.

Hand in hand, they'd dashed back to his RV, and she was half naked before he even got the door closed. Seriously. Keeping her clothes on around this man was practically impossible.

"You know," she said, starting the little fun-facts game that seemed to be their thing. "Before the Greeks gave their gods human forms, the owl was a symbol for Athena. She was the goddess of wisdom and war—a total badass. There are statues of her with an owl at her side so she could see the whole truth."

"I just thought it would be a cool tattoo," he said as he wound a strand of her hair around his finger, his eyes half closed and his breathing steady.

She propped her chin on her hand and stared at him, lifting an eyebrow. "Really?" She scoffed.

"It's the honest truth." He lifted his head and looked down at his tattoo, squinting as if he was trying to picture something else. "But maybe adding Athena into the design would be a good call."

Butterflies broke loose in Thea's chest, and a ridiculous amount of happy hormones flooded her system at the idea that he just might take her idea into consideration, tattooing a permanent reminder of her on his chest, even.

Girl. You need to calm the fuck down.

She would if she could, but being with Kade was like being high. There was a rush and a freeing sense of ease, and her shoulders finally inched down from her earlobes because it didn't feel like anyone could shove her aside on their way to get to someone more important.

"You're thinking hard enough I'm surprised I can't hear

each thought." He drew circles on the bare skin of her lower back in slow, easy movements. "What made you tense up?"

Because the truth—the way he made her feel—was very much not on her list of shit to say out loud, Thea said the first plausible thing that came to mind. "My sister and mom."

"Are they still assigning you Cinderella tasks?"

She flinched at the dig, correct as it was. "They aren't *that* bad."

His circling stopped, and she cringed at getting caught in such an obvious lie.

"Fine," she said with a sigh and laid her cheek down on his chest, taking a moment to listen to the reassuring *thud-thud* of his heart. "They are, but not all the time. In fact, Jackie's actually been looking at me a little differently since the whole foam-heart thing."

He wrapped his arm around her, tucking her close against his side. "When you went all quiet that day and just sort of froze? I did not think that would be the outcome."

"Well, the outcome wasn't the way I would have normally reacted." The surge of adrenaline that had shot through her when Jackie had gone all bridezilla had been enough to steal her breath away.

For more than a few moments, she tried to resign herself to just accepting her part was to suck it up and do what needed to be done. Then she'd heard Dr. Kowecki's voice talking about the experiment and, well, she'd gone a different route. "I would have just gone along with it, no questions asked, no pushback given, because it was easier than dealing with whatever blowups would inevitably happen. But freezing like that? It actually gave me the time I needed to sort out how I was feeling and what exactly I was reacting to that was sending me into panic mode. I guess that's growth."

Thrilling was the wrong word. She hadn't been exactly excited and happy about it, but she was flush with a sense that she had control over things. She didn't have to just accept. She could demand. And she had.

"It wasn't the act of adding the flowers that pissed me off," she said, her blood pressure picking up at the memory. "It was that neither my mom nor Jackie seemed to care enough to ask me." Her voice cracked on that last bit, and she swallowed past the hurt forming a lump in her throat. "They just assumed I'd do it. I mean, they're right, but I still should have been asked."

Kade gave her a squeeze and dropped a kiss on the top of her head. "Seems fair enough."

She melted against him, taking him up on his silent offer of solid comfort.

God, she was going to miss this when she got home.

Sure, she had her girls Astrid and Nola, a great career, and an apartment with an amazing view, but sometimes coming home to the dark, silent apartment wasn't quite all that she wanted it to be. She wanted to be able to cuddle naked in the middle of the afternoon, talk about stupid things like the best Godzilla movie, and have the best sex of her life that left her drained and completely hyped up at the same time. Was that really too much to ask?

She'd have to chat it over with Dr. Kowecki when she got back to Harbor City, the idea of which suddenly had her feeling antsy for reasons that had nothing to do with going to see her therapist. She sat up, curling her legs up to her chest and resting her chin on her knees, not sure what response was best for the anticipatory dread she was starting to feel about this wedding coming to an end in a few days. Fawn? Fight? Flight? Freeze? All of the above?

She was in her early thirties. Wasn't life supposed to be easier by now? First, there was the discovery that she'd still get zits as an adult—and now she had to figure out the right thing to do? It wasn't fair. She sighed.

Kade sat up, cocked his head to the side, and shot her a questioning look.

"Nola is going to be insufferable when I tell her that going to see Dr. Kowecki was just what I needed," she said, coming up with the first truth that popped into her head that had nothing to do with having more feelings (ew, gross) than she knew what to do with.

"You guys are close?" Kade asked as he moved on the bed so he sat behind her.

She nodded. "Since college."

He swept her hair back and began massaging her shoulders, his strong fingers working out the kinks and releasing the tension building up between her shoulder blades. "It's good to have people in your life who are constants."

There was something in how he said it, a lingering wish that he wouldn't let float all the way to the surface, that made her chest ache.

"Do you have that?" she asked, even though she knew the answer already.

He continued to work her shoulders with the same steady pressure and control. "I have Dex and a couple of good friends back home."

There it was again, that echo of something he missed so much he couldn't even say it out loud. It didn't take a genius to figure out what—or, more correctly, *who*—he was talking about. He slid his palms down the outside of her arms and then wrapped his arms around her waist and bracketed her legs with his, cocooning her in his strength.

"And before you ask what about my parents," he said, his voice gruff, "my dad died years ago, and Mom left when I was in high school."

They'd promised not to talk about their moms, but if he was going to shove that rule into the firepit, she wouldn't argue—as long as they were focused on *his* mom.

"She seems to be trying—at least from what I can tell from seeing her here."

"She's an alcoholic. It's kind of her thing. She'll tell you all about the things she's going to try. I'll try not to drink during the week. I'll try to stop at one glass. I'll try not to let it affect you. That last one really isn't true, and it sure fucks up everyone else, too."

And that's where that ribbon of hurt that threaded through his words came from.

The realization made her heart ache for the boy that he'd been and the man he'd become. She pivoted, turning enough that she could look at him. His expression was smoothed into one of absolute neutrality, as if none of this had anything to do with him.

She laid her head in the pocket of his shoulder as she wrapped her arms around him, trying to give back some of that comfort he'd given her. "Is that why you won't talk to her?"

"That part of my life is over." He shrugged, but it was a little too casual to be sincere. "The door is shut. She's the one who slammed it closed. I'm not interested in reconnecting. Second chances are for people who still think there's good in the world. I've got fifteen true-crime bestsellers under my belt that prove that's not the case."

They lay there in companionable silence for a few minutes, each lost in their own thoughts. Then, he shifted so he was behind her again and her ass was nestled up against his cock. He reached around, cupping her breast, rolling her nipples, and tugging them taut.

"So," he said, as if he wasn't making her writhe against him already. "Where do you live?"

"Changing the subject by digging for a little personal information?" she asked, going for nonchalant but coming out breathy and needy instead.

They'd made an agreement. No life stories. No real connection. No taking it beyond the wedding.

"Abso-fucking-lutely." He brushed a kiss across her shoulder. "It's important for our experiment."

"Oh yeah?" she asked. "How?"

"Somehow," he said as he pinched her nipples with just the right amount of pressure that her legs seemed to spread on their own.

Her vibrators didn't stand a chance after this man.

"I live in a fifth-floor apartment." The words came tumbling out as she let her head fall back against him, giving in to the pleasure. "No kids. No cats. No elevator in my building."

"East Coast or West?"

"East." She put her hands on top of his, stilling them. They were about to hit the point of no return, and she had to try one last time, because this man deserved the peace that was so obviously eluding him. "If your mom came all the way out to Colter's Hell, don't you think maybe you should at least hear her out? I'm not saying take her out for a belated Mother's Day dinner, but fifteen minutes to listen with an open mind? See what she has to say?"

"No," he said, the curt tone of his voice ending the conversation.

Thea let out a frustrated huff. "You're the most stubborn person I know."

"As a fellow East Coaster, I'm gonna take that as a point of pride."

Her brain automatically wanted to ask where. The questions came into her head almost as fast as her pulse picked up with excitement. He'd mentioned being an Ice Knights fan—was he close enough to Harbor City that she could fly out to see him or he could come to see her? Was it within driving distance? Was there a chance that maybe this could last beyond the next few days?

"City or small town?" she asked before any of the other questions could slip out first.

He slid his hand down her abdomen, his fingers spread wide as he went south at his usual torturous pace that had her spreading her legs years before he got down to the top of her already wet core and stopped tantalizingly short of her clit.

"I live in a midcentury fixer-upper outside of a city with my dog and a trio of feral cats who seem to show up on my back porch every morning while I'm having coffee."

"So you feed them," she teased.

He kissed her shoulder, somehow making it into one of her top five erogenous zones. "Just some leftovers when I have them."

"Which is every morning?" she teased again.

"Brat," he said as he cleared the last inch to her clit, circling the sensitive nub with his fingertip.

After that, there wasn't any more talking.

Chapter Seventeen

Kade should have stayed in bed with a naked Thea.

But like an asshole, he'd left her there and had shown up on time to the groom's lunch that was being held in a small barn near the skeet shooting range. That's when he'd found out he'd been sandbagged. Instead of the groomsmen sitting with Dex at the table loaded down with burgers and fries, it was their mom.

Oh, and a whole camera crew that were already rolling, catching his every reaction as realization struck.

Kade jerked to a stop inside the door, his guts churning and bile coating the back of his tongue with its foul taste, and looked from a determined-looking Dex to a nervous-looking mom, who had her arms wrapped around her middle. He had half a heartbeat when he felt bad about that, but then almost two decades of resentment went off like cherry bombs in his chest.

Ignoring his mom, he focused all of his fury on his brother, who fucking knew better.

"Are you kidding me with this?" He ground out each word through clenched teeth.

"No," Dex shot back, the level of pissed off in his tone nearly matching Kade's. "It's beyond time you two finally worked this shit out."

"I didn't know about this, either. I just thought I was coming to lunch," his mom said, her voice soft but sure as she stepped between the brothers as if her presence could possibly lessen the tension. "It seems like a good idea, though."

Kade barked out a laugh. *She* thought it was a good idea. Well, she also thought abandoning her family was a good idea, so he'd withhold judgment on that one.

One of the cameramen sneezed, yanking Kade's attention off his family. Usually there was just one cameraperson and a production assistant filming. But there were two camerapeople, three assistants, and the producer, Justine, trying to be as unobtrusive as possible, since they were all squeezed into the same small space. That's when it all made sense to him, and his whole body went ice cold with the knowledge. He knew why Dex was doing this ridiculous wedding. But why their mom had shown up had escaped him. Until now.

He turned his frigid gaze on his mom. "Yeah, I imagine that'll make for great TV. Everyone loves a redemption arc. It doesn't get better than being at the center of that, huh, Mom?" His attention ping-ponged over to his brother. "And the ratings? Through the roof. Perfect for someone willing to do whatever it takes—including getting married—to get as many people as possible to watch his show and get his movie distributed."

"Fuck you, Kade," Dex said, his hands fisted at his sides. "You don't have the slightest clue what you're talking about."

There was only one thing he could do in reaction to that kind of bullshit. He threw back his head and laughed.

"So you love Jackie Pope?" He wiped away pretend tears of amusement, dialing up the asshole factor to a million. "You actually want to be married to a woman who treats her own sister like the shit on the bottom of her shoe?"

Dex had the decency to drop his gaze to the floor and look embarrassed. "We've talked about that. Jackie's got pressures of her own, obligations."

"And her own shitty fucking personality—or is that just a regular personality by Hollywood standards?" Kade was on a roll now. He spent his life being unperturbed, even-keeled, unflappable. Less than five minutes in his long-lost mom's presence, and he sounded like a replica of Dad. Shame twisted his gut, but he couldn't stop. "Is that how you are when I'm not around? Is that why you decided to set up this little reunion that is not *gonna* happen?"

Dex rushed at him, fury twisting his Hollywood good looks into something else entirely. "I'm going to fuck you up."

"Yeah?" Kade rebalanced and shot his brother a mocking grin. "I'd like to see you try."

"Boys!"

Their mom's voice boomed in the small room, jolting Kade and Dex to a complete stop as if they were in grade school about to go ham over a pair of action figures.

"You are both wrong—and right. Dex. You're right that your brother and I need to talk. You're wrong in trying to trick him into doing it when he's not ready—especially in front of cameras." She jabbed a finger in the air toward him. "And you, Kade. You're right this isn't the forum, but you're wrong about why I'm doing this. It isn't about a redemption arc for me. It's only about trying to make things right with you after all I did wrong."

That took some of the pissed off right out of him. He didn't deflate, but he definitely had to take a second to recalibrate. And Dex, being his brother and the person who knew him better than anyone else in the world, swooped in to take advantage.

Dex yanked his mic pack off and tossed it out an open window.

"So we do this the way we should," Dex said. "Just us. No cameras. No mics." He paused and glared at Kade. "Unless, that is, you're afraid you're feeling too tender for it."

Kade shoulda knocked his brother out when he had the chance. That was a low fucking blow, a direct hit right in the ego—his most vulnerable spot. The little asshole.

Still, Kade couldn't help but be a little proud of him for doing what needed to be done to make something happen. Underneath all that charm and good looks, Dex was still a St. James, and they were ruthless when necessary.

"I don't care one way or another about her," he said, clinging to the last thread of hope that he could avoid this.

His brother's smirk was dripping in mockery. "Then listening to what she has to say won't be any skin off your nose."

"Fine." He took off the mic pack he'd put on moments before entering the barn, and it went sailing out the same window as his brother's. "She talks. I listen. Then I leave."

"You two always were so dramatic," Mom said with a sigh as she handed her mic pack to the nearest member of the crew. "Do you mind giving us a few minutes off camera?"

Justine hesitated.

"Please," his mom said.

"Let's take five," Justine said, rounding up her crew and leading them out of the barn and shutting the door behind them.

Good fucking riddance.

Of course, that meant he was now stuck alone with the shambles of his family.

Dex closed the window and then stood in front of it, blocking anyone outside from getting a shot.

Kade sat down at the table and squeezed some ketchup onto the bison burger on the plate. If he was going to be stuck here, he might as well get something out of it. His mom sat down across from him and fidgeted with the silver napkin ring shaped like a bucking bronco.

"I can't even imagine how hard it was for you when I

left like that," she said, her quiet voice trembling. "Please understand, though, that I wouldn't have done it if it wasn't my only option."

Wow.

She was good.

He could see how she'd gotten Dex. The quaking chin. The regretful gaze. The air of absolute misery surrounding her. All of that together would have played on Dex's need to help anyone and everyone who looked like they were in trouble. The guy was a natural-born sucker—and Kade would beat the shit out of anyone who had a big enough case of the stupids to ever say that in front of him, but Dex was his brother and he could say it. Their mom would know it all, though. So she'd obviously played her youngest like an old piano with finger grooves worn into the keys.

"Not even saying goodbye to your *children* was your only option?" Kade scoffed as he lifted up the red plastic cup filled with sun tea in a salute. "Yeah, that seems very likely."

Chapter Eighteen

Kade's gut was churning, but he made damn sure neither his mom nor Dex had any idea. There was no way he was going to add another layer onto the shit sandwich of a lunch by showing this encounter was shredding him.

Meanwhile, Dex was all snarls and glares and fuck-you tension coming off of him in strong enough waves it was like he was a teenaged boy who'd tried to drown himself in body spray. And his mom? An embarrassed flush turned her cheeks beet red.

"Actually, walking away at all was my only option," she said, blinking away unshed tears. "I knew if I didn't stop drinking I was going to die, and the only way I could get sober was to leave. Your father—well, you know what your father was like." She clung to the napkin ring, holding it tight enough that her knuckles were turning white. "So I packed three bags—one for each of us—and made a plan to get out."

She paused, turning her head and looking up at a spot of nothing on the wall as she blinked rapidly.

Then, after a few moments, she let out a shaky breath and turned back to him. "Your father found out. He told me I'd never get custody, that everyone knew I was just a drunk and was obviously an unfit mother. He said you'd both be better off without me."

She leaned toward him, her hands hovering in the air above the table. His first instinct was to reach out, but he squashed that with the force of a man who did what needed to be done. She let out a small sigh and dropped her hands.

"I have spent years of my life wishing that I had done things differently," she went on, no longer looking at him but down at the untouched burger on her plate. "I wish that I'd thought to set aside money so I could hire lawyers to fight your father in court. But I didn't, and with his connections and access to his family's money, I knew I couldn't win." She looked back up at him, her eyes shiny with unshed tears. "Plus there was a part of me that thought he was right. What kind of mother picked vodka or rum or a bottle of merlot over her own kids? The same kind of mother who left her children. The kind of mother that walked away."

This was the perfect moment to slide the knife home. To tell her she was right. That only a bad mother would do that shit.

But he couldn't.

All that hope and want and belief that one day his mom would come back surged to the surface, decades after he thought he'd gotten rid of them for good.

What a fucking sucker you are, St. James. What a fool.

"By the time I'd finished my second stint in rehab and tried to reconnect," she continued, "your father wouldn't even let me talk to you."

"Bullshit," he said, his voice exploding from him, powered by the fact that she'd almost had him. Again. "I heard him. He kept saying you should at least say goodbye and explain why you left."

"No," she said, tears spilling down her cheeks. "You heard him mocking me as I begged to do just that. I never stopped wanting to see you and Dex, to be a part of your life, to make up for how things were when I was drinking. I love you, Kade. I always will."

How many nights had he waited up to hear just those

words? So fucking many. And he wanted to toss all of this into the trash, light the damn thing on fire, and then salt the earth after it was nothing more than ashes. But Mom wasn't wrong. Dad was a prick. He always found fault, always micromanaged every move his sons made, always intimated that whatever they were doing it wasn't enough and never would be. Kade had always chalked it up to the fact that Mom had left, leaving Dad a bitter shell of himself. But thinking back, he realized that wasn't the truth. He'd been like that even before Mom left.

The contradiction knocked him sideways, making his lungs tighten enough that it was hard to breathe, impossible to think, and way too fucking easy to just feel. Fuck that. It was not what he did. So he fell back into what was more comfortable than the uncertainty tearing through him like a tornado of guilt and shame and hurt—so much fucking hurt.

"Is that all?" he asked, keeping his voice cool and even. "Is that everything you wanted to say?"

Mom winced as she wiped away her tears with the back of her hand. "Yeah, I guess it is."

"Okay, then I fulfilled my part of the bargain. I listened." His chair squeaked against the linoleum floor when he pushed it back and stood. "Now, I'm leaving."

Dex snarled, "You giant pain—"

"No." Mom put her hand on Dex's forearm, silencing him. "It's okay. Let him go."

His brother looked like he was going to argue, but instead he crossed his arms and glared at Kade.

Whatever. Dex would get over it.

Just like you did with your mom?

Shut the fuck up, brain.

Kade strode out of the barn, ignoring the camera crew coming in for the after-the-talk shot, and made a beeline for his bike and freedom from this fucking disaster of a wedding.

He was five miles down the road before the irony hit him. He'd spent his entire life swearing he'd never be the one to abandon the people he loved, and yet here he was with half a mind to keep going and never look back.

But he couldn't—wouldn't—do that to Dex.

And Thea?

He wasn't sure he'd ever be ready for that goodbye.

Chapter Nineteen

Thea sat up in Kade's bed with a start, her heart going about four hundred miles a second.

Bridesmaid luncheon.

Today.

"Fuck!"

What time was it?

She grabbed her phone and let out a frustrated "fuckity fuck fuck" when she saw the series of texts from her sister that got longer and more hysterical as they went.

J: *Where are you?*

J: *WHERE*

J: *THE*

J: *FUCK*

J: *ARE*

J: *YOU*

J: *?*

J: *?*

J: *?*

J: *You're not in your RV. Are you OK?*

J: *Thea!*

J: *Theadora Eloise Pope you better answer me even if you're dead.*

J: *I know you're not with that dipshit Kade because he's with Dex. Where are you?*

J: *The producers have my agent on the phone, and they do not give a shit that I am worried about you. I have to go do this bridesmaid luncheon. You better be there when I get there, or you better hope I don't find you.*
J: *THEA!!!!!!!!!*

And this was how things went from bad to worse. Jackie's level of pissed-off panic could always be measured by the number of all caps, exclamation-heavy texts she sent.

Thea flopped back onto the bed and covered her face with Kade's pillow before letting out a loud groan. She needed to get moving. Now. The only problem with that? When she'd inhaled, she'd gotten a good whiff of Kade, and now she wanted to lay in bed, tangled in his sheets and surrounded by his scent.

And *that* realization was what finally got her ass out of bed, because if there was one thing more painful than dealing with Jackie's ire, it was falling for a guy she was just supposed to be anger banging like the petty paleontologist she was—or had become, or always had been and never realized, or—

"Ugh, get *up*, Thea!"

A quick dash to her RV and the world's fastest shower later—yes, she took the time to shave her legs; she had priorities...sexy-times-later priorities—and she was fast walking across the resort, wrestling with getting her hair in a ponytail despite the never-ending wind. She stopped just around the corner from where the sunrise yoga had happened the other day so she could suck in a couple of deep breaths and prep herself for whatever hell was incoming.

"You got this, Thea," she told herself, not believing it even the littlest bit.

Then, she forced her feet forward into the very bowels of doll French braiding hell. Jackie, their mom, and the bridesmaids each had a large dimple-faced doll and were in the process of braiding their yarn hair.

"Oh my God, Thea! Jackie was losing her shit," one of the bridesmaids, Lakin, said, her voice loud enough to be heard in the next state, let alone get picked up by her mic. Then her eyes narrowed as her lips curled into a cruel smirk. "Were you off fucking the best man again?"

Thea jerked to a stop, nervous sweat beading at the nape of her neck as one of the camera operators pivoted to focus on her. This was when her sister would improv some sassy comeback that would leave the other woman grasping for any kind of retort. But Thea was not her sister. Stomach twisting, she clasped her hands together and said—absolutely nothing.

Not a word.

Not a peep.

Not a semi-understandable mumble.

Nothing.

"I can't blame her," the other bridesmaid, Piper, chimed in, her tone sickly sweet. "A woman like her has to grab the opportunities when they come. Good for you!"

Thea could feel the camera's focus on her, as heavy as a thick wool blanket. It made her palms sweaty as she fought the urge to make a half-hearted chuckle of agreement. Really, it wasn't like they were wrong.

"Don't answer where you were!" a member of the production crew yelled as they rushed over, mic pack in hand.

The bridesmaids used the pause to adjust their hair and add another coat of lipstick. Meanwhile, Jackie didn't move an inch—unless you counted the way her tight, narrow gaze combed over Thea as if she was noting every flaw, every not-quite-up-to-par spot, and making notes to herself about areas of improvement. It was an exact replica of every time her mom had looked at Thea, clocking each zit and wild hair slipping free of her ponytail, right before she'd quit acting for good.

"Here," the crew member said after wrapping the mic pack belt around Thea's waist and holding out the mic. "Clip the lav mic on the collar of your shirt, and you'll be good to go."

Her hands were clammy enough that she was afraid she'd drop the mic, but she managed to get it hooked to the bright-yellow Cabbage Patch doll T-shirt that Jackie had made her wear today. Of course, Thea was wearing it long and loose over the electric blue bike shorts Jackie had insisted they wear today, making Thea look like an overgrown toddler. The other bridesmaids and Jackie, however, had done that thing that some people could do to modernize even the most retro of outfits to make it look cool to modern eyes. One of the bridesmaids had tucked the ends of the shirt into her sports bra, giving her an instant crop top that didn't leave her drowning in miles of cotton. Another had tied it into a knot at her waist in a way that highlighted her curves. Jackie, meanwhile, had threaded the long hem through her bra and tied the ends between her breasts so it looked like her Cabbage Patch T-shirt was actually a cute bikini top.

Girding herself for yet another game of which-one-of-these-bridesmaids-doesn't-belong, Thea grabbed all of the hair she'd missed on her walk and stuffed it through the hair tie at the base of her ponytail. This event was going to be fucking delightful.

"Okay," the production crew member said as they whirled around and went behind the camera line, "let's do this."

"Wait!" her mom called out in a stress-strained voice as she rushed over with a freckle-faced Cabbage Patch doll in her hand. "She has to have a doll or the sponsor is going to freak the fuck out."

Thea took the soft-bodied doll with long dark hair that went down to her waist and was dressed in hospital scrubs with a BabyLand General Hospital logo on them. "Thanks, Mom."

Her mom smiled, a grateful curl of her lips, and that frazzled, overwhelmed look in her eyes receded. "Thank you," she said, her voice low. "It has been a morning, let me tell you."

Thea looked around at the bridesmaids who were watching them out of the corners of their eyes like a pride of lions pretending to be asleep as the gazelle that had been separated from its pack wandered by. It took all she had not to take a step back before taking her chances and running for the high ground. That's when her gaze landed on Jackie, whose pinched expression and tense jaw left no doubt about her mood.

"It seems a little tense," she whispered to her mom.

Her mom raised her eyebrows and tilted her head in acknowledgment. "I've been backstage when someone says good luck to the entire cast instead of break a leg and the mood was more relaxed."

"Are we ready?" the production assistant called out before Thea could ask for details.

"Yep," her mom responded, her titanium-level momager mask dropping into place with a nearly audible thump. "Everything is perfect." She gave Thea a quick squeeze. "You got this, champ. It'll be like old times."

Got this? What did she mean *got this*?

Unease skittered along Thea's spine and up the back of her neck, the same kind that haunted her at night when she had a stress dream that put her right back to her most dreaded place to be—the center of attention. The camera crew focused their lenses back on her as her mom backed out of the shot. From her spot a few feet away, Lakin over-enunciated a few vocal exercise tongue twisters as she shook out her arms before turning her attention back onto Thea. Her gaze was glacial and her smile anything but friendly.

Fuck.

Thea felt sick, a wave of nausea knocking her off-kilter as her entire body, from the tiny hairs on her toes to the weird overlong hair that grew out of her right eyebrow, yelled at her to do whatever it took to make this all go away. It was her nervous system equivalent of stop, drop, and roll.

"Like I asked," Lakin said, each word as sharp as knives in a professional kitchen. "Were you off having shy-girl-gone-wild sex with that rough-looking best man?"

"Rough?" Piper said, taking a few steps forward and angling her body so she was centered in the shot. "Really? Come on, Lakin. Some of us prefer guys who look like they could take on a mountain lion and win."

"I guess I like 'em a little more refined." Lakin all but hip-checked Piper out of the best spot in the camera's line of sight and gave Thea a slow up and down before her lips curled upward in a sickly-sweet smile. "Then again, not everyone can be as picky."

On instinct, Thea stepped back, getting out of the line of fire as her brain filled with white noise, and her gaze dropped to the ground as she clutched the soft, oversize doll to her stomach like a shield.

"Lakin," Jackie said, her voice barely above a whisper, but it didn't need to be. Everyone—*absolutely everyone*—turned their attention to the bride. "Stop. Being. A. Bitch."

"What?!" Lakin threw up her arms in frustration, then planted her hands on her hips. "It's a reality TV wedding. I'm not here to make new friends. I have you two, and even if I was looking for a new wing woman, I highly doubt a suitable one could be found in this hellhole." Her voice broke on the last word, and she let out a sad whimper of a groan. "I can't even get the special chef-made meals my agent insists I eat or he'll drop me delivered here, so I'm either bloated or starving because my body hates *everything*."

Her bottom lip trembled, and she sucked in a dramatic,

stuttering, gaspy breath. The move triggered Thea's sympathies because she was a softie and no amount of working on her panic responses was going to change that. Not to mention food sensitivity was no joke. She could have exactly one scoop of ice cream before her whole body sent up flares.

Meanwhile, Jackie stood there, her arms crossed, and waited—not giving an inch.

Lakin made a squeaky huff and continued, "The working conditions are ridiculous, and I am going to have to burn my clothes because there's no way the stench from that river is ever going to come out of it."

The other bridesmaid perked up at this. "Can I have your Birkin, if you're just going to light it on fire?"

"Piper," Lakin said with an eye roll. "No one trashes a Birkin. Stop being such a blonde stereotype."

The other woman blinked her large green eyes. "My hair's black."

"And if anyone's being a stock character, it's you playing the mean girl," Jackie said as she stepped between the bridesmaids. "Take a breath. Enjoy life for thirty seconds. Reevaluate your need to be competitive about everything all the time." She picked up a bowl of chocolate-drizzled popcorn balls from a nearby table. "Take one. They're gluten-free and packed with chia seeds. You'll feel better."

Lakin looked skeptical but exhaled in a huff. "Fine."

She took a bite-size lumpy ball, popped it in her mouth, and her whole body visibly relaxed as she closed her eyes and let out a soft moan of pleasure. Everyone watched in silence as she finished the popcorn ball. Thea rooted for the salty-sweet treat to do its job. Finally, Lakin swallowed the last bite and looked over to Thea.

"I've been such a bitch since I stopped vaping, and I took my withdrawal out on you," she said, sounding sincere in a way that went beyond the possibility of acting. Lakin's cheeks turned pink as she gave Thea an apologetic smile. "I was being awful. I'm sorry."

Thea returned her hesitant smile, not because she had to in order to get her panicked nerves to stop jangling but because she wanted to. It was kind of freeing.

"It's okay," she said.

The production assistant let out a disappointed sigh at her response, but everyone in the bridal party ignored her. Lakin, Piper, and her mom all sat back down at the tables where their Cabbage Patch dolls were waiting, yarn hair going every which way. Thea hung back, not sure where to sit or what to do. Awkward? Oh yes. Her pulse kicked up along with her breathing when she realized Jackie was heading right for her.

Shit. Shit. Shit. She really did not want to deal with her sister's mood. She was confrontationed out.

"Here, sit by me and I'll catch you up." Jackie linked her arm through Thea's. "This challenge is intense. We have to get the doll's hair to look like that." She pointed to the large photos of dolls with elaborate updos and lowered her volume so only Thea could hear. "It's like *Nailed It* but with Cabbage Patch dolls—both are sponsors."

Thea took in the waves and curls and pinned perfection of the dolls' hair in the photographs. "That does not look remotely possible."

"Well," Jackie said with a tired sigh, "I guess the fun for some people is watching others fail."

Fail? Jackie had never failed at anything. She wasn't an A-lister, but she'd made the transition from kid actor to adult actress in a cutthroat business that left 99 percent of people wondering what bus had just run them over and left them broken on the side of the road. Her sister wasn't a failure. She was a tough-as-acrylic-nails badass.

That was true, but there was no denying her too-tight shoulders, the way she squinted even though she wasn't looking into the sun, or the fact that she was doing that middle-finger-to-thumb tapping thing she'd done whenever something was really bothering her since she was a kid.

Jackie might be—okay, was—a total pain in the ass, and yes, Thea was still totally pissed off at her, but she was also still her sister.

"Nah," Thea said, pulling up from her reserves to disagree with her sister instead of just letting Jackie think her pronouncement was the end all, be all. "I think what people like is experiencing the joy of watching someone try and have fun no matter the outcome."

One side of Jackie's mouth curled upward in her actual off-duty smile—the one that her first agent had told her never to do on camera because it made her look deranged. "Don't you sound enlightened."

"Therapy," Thea said with a wry chuckle.

"I might need your therapist's number," her sister said as they walked over to the tables and got to work on their dolls' hair.

A half hour later, Thea looked over the results of the Cabbage Patch hair challenge. The results were as much of a nightmare as she'd expected. Still, she placed her doll with its monstrosity of a French twist next to the others and laughed along with everyone else. Then, after a group photo that would be all over the wedding social media streams within minutes, Jackie and her mom left to go meet with the minister and the other bridesmaids went back to their trailers for some mani/pedi time.

Thea was on her own again, but for the first time since she'd gotten to Colter's Hell, she felt like this week wasn't going to be a total disaster. That's when she spotted Kade coming straight at her, looking like he was pissed off enough to crush boulders with his bare hands.

Chapter Twenty

The sun beat down on Kade as he parked his motorcycle back at the resort, in the exact same spot it had been before he'd left—like someone had saved it for him because they'd known he'd be back.

Just like you knew you would, St. James.

Shut up, asshole.

Great. Now he was not only talking shit to himself but he was responding, too. Usually, he only did that when he had five chapters to go in a book and was writing pretty much twenty-four seven because the words were just flowing in a rush to the final scene. But he wasn't writing. He was back at the resort in the middle of nowhere Wyoming, walking somewhere, but God knew where. He sure as fuck didn't.

His brain had all but checked out for the moment as he strode down the path, not headed to anywhere in particular but knowing he had to move or he just might explode.

And he didn't stop until he was back where they'd held sunrise yoga the other day. Today it was cordoned off for some bridesmaid activity that Thea was supposed to be at. Instead, the place was empty except for some abandoned dolls and a skeleton production crew. He ducked back behind a tree before they spotted him.

He'd *known* there'd be a camera crew here—exactly what he was trying to avoid. So why was he here?

"You look like you're about to go find a buffalo to fight,"

said a familiar voice from behind him.

Yeah. That's right. Thea.

He hadn't planned it. Didn't mean to be here. Still, his feet had taken him right where he wanted to be—with her. Fuck. There was no way that was a good thing.

"That option seems as good as any other," he grumbled as he turned around, more than a little annoyed at himself for even subconsciously wanting what he shouldn't.

She was holding a doll and wearing a ridiculous T-shirt with an illustration of a doll on it that hung loose on her and had him thinking about way too many tempting fantasies focusing on how easy it would be to slip his hands underneath. Her hair was back in her usual ponytail, and he flexed his fingers in an effort to distract himself from the idea of just how good it would feel to wrap the silky strands around his fist. Then there was her smile, as bright as the perfect spring morning that made him feel all soft and warm inside.

All of those things individually were more temptation than a man like him was built to withstand. Together? It just pissed him off, because there was no denying the fact that walking away from Thea Pope at the end of this wedding nightmare was going to suck.

"You know, in therapy, I'm learning how to be mindful and weigh my options," she said, walking over so that she was next to him, her light, summery scent wrapping around him like the softest of bindings. "Maybe it's something you should consider—playing with something more enjoyable than a two-thousand-pound animal with horns and a bad attitude."

He gave her doll a pointed look. "You're not talking about playing with that, are you?"

She shook her head, a blush eating its way up her cheeks as she obviously mentally egged herself on to say something. "No, but adult playtime does sound fun."

With Thea? Fun wasn't the word he'd pick. Mind-blowing? Maybe. Fan-fucking-tastic? Closer. Exactly what he needed, way more than he was used to? Yeah, that was about it. And if he only had a few days left with her, turning down her nervously offered suggestion wasn't even an option.

He meant to tell her at least part of that, but all that came out was a desperate growl of a "fuck yes."

After a quick glance around to make sure the coast was clear, he took Thea's hand, and they headed down the path toward the RVs. He was already picturing exactly how he was going to make her come hard around his dick when they turned the corner and almost ran smack into Justine, the producer, who had her back to them. They skidded to a stop in the middle of the path and exchanged a fuck-no look. The producer started to turn. Kade didn't think; he just moved.

He pulled Thea off the path and behind a small equipment shed barely big enough to hold a riding lawn mower and leaf blower. Thea's eyes went wide as he pressed against her, pinning her to the door.

The last thing a smart man would do under these circumstances was take the opportunity to grind against her, surround himself by her soft curves and her sweet heat. It wasn't the time. It wasn't the place. There were fucking cameras or reality TV people *everywhere* they looked. Good thing he'd never considered himself an overly smart man.

He pressed up close, her soft curves fitting perfectly against his every—very hard—edge. The shock in her eyes faded to a heady desire, and the tip of her pink tongue wet her bottom lip. Fuck. Those lips. Full and soft and just so damn tempting. He had plans for those lips. Lots of plans. However, it turned out so did she, because her hands went to the hem of his shirt, sneaking underneath and going right for the top button of his jeans.

"Impatient," he said, keeping his voice low.

She unsnapped his jeans. "I know what I want."

So did he, but he also had no intention of getting caught. He reached behind her and grabbed the doorknob, twisting it at the same time as he wrapped an arm around her waist to keep her from falling back when the door swung open behind her. In the next breath, he moved them both inside the shed and closed out the rest of the world with one well-placed kick.

"Babe," was all he got out before she had his zipper open and her hands in his pants, wrapping her long fingers around his hard cock.

With his back against the door, he exhaled a harsh breath as she shoved his jeans and boxer briefs halfway down his thighs and freed his dick. She gripped him with just the right amount of pressure to make it impossible to keep his eyes open. It was too good, and if he looked at her as she stroked him he was going to come all over her hand. That was not going to happen—not until he was buried deep inside her and she was already coming down from her orgasm.

Thea, though, seemed to have other plans, because the next thing he felt was her tongue on the head of his cock as she licked the tip in long, slow swipes, following it with her soft lips before taking him in deep into her warm mouth. Christ. The back of his head thunked against the door. He didn't feel it. The only thing he could pay attention to was the way Thea was working him, sucking and teasing and blowing his fucking mind along with his cock. The rest of the world disappeared from the face of the earth as wave after wave of too-damn-good slammed against him, pushing him closer and closer to the edge.

He managed to crack his eyes open and look down at her. It was a mistake. Whatever control he thought he had left snapped the second she looked up, her mouth full of him, and winked. Before he could come in the world's most embarrassingly quick amount of time, he grabbed her ponytail and gently pulled her back.

The loss of her soft mouth was agony, but he was a man

who knew his limits. "Fuck, Thea."

She tightened her grip at the base, squeezing with just the right amount of I-decide-what-happens to put him right back on the edge of coming. "Maybe later, if you're good."

"Is that really want you want?" he asked, surprised he could get the words out, considering she'd gone back to stroking him with one hand and squeezing his balls with the other. "For me to be good?"

Her glasses were tilted and her wet lips swollen when she replied, "Nah, I like it when you're bad."

She slipped the hold he had on her ponytail and stood up, daring him with her expression to react. Oh, she didn't have to worry about that. She wanted more, and he was going to give her just that.

"Turn around," he said, his voice hard and demanding. "Hold on to the shelves."

He grabbed his wallet out of his back pocket as she did so and then rolled the condom on. Then he reached out and grabbed her shorts by the elastic waistband, pulling them down in one swift move. Arching her back and presenting that sweet round ass of hers, she stepped out of her shorts and then looked over her shoulder at him.

His breath caught. She was wearing only an oversize T-shirt with a cartoon doll on it, her glasses were comically cockeyed, and she was surrounded by random lawn-care tools stacked haphazardly on shelves. And Thea was the hottest woman he'd ever seen in his life.

Fuck his life, he was about to tell her that, too, and maybe more, when some emotional survival instinct kicked in, and instead, he grabbed her hips and bent his knees just enough so he could line his dick up with her slick entrance. After that, his brain stopped functioning. All there was to the world was Thea and the tight grip of her pussy on his cock.

It wasn't slow. It wasn't easy. It verged on base instinct, as if his body knew something his brain might never figure out and it wasn't about to miss out on being that close to heaven. He fucked her hard and fast, and she urged him on, meeting his every push forward with her backward move. They didn't flirt or tease—they were both lost in the way their bodies moved together, both reaching for more.

The closer he got to his orgasm, though, the harder it was to keep his sense of control, but he had to. He wasn't about to come before she did. Holding on tight to her hips, he held her in position, hypnotized by the way her ass jiggled with each thrust, mesmerized by the sound of her moans as she begged for him not to stop. He slid one hand around her hip and slipped it between her thighs, rubbing her clit, circling it over and over as her breathing became erratic and she clenched tighter around his dick until she came with a strangled cry.

That was all it took for the last thread of his control to break. He pounded into her over and over as her pussy continued to clasp and let go of his dick. The tension in his body ratcheted up, tightening and strengthening until it seemed like he was either going to snap in half or—

He came in a rush that turned his brain inside out and blasted every semi-thought out of his head. There was just absolute perfect silence and the sense that everything—for once—was right with the world.

By the time he came back into himself, still trying to catch his breath as he withdrew from Thea and got rid of the condom in a trash can filled with yard clippings, he was already fighting tooth and nail to get back to who he was before he met Thea Pope—solitary asshole and beyond fucking happy about it.

But that snarly jerk seemed like a character from another dimension.

Holy hell, St. James, you really have just fucked yourself, haven't you?

Chapter Twenty-One

Thea was never going to look at a leaf blower the same again.

Sure, she'd never gotten a hello-happy-pants feeling about the smell of cut grass *before*, but then again, she'd never gotten straight-up railed the right way while holding onto a wooden shelf stacked with watering cans and gardening tools before, either.

Damn, her thighs were still wobbly.

This was definitely going into her remember-when mental filing cabinet for after the wedding. The one that was happening in two days. The one she'd been counting down the moments until from the instant she'd boarded the plane. The one that she couldn't wait to put in her rearview mirror up until the moment Kade St. James strode into her life with a flask full of Sprite and had anger banged her into some kind of orgasm fiend.

Seriously. She couldn't get enough of the man.

Yeah, well you better. Because in forty-eight hours, you're off to dig up some dinosaurs and he's—

Her brain blanked. Well, she had no idea where he lived. Just like she barely knew anything else about him beyond the fact that he was avoiding his mom, loved his brother, and thought this entire week was a disaster.

Watching the muscles in his forearms as he buttoned his jeans shut—insert mental sigh of disappointment here— she tried to remember all the reasons why she'd insisted on keeping things as anonymous as possible between them.

It had made sense at the time, but the reality was that the only thing that had really done was make her more curious. What city did he live near? How did he take his coffee? Did he make his bed in the morning or just sort of yank the top sheet and blanket up? What was his stance on breakfast for dinner? What was his Sunday morning routine?

These were all things she shouldn't want to know, but she did. She really, really did.

Ugh. Why couldn't anything about her life be easy?

She let the elastic band of her shorts snap back in place with a sharp smack that stung for a second that wasn't even close to long enough to pull her back from the edge of falling for Kade St. James.

Honey, you suck at no-strings flings.

"Everything okay?" Kade asked as he closed the distance between them, reached out, and tucked an errant hair behind her ear.

The tip of his finger brushed the shell of her ear, sending a shiver of desire through her.

"You missed a hair," he said, his gaze dipping down to her still-kiss-swollen lips.

If her internal warning system made a sound, it would be deafening right now, sonic booms of girl-you're-about-to-go-down-like-the-*Titanic*.

Heart hammering in her chest, she said the first thing that came to mind just to cover up all of the jittery freak-out going on. "You seem less likely to go on a buffalo rampage."

His hand was still by her ear, and he trailed his fingers down the side of her neck, looking at her as if he couldn't believe she was real. "Amazing how being with you will fix that."

"I'm glad I could help." An embarrassed flush burned her cheeks, but she forced herself not to drop her gaze to his feet. "I like helping you."

Whoa, girl. What are you doing, telling the truth? Might as well start doodling his name on every possible writing surface like you're in middle school all over again.

"That's kind of what we've got going here, right?" He grinned at her as he took a step back, breaking contact. "You help me. I help you. We both survive this wedding from hell."

Her chest was too tight all of a sudden. They had rules. They had a time limit. This was not about building a bond. This was an *arrangement.*

"Oh yeah," she said, her tone too loudly jovial, too yes-please-pick-me-please, too fast-talking frenzied—but she couldn't help herself. "That's exactly it. Just two buddies doing each other a solid."

She slammed her mouth shut before any more inanities could come out.

Buddies?

Doing each other a solid?

What the fuck, Thea? You have a PhD. You can talk without sounding like a fool.

And that was before she registered the fact that her voice had gone up in pitch, and she couldn't get the uncomfortably big maybe-she's-a-stalker smile off her face.

One side of Kade's mouth kicked up in an indulgent half smile. "Are you about to fight me, run away, agree with me, or freeze?"

Considering she had so much adrenaline running through her veins at the moment that it felt like she just might start levitating, there was only one thing she could say to that. "All of the above."

"Yeah, sometimes really amazing sex will do that to a person," he said, his voice low and intense.

She flinched, imagining all the other women he'd been with who'd made him feel like that. "You speak from experience?"

Why did the idea of him being with other people make her gut churn? This wasn't a relationship. It was just temporary fun.

"Yeah." He stepped in close, looking down at her with an intensity that made her breath catch. "Happened to me for the first time a couple of minutes ago."

Breathing was no longer something her body did automatically, because all she could do was stare while two words screamed through her head.

Holy shit.

Holy. Shit.

HOLY SHIT!

Her heart was going just-downed-a-dozen-iced-coffees fast, and she probably could have powered a small city with the amount of nervous energy coursing through her. What was she supposed to say to *that*?

"So lunch with your brother went bad?" she asked, the absolute worst words (besides *I could totally fall in love with you, let's go have babies and name them after dinosaurs*) coming out in a panicked rush.

Kade stilled, his gaze sharpening as he scanned her face. Her stomach flopped. Yeah, it didn't take a genius to realize that had been the very wrong thing to say, not just after he'd said *that* to her but in general.

"That's putting it mildly," he said as he took a step back, getting as much distance between them as possible, given the equipment shed was the size of a large walk-in closet.

She grimaced, cringing all the way down to the marrow in her tiny toe bones. *Way to go, Thea.*

"Dex set me up," Kade said, the muscles in his jaw flexing as he crossed his arms as if he needed a shield. "My mom was there."

"Oh." Without thinking of what she was doing, she

walked over to him and reached out and laid her hand on his forearm, stopping herself—barely—from wrapping her arms around him and holding him tight. "And it went badly?"

The expression on his face darkened as he ground his molars together. Tension made the air electric, marching across her skin like a line of ants and making her shiver in a very not good way. She was about to tell him to ignore her question. It wasn't her business. But before she could, he shoved his fingers through his hair, making it stand up on end so it went every which way.

"She wants a second chance. For what, I have no fucking clue. Didn't she fuck me up enough the first time?" He winced and locked her into place with the plea in his eyes. "Forget I said that. I didn't mean it."

Yeah, that wasn't going to happen. Acting on instinct and the way the hurt in his eyes made her want to fight the world on his behalf, she gave in a little and wrapped her arms around him from the side. His body tensed for a breath before relaxing against her.

She pressed her cheek against his arm. "I know there's history there but—"

"She left us," he said as he broke free and strode the three steps to the other side of the shed. "She just walked out the door one day and never came back." He whirled around and looked at Thea, the pain—still so fresh after all these years—shining in his eyes. "She didn't call, didn't email, didn't text. Nothing. For years. Decades." His voice broke on the last word, and he dropped his gaze, looking at the floor while he fisted and unfisted his hands.

After a few beats, he let out a harsh breath and looked back up. His face was carefully blank, and an air of don't-fuck-with-me encircled him like a force field. "Then a few years ago she reached out. Dex picked up and talked to her. I hung up as soon as I heard her voice."

"Oh, Kade," she said, fighting to stay still because it was obvious that he did not want to think he needed the comfort. "I'm so sorry."

"It is what it is," he said with a shrug. "I'm over it."

As if she could—or would—ever believe that. She too knew the seductive power of denial. How many times had she agreed to go along with some plan of her mother's or dream of her sister's or wrong-headed promotional decisions of her boss at work because it seemed easier than the confrontation she'd built up in her mind? Too many to count. Kade may not be fawning out of panic, but he was lying to himself about how much he still wanted a relationship with his mom and how much that scared him.

"How old were you?" she asked.

His jaw tightened. "Fourteen."

Wrapping her hands around her middle, she held herself, since he was—and was staying—out of reach. God, her chest ached for him. "And she didn't give any explanation?"

"She did, but not until today." He paused, and then let out a facsimile of a laugh that would only sound happy to a serial killer. "She said she tried to talk to us but that my dad blocked her while she was in rehab—something I can see him doing—and afterward we refused to take her calls. It was too late. We were fine without her." He looked at the shed's lone dirt-encrusted window. "I don't need people in my life that leave, but Dex says she deserves a second chance."

"But you don't think so?" Nothing like stating the obvious—or at least what she was damn sure he *believed* to be obvious. "No second chances for you?"

He jerked his head around, his focus like a laser beam aimed right at her. "Is this where you tell me I'm wrong? Because I'm not."

"It's not my place to say if you're right or wrong or what you should do." She let out a shaky breath as she tried to thread her thoughts into one coherent idea, her pulse wild with anxiety at actually pushing a point rather than just accepting. "Still, you have to admit that we all fuck up. Sometimes it's a small thing, sometimes it's a huge thing. I'm not saying to forgive her, but maybe giving her a second chance is worth thinking about. Just something to consider."

Her lungs were tight, and she could barely breathe, but she held her ground under the severe heat of Kade's glare. They stayed like that for one heartbeat, then another, and another as every nerve in her body seized up. Then, Kade let out a breath and some of the tension eased out of his rigid shoulders.

"I don't think you're right," he said, his tone nearly back to normal, "but I appreciate the input."

Oxygen whooshed back into Thea's lungs on a wave of relief.

"Families are hard." Wasn't that the fucking truth. There were a million more things she wanted to say about Kade and his mom, but the man had the pinched face of someone on the edge, and she didn't want to be the one to push him over. A change in subject seemed the kindest thing she could do. "We better get going before they send out a search party looking for us."

"This wedding is the worst," he grumbled, but with the beginning of a real grin as he crossed over to the door and opened it a crack, no doubt to make sure they weren't going to be ambushed by a camera crew the instant they walked out.

"Yeah," she said, the words coming out before she could stop them, "but at least I got to meet you."

He glanced back at her and winked. "We'll be doing more *meeting* later tonight, if I have anything to say about it."

"That sounds like the one thing that will get me through whatever they have planned for the bachelorette party." Sort of like how she looked forward to an oversize spoonful of the emergency Betty Crocker chocolate frosting at the end of a hard day.

"Great minds." He opened the door the rest of the way and stepped out, then held out his hand for her. "Now, once more unto the breach."

Chapter Twenty-Two

A few hours later, Kade was mic'd up again and had one camera focused only on him, even though it was Dex's groomsmen who were failing at flirting with the bored bartender.

Dex's bachelor party wasn't like any other he'd ever been to or heard of. No strippers, no ax throwing, no Vegas, no intensive yoga retreat that included a drumming circle, no pub crawl through London. Instead, it was Dex and his buddies doing shots and holding an impromptu movie trivia contest. In between rounds of guessing the movie this line came from, the groomsmen were doing their best to impress the bartender—a woman who looked like she had been putting up with annoying tourist behavior for years and was beyond unimpressed with it all.

Watching these pretty boys flame out was almost enough to put a smile on Kade's face—not like the kind he couldn't seem to stop whenever he was around Thea, but close. He should be more worried about that than he was.

Sometime between agreeing to her anger bang plan and this afternoon in that lawn equipment shed, he'd started to pretend that there wasn't a clock ticking on going home. Oh, he knew he was full of shit, but pretending to believe his own bullshit was better than acknowledging that in forty-eight hours he'd be on a plane home.

Alone.

That was exactly what he didn't want to be thinking about. So instead, he was leaning in against the bar in the big barn where the first reception party had been held. There were cameras everywhere, and the mic attached to the collar of his shirt kept itching his collarbone. Trying to distract himself, he twisted a bit so he could better eavesdrop on the bartender as she gave the Hollywood types the what for when it came to hockey (how in the hell was she an Ice Knights fan clear out here?) compared to the L.A. Inferno. That's when Dex bellied up to the bar next to Kade and set down four shots hard enough that some of the brown liquid inside them sloshed over the sides.

His younger brother's usually picture-perfect hair was going six ways to Sunday, and one eyelid drooped lower than the other. Unlike Kade, Dex did drink every once in a while, but he'd never seen him drunk before. He wasn't ski-slope drunk, where he had to lean forward to keep his balance, but Dex was weaving just enough that Kade used his forearm to move the shot glasses out of the way in case his brother went timber.

Dex huffed out a breath and picked up one of the shot glasses. "We're doing these shots."

How drunk was his brother to forget Kade didn't drink? "I don't—"

Dex shoved the shot glass practically into his mouth. "Drink it!"

That's when Kade caught on to the fact that the brown liquid in the shot glass had tiny little bubbles popping when they hit the surface and had the distinctive fruity cola smell of Dr Pepper.

"Here, let me," Kade said, taking the glass from his brother.

The little glass had *Dex Hearts Jackie* etched onto it inside a heart. Kade gave the drink another sniff. It smelled like straight-up Dr Pepper, but who in the hell knew what kind of shit the production crew was up to?

"Thass it," Dex slurred and then picked up his own shot from the bar. "To love true ever for."

What the—

Kade didn't even have time to finish the thought before Dex was tossing back his shot as he stumbled a step forward. The move brought him close enough that his elbow hit the bottom of Kade's shot glass, sending the liquid flying. At the same time, Dex let out the mother of all burps, which made his head bobble, and he ended up spilling his shot, soaking the collar of his own T-shirt—the exact same spot where Kade's shot had landed.

Oh yeah, and that was where the mic was hooked to their shirts. The ones that had emitted a little crackle sound when they'd gotten soaked.

Some people believed in coincidences. Kade did not—especially not when it came to his brother. That little fucker. He was about as toasted as Kade was. A snort-laugh escaped before he could stop it. Dex's hand came down hard on his shoulder, and something that read a lot like shut-the-fuck-up-asshole flashed in his supposedly inebriated brother's eyes before they faded back into a drunken haze.

"Shit," Dex mumbled, leaning forward enough that he pushed Kade back a few inches. "Thas sucks."

"Okay. Okay. I get it," he said, his voice low enough that only his brother could hear before pivoting so he was next to Dex so he could sling his hand over his shoulder. "I think you need to sit down."

"Thass a good idea." Dex wobble-walked alongside Kade over to the couch in the section of the barn the production crew had warned earlier had shit reception for the wireless mics. "Perfect."

One of the cameras was focused on them, but the sound

guy kept adjusting the knobs on his equipment while another crew member sent him death glares.

"That was quite a show," Kade said.

Dex relaxed against the back of the seat, slumping a little but twisting his body so that his back was to the rest of the room. His gaze sharpened immediately. "I thought you were never going to catch on. You're supposed to be the smart one."

Kade shrugged. "We're all stupid sometimes."

"No fucking shit," Dex grumbled, looking like a man who could really use something stronger than the Sprite in Kade's flask. "What in the hell was I thinking?"

"With the wedding or with that bullshit you pulled with Mom at lunch today?" Was he an asshole for putting it that way? Maybe, but he didn't give a fuck.

"You're being the dummy with Mom," Dex shot back. "I'm talking about the wedding."

Yeah, he was full of shit on that one, but Kade had had enough battling today so he skipped past it. "A PR wedding doesn't seem like such a great idea all of a sudden, huh?"

Dex sank lower in his seat. "Not when you're in love."

Kade started. "Fuck. Who?"

It sure as hell wasn't Jackie. There was no way his brother—even as soft as he was—would fall for someone like her.

His brother shrugged, a pinched and pained expression on his face. "It doesn't matter."

How many times had he talked to Dex about how ridiculous this wedding was? About a million before they'd even gotten to Wyoming. At absolutely no point in any of those conversations had his brother even hinted at being in love.

"You can't go through with this," Kade said, glancing over at the camera crew to make sure they were still all-seeing but not listening.

"I can't *not*," Dex said, following Kade's cue and taking an intoxicated-looking slow head roll that didn't give away the game.

The sound guy was exchanging oh-yeah-fuck-you-too words with the camera operators.

"Contracts have been signed," Dex said when he turned back around. "Funds exchanged. My agent called today because he heard a distributor is interested in my movie. Plus the TV show has been renewed for another season. Jackie and I are getting everything we want."

"Not everything," Kade said, pointing out the obvious that his brother was missing even though it was slapping him across the face.

"No one gets *everything*, at least not in the real world," Dex said. "When the cameras are off, you have to be happy with the scraps."

That was fucking bleak coming from his younger brother. "Holy shit, you sound like Dad."

Dex toyed with a wedding napkin someone had left on the table, twisting it up and shredding it into small strips. "Even an asshole wrong clock is right twice a day."

"You can't go through with the wedding," he said loud enough to get a glare from his little brother. Kade punched down his frustration at having to watch the one person who'd always been there for him make a life-altering mistake. "Then you really will be like Dad. He never loved Mom. If he had, he wouldn't have treated her like he did."

One of Dex's eyebrows shot up. "Almost sounds like you're sticking up for her."

"I'm not, I just…" Kade's voice died away as he tried to figure out what in the fuck he wanted to say. "Someone pointed out that maybe it wouldn't hurt to see things from her perspective, to consider the extenuating circumstances."

"Like our dick of a dad?" Dex scoffed.

Now it was Kade's turn to shrug. "Something like that."

His brother wasn't wrong. Their dad was a piece of work, always looking out for himself first, warning the boys not to do anything that would reflect badly on him, and reminding them that no matter what they did, it wouldn't be enough. All of that, and no one would have believed it from the outside. Their dad had been the ultimate diplomat, office buddy, and golf partner to them. The man was a borderline narcissist and probably the reason why Kade was obsessed about the real person people were behind the facades.

"You know, I remember when she left," Dex said, continuing to tear up the napkin into smaller and smaller pieces. "I was out in the side yard, and I saw the cars pull up. These huge dudes got out, hustled inside the front doors, and then a few minutes later came out flanking Mom on both sides. She didn't fight it, but she was crying. I called out to her, and she turned around. Her mascara had run down her face, and she had that glassy look of being three-quarters of a wine bottle in, but she smiled at me, and it was like the sun coming out after a thunderstorm."

Kade remembered that smile. He could picture it now without even trying, and for half a second his entire chest was filled with bright hope. That smile had been the bane of his existence. It was the one that made all the promises that this time would be different. It never was.

"Then one of the guys grabbed her by the elbow and whirled her around, strong-arming her forward," his brother went on, the vein in his temple pulsing as he decimated the napkin. "I yelled out for her to stop, but she just looked at me over her shoulder, her eyes all watery. I started to run toward her, but Dad appeared out of nowhere, it seemed, and grabbed me by the back of the shirt. By the time I looked back toward Mom, the car was pulling out of the drive."

It hadn't happened that way for Kade. He'd come home from a friend's house, and their mom was just gone. For years, he thought he'd gotten the short end of that stick. Looking at his brother, though, he wasn't so sure anymore. Fuck.

Now *he* wanted a damn drink or to kick his father or to give his brother a giant fucking hug that would make everything all right. None of that was possible, though, not with him not drinking, their dad being dead, and the camera crew looking for any sign of emotions they could wring dry for ratings.

So instead, Kade reached out and did that awkward man-to-man shoulder-pat thing. "I never knew that."

Dex gave a dry chuckle empty of humor. "Well, kinda hard for you to know when I stopped talking."

"Christ." Kade closed his eyes and let his head fall back and hit the wall with a thud that felt better than the dread filling him up. He thought he'd protected Dex better than that. He hadn't. "So what are you going to do?"

"Marry Jackie," Dex said without hesitation or enthusiasm.

"Whatever they're paying you to be with her," Kade said, wishing like hell he could just snap his fingers and fix this for his brother, "I'm not sure it's worth it."

Dex gave him a twisted, sad smile—the same one their mom had given him at lunch.

"Yo Dex," one of the groomsmen hollered. "Time for another round of shots!"

Dex grimaced. "I really could have done without the whole alcohol sponsorship deal."

That explained why in addition to stirring up trouble, the production team was so hell-bent on having them drink all the time.

"How much did you spot the bartender to sneak you Dr Pepper shots?" Kade asked.

"Front row seats whenever the Ice Knights play Denver for the next season," Dex said. "You coming?"

To go pretend to do shots with a bunch of knuckleheads and argue hockey? That sounded about as much fun as dunking his head in honey and then laying down on an anthill.

"Nah." Kade shook his head. "I wanna change my shirt."

"How much does that have to do with the fact that the bachelorette party should be breaking up about now?" his brother asked with a knowing grin.

There wasn't any point in denying that, so Kade didn't.

"Don't do anything I wouldn't," Dex said with a chuckle that sounded almost like his old self.

Then he stood up, and, almost like magic, his brother's right eyelid came down just a bit, his mouth slackened, and he unfocused his gaze just enough to look like he was drunk enough to fry two mics by accident.

"Shee ya, brother," he slurred before turning around and weaving his way back over to the groomsmen already holding up shots.

The group made a big production out of taking their shots, then broke into a loud rendition of the L.A. Inferno's fight song led by a very inebriated-sounding Dex. And that was Kade's cue. He unhooked his mic pack and left it on the table along with the Dr Pepper–soaked mic before making his way outside to find Thea.

Chapter Twenty-Three

That evening, Thea couldn't have felt farther away from the lawn shed of lust than if she was on the moon.

After an hour spent with Jackie and the bridesmaids getting eighties makeovers for the bachelorette party, she was dressed in a shiny teal-and-magenta monstrosity of a prom dress that looked like it was made out of highly flammable wrapping paper. The sleeves were puffed. The skirt was tiered. The waist was dropped. And her hair? Thanks to a mountain of teased-out temporary extensions, it was ten miles high and pulled into a high side ponytail. And she didn't even want to think about her makeup. Her eyeshadow matched the dress, shade for shade, and her mascara was a bold electric blue that fought for dominance with her bright-pink lipstick.

Of course, it could be worse. She could be wearing Jackie's outfit. Her sister was wearing a grape-Kool-Aid-colored dress with a sweetheart neckline made out of the same cheap metallic material as Thea's. However, Jackie's tiered skirt abomination had been styled with a black satin bow and a copious amount of ebony tulle under her skirt.

Between the dresses and the amount of hair spray locking everyone's eighties hairstyles in place, it was no surprise production had warned them all not to go near any open flames.

Maybe they should have warned them to stay away from Jell-O shots. Instead, Lakin, Pepper, Jackie, and Thea had drowned their dress sorrows in sugar-free gelatin spiked with vodka while playing throwback games like lawn darts and bocce ball. By the time the crew finally let them take ten precious off-camera minutes to shake off their "being on" personas, most of the Jell-O shots were gone.

"This is a fucking nightmare," Jackie groaned as she sat down on the iron bench where Thea was. She held out a small tray loaded down with tiny plastic cups filled with green and blue gelatin. "Jell-O shot?"

Thea grabbed a lime-flavored alcohol treat and slurped it down. "*This* is a nightmare?" she asked as she gestured toward the makeshift dance floor under the stars where Lakin and Pepper were chatting with the production crew. "You wanted all of it."

"Not this. It's just the shit I *have* to do." Jackie's shoulders slumped as she rested the tray on her lap and she let out a harrumph of a sigh before letting her head rest on her sister's shoulder. "It's not all roses for me, you know."

Thea didn't. Everything seemed to come easily for Jackie, and if it didn't go her way she strong-armed it into submission. She was a force of nature and always had been.

Still, sitting here feeling the light floatiness of being tipsy off Jell-O shots with her sister by her side made Thea remember the days when they'd been closer. The times when they could talk to each other without saying a word or when there was never any doubt that they had each other's backs. It had been years since that was their reality, but at this moment, it felt like not a day passed since they'd last spent an all-nighter watching scary movies while huddled together under the same giant blanket. God. Thea hadn't realized just how much she'd missed that up until now.

Emotion clogged her throat as she blinked away unexpected tears and tilted her head so it rested against the top of Jackie's.

"So why do you do it?" Thea asked her sister.

"Because I love it." Jackie gave a shaky laugh that teetered on the edge of tipping over into tears. "I love trying on a character for a while and getting lost in it, the opportunity to let someone watching escape into a new world, and that sense of community that comes when you make something together." She sniffled and sat up, pivoting in her seat so they faced each other. She lifted her chin in defiance. "People make light of it, but life is fucking hard, and we need to have a place to let ourselves believe that our hope for something better isn't misplaced. I know my shows are silly, that it's not important like what you do at the museum, but..." She ended the sentence with a loose-limbed shrug as her chin dipped back down and another sniffle snuck out.

Thea scrunched up her face in an effort not to let how much she ached for her sister spill out into tears. God, she knew that feeling. The not-enough feeling. The not-meeting-expectations feeling. The hollow, achy, you-could-be-more feeling. She never expected to find out her sister experienced it, too, and the guilt for that oversight hardened the spiked Jell-O sloshing around in her stomach.

"What you do is important." She put her arms around her sister's shoulders and squeezed, hoping she'd feel the truth in her touch if she didn't catch it in her voice because Thea meant every word. "It's not an either-or. It's a both."

"Both?" Jackie's chin trembled, and she started blinking rapidly as she looked at an empty spot on the wall. "I can't even have a world where the guy I love thinks of me as anything more than a friend."

Thea gasped, surprise flooding her system so fast her jaw went slack. "What?"

"Fuck. I should stop with these now." Jackie grabbed another plastic Jell-O shot cup from the tray on her lap and sucked it dry. "Or maybe I should get a few more."

"Tell me everything."

"There's nothing to tell," Jackie said with a shrug. "He loved me. I said I only had time for my career. He said he understood, and we became friends, and then I realized that I'd biffed it. He was amazing. Of course he moved on. That's what great guys do—they find people who have it in them to have feelings." She looked around as if flabbergasted by everything she saw. "And now here I am, with the kind of wedding every girl dreams about, acting like the queen of bitches while trying not to cry my eyes out because the last thing I fucking need on top of it all is for social media to analyze all of the ways I'm a haggard old crone who always looks tired."

What the fuck? "You're not even thirty."

"Exactly! I'll be playing the mother to some guy a few years older than me in a few seasons." Jackie set the tray down on the floor and nudged it under the bench with the heel of her bright-blue satin high heels and then took Thea's hands in her own, holding onto them tight. Her eyes glimmered with unshed tears and determination. "But it's not too late for you. Don't make the same mistake I did. Promise me. You'll regret it, and then you'll find yourself in acid-washed overalls and a sports bra in the middle of nowhere Wyoming where it smells like sulfur and lime Jello-O, getting shitfaced on the eve of your wedding."

"That was very specific." And a lot to process. All of the new information was swimming around in Thea's head like rabid sharks in a feeding frenzy.

"I'm serious, Thea." Jackie grabbed Thea's hands, clasping them tight in her own. "Promise me."

"I promise," she said between gritted teeth because of how her sister was squeezing her knuckles together.

Jackie lifted a perfectly shaped eyebrow.

Thea let out a pained huff of breath. "I promise not to let

someone I love go."

The pressure on her hand eased, but Jackie didn't let go. Instead, she swallowed and looked up at Thea with big, rounded eyes.

"That includes me?" she asked.

The tip of Thea's nose tickled with the rush of emotion. It had been years since she'd experienced that sisterly connection like they used to have. But somehow in all this craziness, they'd found a way to excavate, brush off years of dirt, and shine it to a perfect sheen.

"Yeah," Thea said, her voice breaking, "that includes you."

Jackie threw her arms around Thea in an awkward sideways sitting-on-the-bench hug. "I love you, too."

By the time her sister sat back, they were both wiping away fat tears from their cheeks with the backs of their hands, but they were smiling. Huge grins. The kind that made a person's cheeks hurt.

An old eighties song about it raining men blasted through the speakers. The bridesmaids let loose with some high-pitched, drunken "wooooooooooos" of approval and started calling for Jackie to join them.

She got up and took a step toward the dance floor before turning and looking at Thea with a grin. "So are you going to blow them away with your moves or what, Tiffany?"

Thea snorted at the idea of playing her last TV role one last time. "Tiffany Twist is retired."

"So is Crystal Cancan." Jackie smiled and jerked her head toward the dance floor. "For old times' sake."

Thea had never been a rush-out-on-the-dance-floor kind of person. She liked to chair dance, maybe stand in a corner half hidden by a fake tree or something and break out those old Tiffany Twist moves that she still knew two decades after that show ended. But her foot was tapping against the ground, and Jackie was giving her *that* look—the one that when they were growing up had always led to trouble and a helluva lotta fun.

"My name is Crystal," Jackie said in a singsong voice that made her part of the theme song sound even dorkier than it had been with backing vocals and the house band. "I like to cancan on the dance floor. Are you with me?" She planted her hands on her hips before singing her line again. "I like to cancan on the dance floor—are you with me?"

Shaking her head, Thea mumbled the scripted response back.

Jackie made a tsk-tsk sound and waved her finger in time with the beat they both knew by heart. "Tiffany Twist, your dance floor awaits."

Thea rolled her eyes. "No more Jell-O shots for you."

But she got up anyway and walked arm in arm with her sister out to the dance floor, not because she felt she had to so she could avoid a blowup but because she wanted to. Thea didn't miss the cameras or the yelling directors or the pressure of being a child star, but she did miss silly moments like this with her sister.

So she took the dance floor with her sister, and they reenacted the opening dance sequence to the one kids' show they'd been on together, portraying sisters with more enthusiasm than skill at an all-girls dance academy. It had been one of the best summers of her life, filming those episodes with her sister. The show had only lasted a few episodes before cancelation, but Thea and Jackie still knew the moves by heart.

That's the way it worked on the really good days. The palpable sense of happiness and feeling that things were going to be better from now on found a way to burrow into a person's heart and power them forward. Tonight didn't just feel like one of those good days. It felt like the best of them.

And the only thing that could have made it better would be if Kade was here, too—which was pretty much the last thing Thea should be thinking but was still the only thing on her mind.

Thea ignored the tightness in her chest as she swung around into the next sequence of choreographed steps without thinking—all the while praying she wasn't going to have to keep her promise to her sister later tonight and tell Kade she was starting to fall for him. At best, he'd feel sorry for her and pretend until the bride and groom said "I do" so he wouldn't hurt her feelings. At worst... Well, the "at best" was pretty bad, so there was no way she'd even try to imagine the worst. Instead, she'd just dance and pretend that the wedding was still a week away.

Chapter Twenty-Four

Kade had no fucking clue what he was doing.

For the past ten minutes, he'd been lurking on the path that led to the pavilion where the bachelorette party was in full karaoke mode, by the sounds of it, trying to decide if he should follow it or just wait for Thea to leave the bachelorette party. It wasn't that he'd planned on coming down here to find her—he'd just gone for a walk and had ended up here, leaning against one of the trees and straining to hear her voice in the screechtacular version of "We Got The Beat."

He closed his eyes so he could better focus on each individual voice. The high-pitched one had to be the short bridesmaid. What was her name? Pansy? Pepper? Piper—that was it. The low, I've-been-done-wrong one couldn't be anyone other than Jackie, and it was tinged with enough true emotion to make him wonder if there was more to her than just being a bitchy bride. That left the hesitant middle voice that always came in with the lyrics half a beat behind. He tried to imagine that singing voice coming out of Thea's mouth, and for some reason, it just didn't fit.

"Just the man I was hoping to see."

His eyes snapped open at the sound of Thea's voice.

She was standing a few feet away from where the path curved around a large growth of sagebrush. Her hand was on her hip, and the glow from the path sconces bathed her in soft, golden light. She had this relieved look on her face as if she was so fucking happy to see him, and everything inside him settled. All the questions about what he was doing, how long he'd skulked around, and where he should go next were answered in a heartbeat. He was waiting for Thea, for as long as it took and wherever she wanted.

The realization had just enough time to hit his brain before he was moving again, striding toward her. He was moving quickly, but it wasn't fast enough. The need to be near her, touching her, with her, was an overwhelming, primal, gut-level insistence that he couldn't deny if he'd wanted.

As soon as he was within arm's reach, his heart hammering in his chest as if he'd just run a sub-four-minute mile, the whole world faded away. The awful singing. The sound of the crickets. A coyote somewhere in the distance. There was just Thea and him. The air around them was thick with promises and possibility, and he'd never in his life felt more like he was exactly where he was supposed to be.

Then, the sound of a branch snapping registered half a second after Kade brushed his thumb across her plump bottom lip, and the rest of the world came rushing back. He looked down the path, and his gut tightened.

Camera operators.

Production crew.

A guy holding a damn boom mic.

They were all coming out of the RV that acted as their command center and hadn't noticed him and Thea yet. One of the camera guys took a hit off his vape while two crew members groaned and one told him to fuck off away from them.

"We gotta get the hell out of here," Kade muttered, taking her hand and stepping into the shadows so they were somewhat hidden from view.

Thea nodded. "Preferably before they spot us."

"What happened to the woman who was so concerned

that first night with not meeting her contractual obligations not to sneak around to avoid the cameras?" he teased.

She lifted an eyebrow. "Do you really want to have that conversation right here, right now, or do you want to go to your RV without us ending up on the live stream?" She freed her hand and gave him a flirty wink. "Race ya."

She took off, running through the trees away from the crew. He didn't hesitate. He didn't have to. Following Thea was just the right thing to do.

By the time he yanked open the door to his RV, they were both a little out of breath from how fast they'd sprinted. He barely got the door closed behind them before they both burst out in gasping laughs. The giant belly kind of laughs that barely made any noise because you couldn't get enough air in. Usually, it was the kind of manic giggles that happened when something was just hysterically funny and unexpected. However, it also happened at those times when a person had been wrung out and there was nothing left to do but let it all fucking go. This was that time. The wedding. Her sister. His mother. The cameras that were always everywhere. All of it combined to make a real hell in a place that was just named one where everything was a nightmare.

Except for her.

Except for Thea.

In half a heartbeat, his laughter turned to lust. He had her up against the RV's closed door. His hungry, desperate mouth was on hers, kissing her everywhere but her mouth, claiming her in a way that he hadn't realized until that moment that he wanted to. No. Check that. He needed to. And judging by the way she was responding, her body demanding everything that he could give, he wasn't the only one on the edge of something that couldn't be controlled.

He flipped her around, putting her palms flat on the door, and then he lowered the zipper of her dress, letting it drop to the floor. The only thing she had on underneath was a pair of pale blue sheer panties that barely covered her perfect, round ass. They were temptation come to life, giving him just enough of a look to make him desperate for more.

"Take them off," he practically growled out, "or I'm gonna rip them off you."

She dropped her hands, hooking her thumbs into the waistband and sliding them over her hips. They slid down her legs to her ankles, and she kicked them off before arching her back, presenting her ass to him.

He palmed her ass, caressing it and squeezing it enough that she let out an appreciative moan as she spread her legs. He slipped his hand between her thighs and plunged two fingers inside her, stroking her pussy just like he was going to fuck it—but not yet. He withdrew his hand to her grumbled complaints, grasped her hips, and turned her around so she faced him.

"What are we doing?" he asked, the words coming out before he had a chance to think better.

A flush spread up her cheeks, and her gaze dropped down to his hand spanning the width of her bare thigh. "Anger banging."

"Bullshit," he said, his tone harsher than he meant.

She watched him for a second, her eyes wary. "You're saying there's more?" she asked and leaned back against the door as if she wanted him to believe she didn't think there was.

Too bad he knew better, and he was going to prove it.

"Fuck yeah." He spread her legs wide and settled on his knees between them, a man ready to worship. The sight of her wet pussy so soft and swollen for him made his brain go blank for a second. He reached out as if in a trance, tracing the pad of his thumb around her clit so lightly that there was barely any contact. Still, her moan of yes-but-more made his dick

ache. "We broke your rule about not making it personal."
He looked up at her face, taking in her parted lips, the dark
desire in her eyes behind her cockeyed glasses. God, she was
beautiful. "I know you." He increased the pressure of his
thumb, giving her almost as much as she wanted, drawing the
anticipation out. "You know me. We don't know everything
about each other, but it's enough for a start, for something
more than just fucking to piss off your sister." He stopped,
his thumb hovering in the air above her clit. "We're friends."

"Yes," she said, the word coming out like a plea.

"Are you just saying that because you want me to touch
you?" Using his thumb and pointer finger, he spread her lips
wide, stretching her, completely exposing her swollen, needy
clit to the cool air conditioning. "Because you know I will. If
you want it, I'll do it—lick you, fuck you, make you come on
my hand, my thigh, my cock that's so hard it fucking hurts."

He dipped his head between her thighs, pausing just long
enough to inhale her scent, and then he lapped at her clit. He
licked it, sucked it, and kissed it, lavishing all of his attention
on that one sensitive spot. Her head fell back against the door
with a metallic thunk, and when he moved his head to glance
up and make sure she was okay, she sank her fingers into his
hair and held him in place.

That was fine with him. Being between her legs was
pretty much the best place in the whole world to him. He
slipped a finger inside her slick entrance, and then another,
finger-fucking her as his mouth stayed busy with her clit. She
clenched around him, and he curled his fingers inside her,
rubbing and circling as her thighs started to shake on either
side of his face.

She let out a lusty moan, then begged and pleaded for him
not to stop, her grip on his hair loosening. She didn't have to
worry. He'd give her what she wanted—just not quite yet.

He pulled back but kept slowly fucking her with his

fingers, stretching them apart as he thrust forward and retreated.

"And you know what I'll do after I make you come where I want?" He licked the glorious taste of her off his lips. "Then I'll make you come again. And again. And again. I'll keep making you come until you can't even pick your head up off the pillow, and you won't care because you'll feel too fucking good."

His gaze dropped to where his fingers were going in and out of her, every single part of him focused on Thea as if the world began and ended between her thighs. "And why can I do that?" He pressed his thumb to her clit while his fingers continued to work her harder, faster, while he watched her face. Her eyes were closed, her mouth open, and her breathing erratic as she reached for that orgasm she was on the edge of. "Because I *know* you, Thea Pope. I knew you the first moment I laid eyes on you outside your sister's RV."

She bit down on her lip as her core clenched around his fingers, her orgasm making her whole body tight. He waited, watching the pleasure roll over her as if it was the most magnificent thing he'd ever see—and it probably would be. And when it started to ebb, when her eyes began to open, he went back for more. He was softer this time, cognizant of the way she may be more sensitive, but he teased her still-pulsing clit with his tongue as she begged and pleaded for relief until she found it in another climax, bucking her hips forward with the urgency of it. Losing contact with that sweet pussy of hers was at the top of his things-I-hate list, but she needed the break, so he did, even as he stayed kneeling between her legs, his cheek resting against the inside of her thigh that was slick with her own pleasure.

"Thea Pope," he whispered, too quiet for her to hear, not realizing the words were a solemn promise until he started talking. "I don't ever want to *not* know you."

Chapter Twenty-Five

Even though Thea was as blissed-out as a human could possibly be, the look in Kade's eyes as he watched her, her satisfaction making his chin all shiny, sent a shiver down her spine. She had no idea what in the world he was going to do to top two orgasms, but damn if she wasn't ready to believe that whatever it was, it was going to rock her world.

"I'm not sure my legs are going to hold me up for much longer."

He stood, a self-satisfied grin on his face. "I got you."

Then in one swift move, he picked her up so her core was pressed against his long, hard length under his jeans and his gaze caught hers. Something passed between them in that moment, something she couldn't pinpoint or explain, but it stole her breath, and she just knew. If she didn't kiss him right here, right now, she'd regret it for the remaining decades of her life without him.

"Kade." She cupped his face. "I know we agreed, but would it be all right if I kissed you?"

He froze with his arms locked tight around her, and the smile faded from his face.

Thea's heart started to race, and embarrassment beat her cheeks red. Oh. God. OH. GOD. What had she done? She'd ruined it. She knew the rules. No kissing. Never on the mouth. That was their deal. It was their safety net to remember that this was just an arrangement. Nothing more.

And she'd fucked it all up. She started to squirm in Kade's arms, pressed her palms against his chest in an effort to get space between them before she imploded from humiliation, but there was no moving him.

"Thea," he said, sounding like a man who was not going to say it twice. "Stop."

"Why?"

"Yes, you can kiss me."

"I can?"

"Not if you take much longer."

Nerves jittery, she let out an anxious squeak of a sound, squeezed her eyes shut, and gave him a hurried kiss. It was so brief of a peck that she wasn't sure it even qualified. She opened her eyes, and all she could see was the annoyed look on Kade's face.

Way to go, Theadora Eloise Pope. You are masterful at this.

"You did it wrong," Kade said, his voice low and growly. "*This* is how we kiss."

While he held her ass with one hand, he used the other to grab her ponytail and pull her face close to his. And then he kissed her stupid. Seriously. The moment that man brushed his lips against hers, she lost track of most things. But when he started kissing her the way he was now, the way that promised anything and everything she'd ever even thought about wanting? It obliterated anything else from happening except for kissing him back with everything she had. She wrapped her legs around his hips, locking herself in place as he strode down the RV's narrow walkway between the sitting area and the kitchen to end up in his bedroom in the back. The room was dominated by a huge bed, and she had no doubts that they were going to use every single inch of it before they were done.

Kade broke the kiss and tossed her down on the bed.

"Stay there."

"Am I allowed to move?" she asked, trailing her fingers over her breasts. "Is this okay?"

His eyes darkened as he watched. He clenched his jaw hard enough that the muscles flexed as he ground his teeth, but he didn't say anything.

Well then, she'd take that as a yes. She grasped her puckered nipples, rolling them into even tighter tips, and then tugged on them, the sting of pleasure making her bite down on her bottom lip to keep from moaning. It wasn't that she didn't feel like she could make noise so much that she didn't want to pull him out of whatever trance he was in as he stayed focused on her. His nostrils flared when she gave her left nipple a little twist, and he let out a harsh breath, his hands fisting at his sides.

Whether or not Kade was enjoying the show wasn't a question. The man looked like he was so close to losing it. But was he inches close or millimeters close? There was only one way to find out.

She spread her legs, opening herself up to him so he could look his fill as she traced a lazy, meandering line down her belly. He watched her progress like a starving man observing the preparation of a nine-course meal.

"Stop," he ordered, the vein in his temple throbbing.

Oh, he was millimeters close. She was tempted to ignore him and keep going, but she ignored the impulse. Not because she was fawning, but because whatever he had planned was going to get her off so hard she might not be able to uncurl her toes in time for Jackie's wedding.

His hand went to the top button of his jeans, and he paused, one side of his mouth rising in a smirk. Then he toyed with that button, dragging his thumb over the surface, circling it like she wanted him to do with her aching clit. The asshole. He knew what he was doing. Thea held her breath, watching, waiting, desperate for him to flick it open. She'd just had two orgasms, and she could feel her heartbeat in her core as desire flooded her body.

"Kade," she pleaded, "torture me another time. Right now I need you."

"You need me?" He undid his jeans and lowered the zipper. "Or you need my cock?"

Thea was too far gone to lie. "Both."

He kicked off his shoes and then started unbuttoning his shirt one teeny-tiny little button at a time. Letting out a groan of frustration, she shot him a dirty look that only made him laugh. She'd make him pay for that.

"Because we're friends?" he asked once he finally finished undoing his shirt. "The kind of friends who fuck and flirt and kiss?"

She nodded, gliding her hand lower so it brushed the top of her mound.

"Thea, I told you to stop."

The sandpaper roughness in his voice only made what she was doing more thrilling. "Why?"

"Because sometimes the things that feel the best are the things you don't get right away," he said, his gaze following every slow circle she made around her clit. "The things you have to really want until it's all you can think about or feel or hear. I want you so focused on what you want that nothing else can get in." He pulled his cock out of his jeans and started stroking it as he watched her. "No doubts. No questions. No need to put someone else first. It's just what you want at that moment."

She stopped touching herself, leaving the tip of her middle finger on her clit, a reminder and a promise. "What if what I want is to play with myself?"

"That changes everything," he said with a wink. "Do it."

She slipped her fingers between her slick folds, and he

let out an appreciative groan before letting go of his dick, getting rid of the rest of his clothes, grabbing a condom from his bedside table, and rolling it on with what seemed like superhuman speed.

In the next heartbeat, he was on the bed, braced on his forearms and hovering over her.

"Let me taste you," he said with a fierceness that took her breath away.

It took her a second to realize what he was asking for. Once she did, she withdrew her fingers from between her legs and brought them up to his open mouth. He dipped his head lower and sucked her fingers dry while making her pussy so fucking wet.

"Damn, you taste good." He reached between them and used his hand to line himself up with her entrance, the tip of his dick just pressed up against her like a tease. "But you feel even better."

He sank into her, filling her completely before withdrawing with torturous slowness and then pushing forward again. Thea planted her feet on the mattress and lifted her hips, angling herself so that when she met his every advance, his dick hit at just the angle that had her halfway to heaven within minutes. She could hear herself begging and babbling for more, but she didn't care. It was so much, and it felt so good that nothing else mattered.

Then, he rolled over onto his back, taking her with him. "Do what you want."

For a moment, she was frozen by all of the choices. Then, the feel of his chest hair against her fingertips registered. With a fascinated reverence, she glided her hands over his chest, tracing a path to the flat discs of his nipples. The second she brushed her thumb across one, his cock twitched inside her. She did it again. The same thing happened. So she leaned down and licked and kissed her way from the line of his collarbone to the tip of his nipple before sucking on the now-hard nub.

Kade let out a harsh hiss of breath and started lifting his hips underneath her, fucking her in a slow rhythm that showed just how much control he had.

And that's when she realized what she wanted—to see him lose it in the best way possible.

She inched her thighs out a bit wider and pressed her palms to his chest and leaned forward, changing the angle enough that when she lowered herself down on his thick cock and bottomed out, her swollen clit was rubbing against him. She rocked forward and back, lifted her hips, and brought them back down over and over again. Each time brought her closer to orgasm even as her thighs burned with the effort. She let her head fall forward, losing herself in the moment, in the feeling of being with Kade. How he filled her. How her body reacted to his. How it felt like everything she'd ever wanted was only a few breaths away.

"Thea," he groaned, his gaze locked on her face as he tightened his grip on her hips, holding her in place as he lifted his ass and thrust into her hard and fast from below. "I—"

Whatever else he was about to say got lost in a harsh groan as he surged upward and came, his orgasm forcing his eyes shut as his entire body tensed below her. It was the hottest thing she'd ever seen—but she wasn't done.

Sliding her hands higher, she grabbed ahold of his shoulders and ground herself against him as his climax kept him rigid beneath her. She rode him, fucked him right to the edge of her orgasm, and then went straight over, milking every last bit of his climax from him as pleasure flooded her entire body until she couldn't take it anymore and collapsed on top of him.

She was brainless, boneless, and beyond blissed-out. The wiry hair on his chest tickled her nose, but there was no way she could move.

Later, as she lay there in Kade's bed, his sinewy arm wrapped around her, holding her tight against him as he spooned her, Thea tried to keep her breathing steady and slow. Maybe if he thought she was sleeping, he wouldn't ask her why she'd gone so quiet. Why she was blinking as fast as she could to keep the panic tears at bay.

She shouldn't be crying.

Who did that after having the best sex of their life?

People who were in the middle of a well-deserved panic attack because what was supposed to be an anger bang situation to get back at her sister turned slow or fast experiment had become so much more and she had no clue what to do.

Fuck, she was screwed.

Honestly, it's not like she'd ever see Kade again after the wedding. He lived…wherever he did. There! That was the easiest example of how not real this was. If it was real—if a relationship with Kade could actually work—she'd know where he lived.

There.

Infallible logic.

It was all right there.

Yeah, keep telling yourself that, Thea.

God, she wished she could tell the little know-it-all voice in her head to shut right up, but the thing was, this could happen. They could make it work.

They could have a long-distance relationship. What in the hell was technology for, if not naked video chats and sexting between telling each other stories about the funny guy she'd run into on the train on her way to work and the interesting factoid he'd come across while researching a book? The more she thought about it, the more the knots in her shoulders started to unravel. Maybe instead of just going along with their original plan because everyone was comfortable with it, or running away from her feelings, or getting locked into place because of indecision, or self-sabotaging with some kind of fight over something dumb, she could be an adult about it.

Tell him how she felt.

Open up.

Be vulnerable.

Go from fawn to fight—for what this thing between them could be.

Her pulse revved up like she was thirteen again with a huge zit the TV makeup person had told her couldn't be covered up. She was as twitchy as that moment when she was about to step in front of the cameras and ask the whole world to look at her and her giant zit.

But she wasn't thirteen anymore. She wasn't asking the world to glance her way. It was only Kade—and he saw her (really saw her) already.

This could work.

God, she hoped it could work.

Chapter Twenty-Six

The next morning, Kade work up to an empty bed, except for a note from Thea written on the back of the welcome note production had left with the untouched basket of alcohol.

HAD TO MAKE AN EARLY CALL TIME FOR MY DAY-BEFORE-THE-WEDDING CONFESSIONAL INTERVIEW. SAVE MY SPOT IN BED. BE BACK AS SOON AS I CAN.

XOXO,
T

P.S.
YOUR SNORE IS ADORABLE.

Like a jackass, Kade sat buck naked on the edge of his bed with a dumb-ass grin on his face as he read the note again.

At least no one was here to give him shit for it.

His phone buzzed on the nightstand. Glancing over, he clocked his brother's face on the screen. It wasn't one of his Hollywood pics. Instead, it was a shot of Dex in an Ice Knights jersey, screaming his head off at a game. The man was serious about his hockey.

Kade swiped the text notification.

DEX: *Dickhead, you're supposed to be here for our pre-wedding brother bonding. Production is getting all pissy.*

Fuck. He'd been so distracted by the series of Xs and Os in Thea's note, along with the promise that she'd come back, that he had totally blanked on the time. He was supposed to go give his baby brother advice about love and marriage. As if he knew a damn thing about any of that.

DEX: *Asswipe, are you alive? If so, I'm gonna kill you if you don't get here ASAP.*

KADE: *On my way.*

He took a quick shower and got dressed according to the production crew's detailed wardrobe plan for each day. Since it was the day before the wedding, they'd kicked up the requirements from T-shirts and stuff that sorta looked like it came from this century to full-on eighties crap. Grumbling to himself, he put on a pair of acid-washed jeans and two pastel golf shirts (one on top of the other), popping the collars of them both. He glanced at himself in the mirror and grimaced. He looked like some dipshit from an old movie—and not even a cool one like *The Goonies.*

He was three-fourths of the way to a full-on snarl when, out of the corner of his eye, he caught sight of Thea's note. He was smiling again before he realized it and way before he had enough time not to catch his goofy-ass grin in the mirror.

"Fuck," he said in the world's worst attempt to get back to his usual salty self.

The smile remained.

What in the hell was he going to do now? Thea was more than clear last night. She only wanted an anger bang. He'd practically had to get her dick drunk to agree that they were friends. Getting her to see they could be something more? Not a snowflake's chance in Scottsdale.

Now *that* brought back his scowl.

He stomped out of the RV and headed over to the

outdoor pavilion where the bachelorette party had been last night. The camera crew was still setting up, and Dex stood off to the side in a grassy area, tossing a baseball into the air and catching it with a glove bearing the logo of one of the reality TV wedding's sponsors.

"Think fast," Dex yelled as soon as he spotted him.

Kade caught the ball with ease. It had been years since they'd tossed the ball in the backyard, but some things came back without any effort.

"About time you got here, asshole," Dex said.

"Did you spend the last half hour trying to think up that insult?" Kade asked before putting his little brother in a headlock and giving him a noogie.

Really, there weren't a ton of benefits to being the oldest brother, but being able to do that for pretty much forever was definitely one of them. Dex shoved him away and then flipped him off.

"I'm a Hollywood star," his brother said with a smirk. "I had some writers come up with it."

Kade's laugh boomed out of him with enough gusto that his little brother gave him a weird look. Yeah, the joke wasn't *that* funny. Hell, it wasn't really funny at all, but Kade was just in that much of a good mood. Shit, it had been like that for him ever since he'd read Thea's note.

"Oh good," Justine the producer said, walking up on them and looking from one St. James brother to the other. "So you and Dex will have a little man-to-man pre-wedding chat out here while tossing the ball back and forth. I'm not telling you *what* to say, but if you can bring the convo around to any concerns you may have about whether the wedding will last, what kind of a wife Jackie will make, or anything else, that would be great."

A few days ago, he would have seen the direction as the last opportunity he may have to save his brother from a massive mistake. But something had changed over the past few days. Maybe it was Thea's influence. Maybe it was last night's talk with his brother. Maybe it was him feeling like all he wanted was to spend time with Thea (preferably naked) that had him thinking maybe Dex wasn't twelve anymore and if he wanted to make a huge mistake then it was his right to make it.

"Before we get to that, though," Justine went on, "we need to take care of Dex's pre-wedding interview."

"Please tell me I don't have to be a part of hearing him talk some shit about the universe finding a way and soulmates and whatever other bullshit you came up with for him to say."

"Stellar attitude," Justine said, blasting him with the fakest of smiles. "Let me just walk you over to the waiting area. That way you're close by when he's done. Come on."

She led him over to the covered section of the pavilion, where there were two picnic tables. The first one was covered with the crew's equipment. The second was empty—except for his mom. She had her hair pulled back into a long braid that went down her back like she used to when he was growing up, and the way the late-morning sun was coming in reminded him of the good mornings growing up. That was when he and Dex would come downstairs and find her and dozens of pancakes that they'd all scarf down.

All of a sudden, he was a boy again—the nostalgia of those mornings, the casual ease of it, the settled belief that this time would be different, that this time would work crashed into him with such a force he nearly stumbled back on his heels. Then he remembered where and when he was. His pulse shot off like a rocket, adrenaline rushing through him and making his whole body tight until he was at the breaking point.

His first instinct was to turn around and leave, walk away without ever looking back. He almost gave in to the urge, but then he remembered that first night with Thea and her talking to him about the challenge her therapist had given her. What if he tried that? He'd already chosen flight. He'd tried out fight. And freeze had done shit all. But fawn? What did he have to lose?

"Hello, Mom," he said, sitting down across from her at the table. "What are you doing here?"

She braced her shoulders and looked him square in the eyes. "I wanted to talk to you. Alone. No Dex. No cameras."

Uncertainty made his gut twist. "Why?"

His mom let out a little huff of a breath and clasped her hands together on the table. "Because it's apparent that you have things you need to work through, and you're not going to do it by yourself."

The laugh that came out of him this time was nothing like before with Dex. It was cold, unbelieving, mocking. "And my long-lost mother is the one who is supposed to guide me through it all?"

"If it's easier, don't think of me as your mom," she said without flinching. "Just think of me as some random person if you want."

"It's who you are."

Now she flinched, jerking back before regaining her calm demeanor that probably went half an inch deep, considering how hard and fast she was blinking away the moisture in her eyes.

Way to go, St. James. You are a real asshole. The woman is just trying to make a connection. Would it kill you to not be yourself for five minutes?

No. Yes. He didn't fucking know.

"And anyway, I don't have anything to talk about," he grumbled, falling back into his old surly habits. "Everything is fine. I have a dog. A great house. Book contracts that are going to keep me busy for the foreseeable future. I have the perfect life."

His mom sighed and looked at him as if he wasn't the son who'd brought home straight As every school year. "Except you're going to leave here in forty-eight hours, and you'll be going back to that life alone." Her expression softened, and her lips curled into a sympathetic smile. "I see how close you're getting with Thea. The whole world can see it. You do realize that all of the sneaking away you and Thea have been doing has been well documented."

He groaned. "That's not true."

"Really?" she scoffed as she swiped her phone off the lock screen and pulled up a Google search of Kade's name.

It used to be that the first hundred or so hits were all about his books, followed by links for some poor guy trying to make it as a children's party clown that happened to have the same name. He'd gotten a few of the emails meant for the clown and had to explain that a true-crime writer was probably the last form of entertainment they wanted for little Suzie's fifth birthday party.

Now, though, it was just page after page of Reddit threads, blog posts, and social media conversations about him and Thea. There were grainy pictures from long shots of them holding hands, GIFs of them kissing, memes of him looking at Thea with so much want on his face it gave Kade secondhand embarrassment even though the pic was of him.

His brain struggled to catch up as he tried to work out what in the fuck was happening. Yeah, he knew that first night with Thea had gotten attention just because of the unexpectedness of it. But people had to have forgotten about them. There were actual people who made regular appearances on red carpets here. It made absolutely no sense *why* people would care about him and Thea.

"I know that look," his mom said with a chuckle. "People know the real thing when they see it. You two are everywhere online. The ratings are through the roof for the live stream. People are rooting for you two. My question is, what are you going to do about it?"

His lungs tightened, and all of a sudden it was like he was trapped in a dark room feeling little creepy-crawly things climb all over him. He needed to itch. He wanted to fling his mom's phone across the room. And if he was feeling like that, Thea was going to have an even stronger reaction. The woman despised being the center of attention. She was not going to like this—not in the least little bit.

"Do about it?" he whisper-shouted. "Nothing. It's no one's business, and these people are creepy as fuck for caring so much."

"I'm not talking about them." She grimaced and let out a calming breath before talking again in the slow, too casual tone used for small kids or too-stubborn-to-understand adults. "I'm asking about *you*. What are *you* going to do about Thea?"

His mouth went dry as his stomach churned, sending what felt like battery acid mixed with lava swirling around inside him. He handed over her phone with the care of a man holding a live grenade.

"We're just having fun," he said, fighting to keep his tone even, unbothered, because if any of what he was feeling slipped through, he wouldn't be able to stop it from all rushing out. "It's a fling." He swallowed past the anticipatory hurt that would swamp him when Thea walked away. "We're just banging with an expiration date." He looked over and saw that his mom's cheeks were red with embarrassment. "Sorry, Mom."

"No." She shook her head. "I'm just some random person, remember?"

"So what would your advice be?" He fisted his hands, needing to do something to keep them from shaking as hard as his leg was jiggling under the table.

Something sad filled his mom's eyes as she watched him for a few seconds before speaking. "Well, as someone who has made more than her fair share of mistakes—including some that I'm going to regret for the rest of my life—all I can tell you is that this life is hard. It is unfair and cruel, and you seldom get what you want out of it."

"Now I see where I get my cheerful outlook from," he said, deflecting to self-deprecating humor as his breathing kicked it up into running-from-zombies levels.

She chuckled, her whole face lighting up.

"But that's it." She reached across the table and laid her hand on his, giving it an encouraging squeeze. "That's what makes even opening yourself up to falling in love such an act of absolute badassery. Showing people how you feel. Giving folks a chance. Trusting someone not to heart-stomp you. It is the scariest thing you can do, but it is so incredibly worth it. Don't take the easy choice. Don't walk away."

But that was the thing. He didn't walk away. Other people did. He stayed in the same fucking place, and everyone else left. His mom when he was young. His dad was emotionally gone even if the bastard made a point of staying physically for years until his death. His brother who wanted to get away from everything so badly that he got the one job that required him to be someone—anyone—else than Kade's little brother.

And now Thea. Even if she wasn't gone yet, she would be as soon as the wedding was over. It shouldn't matter. They'd only known each other a few days, but the sad fucking truth of the matter was it did. It mattered a lot.

He was holding on by the skin of his teeth, trying to find something to focus on that wasn't his impending doom, when he spotted it and everything went from hot, sticky panic to an icy numbness.

One of the cameras on the other picnic table had a red

light on above the lens. Whether it was being operated by
remote or had been left on, their entire little conversation
had been recorded. No doubt it wasn't being live streamed
already—it would be a part of the edited version of the show
later. Like a chump, he'd forgotten that his mom was here for
her redemption arc, not because she actually gave a shit.

You stupid fucking dumb-ass, St. James.

Shoving back from the table, he fell back into that safe
place—the one where no one and nothing could touch him.
The place where he didn't give a shit about anything.

"Nice speech," he said, covering all of the anticipatory
agony with ten feet of sarcasm. "How long did it take you to
come up with that? And the last line, leaving the 'like I did'
left unsaid?" He pinched his fingers together and kissed the
tips in the chef's-kiss gesture. "It's the kind of dialogue that
sticks with the reader even after they've finished the book.
You've got a real gift there. Have you thought about writing?"

Her shoulders slumped, and her gaze dropped to the
table. "Kade."

"Don't worry about it, Mom—oh, wait, let me try that
again." He flashed an angry smile at the camera on the table
and continued, "Don't worry about some random stranger
giving me advice while we're alone. I don't need your advice.
Never did. None of this matters." He stood up and started
pacing, all of the hurt energy needing an outlet. "Just like
whatever is happening with Thea doesn't matter. We're just
fucking to piss off her bridezilla of a sister." It was true. She'd
said it last night, but, like a fool, he'd convinced himself that
he could change her mind, make her believe that staying with
him was worth it. Even worse, with that kiss he'd thought
he'd made it happen. Why did he do that? Why did he always
think that this time would be different? No matter what he
told himself, he hadn't learned anything from years of his
mom's fake promises that everything would change. Like a

fool, he always believed.

"After the wedding tomorrow, I'll never see Thea again. I'll probably even forget her name eventually. She'll just be that one girl at Dex's wedding—hopefully for his starter marriage, because there's no way this is going to work out between him and Jackie." The lies streamed out of him at full volume as he got closer and closer to his appearance of control disappearing so that the world could see who he really was. "And a few years after that, I probably won't even recall that much. It's a blip, a glitch, a weird coincidence—just like you showing up here." He looked at his mother, who was now crying silent tears, and nearly stopped, but he couldn't. He was too far gone. "None of it matters. None of it means a thing."

Fuck. He needed some air. His entire body felt like it was filled with knives. He turned to get the fuck out of there, and that's when he saw her.

He stopped dead in his tracks, and his chest felt like it was about to implode.

Thea stood in the doorway, her eyes wide with shock and her lips—the ones he'd spent hours kissing last night—pressed tightly together.

All of the air in his lungs whooshed out of him as if the entire universe had just sucker-punched him in the kidneys. Everything he'd just said, every lie, every bullshit word of it came rushing back to him. He wanted to sprint over to her, but he couldn't fucking move. He was frozen to the spot, first by the raw hurt he saw in her eyes and then by the way she made it smooth out and disappear as if it had never been there, as if she'd always been this utterly calm and unflappable woman that no one could touch—especially not someone like him.

"Don't worry about it," she said, each word clipped and cold. "It's fine."

"Thea," he pleaded without even a hint of a clue about

what he'd say next.

Not that it mattered.

If she heard him, she didn't respond. At least not verbally. Instead, she turned around and walked away, her head held high, not even the tiniest bit of a falter in her step.

In all honesty, that was probably all of the response he deserved.

Chapter Twenty-Seven

Once, when she was still acting, her foot had been run over by one of the golf carts that ferried the important people around the back lot. She'd had her nose in a book—it was her fourth or fifth rereading of *Jurassic Park*—and was walking to their mom's car when Jackie grabbed her by the the shirt and yanked her back. It was enough to save Thea from getting plowed into but not enough to save two of her toes from being crushed.

Ever since then, whenever she got injured, she compared it to that. Did it hurt more or less than having a golf cart break her toes?

Hearing Kade hurt more. Way more.

She felt the ache everywhere, all the way down to the marrow of her bones. It burned. It was freezing. It was sharp jabs of agony. It was that low-level throb of pain that reminded you every moment exactly how many muscles you never thought about got used just to pull air into your lungs.

And she had about five minutes—tops—before shock's gift of an outer shell of numbness wore off. After that? She was going to be a mess, and the last thing she wanted was for all of that to be caught on camera—which seemed to be everywhere.

She ignored the producer's call about needing to do a quick on-camera pre-wedding interview and quickly walked away from the pavilion, berating herself with every step.

She'd been so full of stupid hope about what could happen after the wedding that she'd frozen completely in the door as Kade ranted. She didn't matter. *He wouldn't even remember her name.* She'd wanted to move when he'd said that. She'd *tried* to move. But her feet refused to respond, though, and she was stuck there listening to all of those ugly words coming out of Kade's mouth.

Thea stumbled over a small rock on the gravel path but quickly righted herself. Yeah, that was all she needed to go with all of the humiliations she'd endured during this wedding—to fall flat on her face.

She marched all the way to her RV, powered by a slowly waking fury and the instinctual urge to get as far away from every other living soul as she could. The cool air from the air conditioning hit her in the face as soon as she closed the door behind her. Leaning back against the hard metal, she clamped her jaw together tight, trying to give herself another few moments before she fell apart.

As soon as the knock came, though, she realized her mistake.

"Thea," Justine the producer said in a sickly-sweet tone. "I know you may not want to talk right now, but it really could help. Let's talk, just you and me. You won't even see the cameras. I swear, it will help."

Yeah, it will help their ratings and ruin her career. No one would take her seriously at the museum after an interview like that. She'd forever be that woman who cried like a baby on a reality TV show. Forget her PhD. Forget her years of experience. Forget the fact that she could name all three hundred stegosaurus bones and had published more articles than any man in her department. She'd just be the hysterical woman who couldn't keep her shit together.

Desperate to get out of there but with her escape blocked, Thea scanned the RV.

Her gaze landed on the window above the bed, and an idea began to form.

Justine's knocking grew more intense. "Thea, open the door."

No. She wasn't going to do that.

She stared at the window again, cocking her head to the side and doing a few mental calculations. It would be tight, but she could get through. Fuck that. She *would* get through it.

Mind made up, she swiped a bottle of who-the-fuck-knows from the free alcohol basket and opened the window. She was halfway out before she realized just how high up the window was. At about five feet off the ground, the fall wouldn't do much damage but had made the decision to go out of the window headfirst quite foolish.

Way to go, Thea.

She was just doing an awkward crawl-backward move to get back into her room when Justine's radio crackled to life. The staticky sound cut through the initial panic buzzing in Thea's ears.

"Hey Justine, they found the camera on the picnic table," a man on the other end said. "You're gonna have to file a damage report."

"Just great," she grumbled. "Wait. Are you set up out back of Thea's RV?"

"Negative," the man said. "I'm still set up at the pavilion."

"Are you fucking kidding me?" Justine snarled, accompanied by a groan of frustration. "Do I have to do everything myself?"

Shit.

Thea had to get out of here now or spend the next stretch of eternity hunkered down in the RV. Spurred on by a blast of adrenaline, she grabbed her phone and then went feetfirst out the window and took off toward the one place everyone in the wedding avoided like the plague—the Stinkingwater River.

Chapter Twenty-Eight

Kade was pissed off at everything.

He was mad that he was in Wyoming instead of his house, spending some quality time with his laptop, plotting out his next book.

He was annoyed as fuck with the fact that he couldn't get his mom's advice out of his head.

Most of all, he was beyond furious that he smelled Thea's perfume with every inhale, saw her out of the corner of his eye every time he turned around, and couldn't escape from himself.

Pacing from one end of his RV to the other, he glared at Dex, who was scrolling on his phone, a surly expression on his pretty-boy face.

Good. If Kade was going to be abso-fucking-lutely miserable, then his baby brother could join him. After all, everything was Dex's fault. If he hadn't decided to get married for PR reasons to a woman who was such a pain in the ass she'd make her own diamonds if she had a piece of coal stuck up her ass, then Kade wouldn't have met Thea. If he hadn't met her, then he wouldn't feel like he'd just repeatedly kidney-punched himself.

He glared at his brother. "This is your fault."

Dex didn't even bother to look up from his phone. "When has you being a super dickhead ever been my fault?"

"You invited Mom." Yeah. His brother was the one

human being that Kade had looked out for and taught how to throw a ball and had even run lines with the little shithead when Dex had been too nervous to ask anyone else, and he'd fucked Kade over like no one else ever had with that move.

"So what?" This time Dex did look up, no doubt so that Kade could better enjoy his oh-so-mature eye roll. "You're the one acting like a twelve-year-old about it."

Kade stopped himself, just barely, before he said something inane like "nuh-uh" or "I know you are." He was too old for that shit, even if the only thing he could come up with in retort was, "You're marrying for the wrong reasons."

"Yeah, well that's my choice to make, you prick," Dex snapped back. "Why don't you admit the real reason you're so mad and *who* you're actually mad at?"

Kade stopped pacing at that and crossed his arms over his chest—the better to glare at the brother he'd mistakenly thought wasn't a total dumb fuck. "I'm not ticked off with Thea."

"No shit, numbnuts." Dex dropped his phone on the couch cushion and leaned forward, resting his forearms on his thighs, his expression hard. "You're mad at yourself for being a scared little bitch."

There was a buzzing in Kade's ear, so high-pitched and loud that it vibrated through his whole body as he took a step toward his brother. "You better watch your mouth."

Dex stood up, straightening to his full height. "Or what?"

"There's no stuntman here to swap places with, Hollywood," Kade snarled, puffing up his chest as he stepped forward.

"Like I need one to beat your ass," Dex scoffed before picking his phone up off the couch, flipping it around, and shoving it in Kade's face.

Some self-preserving instinct was screaming at him not to look, but he did anyway. He knew Thea was going to be on the screen, and he could never stop himself from seeing her. It was a GIF someone had made off the live stream of Kade smiling at Thea with his whole soul—and she was returning it.

"Look at her. Look at you. Look at you looking at her," Dex practically yelled. "Are you such a self-sabotaging jackass that you'll let your fear dictate the rest of your life even if it means losing Thea?"

The loop of them smiling at each other played over and over. He could have watched it forever, but he finally made himself glance away. "I never had her."

"Really, asshole?" Dex threw his phone back down on the couch in disgust. "It sure doesn't seem like that to anyone with the ability to see past their ego."

Heat blasted through Kade. "It's not ego."

Dex looked like he was about to yell again, but then he let out a long sigh. His shoulders loosened. His face relaxed. The tension visibly ebbed out of him.

"You're right. It's not ego." Dex shoved his fingers roughly through his hair and gave his brother a pitying smile. "It's fear. You did what you did because you were scared of what was happening between you two. And now you're sitting here like some asshole who can't stop feeling sorry for himself because deep down you think if you don't go after her then you don't have to worry that she'll leave you someday."

Kade didn't flinch. Instead, he went into lockdown mode, shoving every thought and emotion down so far that it wouldn't break the surface for a million years. And once he was ice all the way through, breathing normally, heart rate steady, molars ground down enough that he was going to have to make an appointment with his dentist, he looked at his brother and shrugged.

"Oh my God, Kade," Dex said, back with the what-the-fuck-is-wrong-with-you almost yelling. "Welcome to real life, assface. Sometimes people leave. Sometimes they stay. You don't always get exactly what you want. Grow up."

"Like you?" Kade asked, matching the not-shouting energy. "I should become the kind of guy who gets married for work reasons?" He stepped forward, getting right in his brother's face. "Yeah, come talk to me about my shit when yours doesn't reek to high heaven."

That's when the punch should have come, and Kade was ready for it. Hell, he would have welcomed the pain and the distraction of it. But there wasn't one.

Dex sat back down on the couch and dropped his head into his hands. "It's not just for work."

"What?" Kade chuckled dismissively. "You actually saying you *love* Jackie?"

When his brother didn't say anything, didn't even bother to flip him off, Kade realized what his brother had been telling him this whole time.

Dex ordering Kade to take it easy on Jackie. Dex agreeing to this absolutely batshit bizarre eighties-themed wedding. The way his brother had put everything else in his career on hold so he could get married. The fact that Dex had been insistent on having their mom here and trying to broker some kind of reconciliation.

For all of the muscled-up dude-bros Dex always ended up playing on TV, the man was a soft touch who really believed in happily ever afters.

"Holy fucking shit," Kade said, sitting down on the couch by his brother. "You love Jackie."

"Only for the past ten years," he said, sitting up and grabbing his phone. He didn't start scrolling—it was as if he just needed to have something to anchor him. "You know we dated back in the day. Well, she broke it off and said she had to concentrate on her career. I went out and got shitfaced out of my mind. Me! Can you fucking believe it?"

Kade could and he couldn't. Yeah, neither of them drank much after watching their mom fall into bottle after bottle, but that didn't mean Dex *never* had a drink.

"I just couldn't function," Dex went on, his misery apparent. "And after that night, I still couldn't function but I had the mother of all hangovers. That went away, but I never got over how I felt about her." He sighed and collapsed back against the couch cushions. "So when the publicist suggested this, I figured it was as close to the real thing with her as I'd ever get, so I went for it."

And like the jerk he was, Kade had never realized. He'd left the one person in the world he was supposed to take care of alone, in spirit if not physically. "Fuck, I'm sorry, Dex."

His brother let loose with a sad excuse for a self-deprecating laugh. "I just know there's no one else for me but Jackie. And if this is as much of her as I get, then I'll take it. And maybe all of those feelings she had for me back then will return." He shoved his hands through his hair hard enough that it was standing up. "I'm not gonna pressure her or be some kind of dickhead, but strong lifelong marriages have been built on less. We already like each other as people, we're compatible, and we respect each other." He glared at Kade, jabbing a finger in the air near his face. "And don't fucking say it. I already know. I'm a fool for believing."

"You're an idiot," Kade said with a shake of his head, "but not for this."

His brother flipped him off. "Fuck you."

"No, I mean it." God, Kade couldn't believe he was about to say this—seriously, his stomach was lurching—but it was the ugly, awful truth. "As someone told me today, opening yourself up to love—or even the possibility of it—is some next-level badassery."

Kade's fuck-you energy went down a few notches.

Dex blinked up at him. "Thea told you that?"

Kade shook his head. "Mom."

Both sat there in silence and let that one word fill the space between them.

They were two guys with the same scar. But Kade had spent his life guarding his, picking at the scab. And eventually chose to make a living writing about tragedy and those who overcame it. Now he knew why—he wanted to understand how they'd survived, moved on from the betrayal and pain, like his brother.

Dex had cared for his scars, letting them heal and become a part of himself—but not the definition of who he was. Looking at his brother, Kade realized that while he'd taken on his role as the oldest without question, guiding and educating Dex as best he could, there were quite a few things he could probably learn from his younger brother.

Kade took one short trip to Wyoming, and the entire world as he knew it changed. Christ, now *he* wanted a drink.

"She's not so bad, you know," Dex said.

Kade didn't need to ask who his brother was talking about. "I know."

"And are *you* going to take her advice?"

He rubbed the back of his neck, trying to work out the tension of realizing he'd fucked up beyond redemption. "It's too late."

"Never give up. Never surrender," Dex said, quoting the old movie they must have watched a million times growing up. "You've got to fix this with Thea."

Yeah. Too bad there wasn't a way to do that. Gut twisting, he shot up from the couch and started pacing the RV again, racking his brain for a solution and coming up with jack shit. What in the hell? He was a writer. He came up with plots. He investigated the facts. He researched and created and made things happen.

But not now. Not when it counted.

"You got a time machine?" he asked in frustration.

"I'm not a doctor, but I sure would like to play one on TV," Dex said.

Kade reached inside the mini-fridge and grabbed a can of Sprite and another of Dr Pepper. "They ever cast an American as Doctor Who, there would be a riot."

"And you'd be right there in the middle of it?" Dex asked with a chuckle.

He handed his brother his soda. "Fuck yeah."

The sound of the cans being popped open and the sizzle of the caffeinated bubbles filled the RV a second before they both drank half their can in one gulp.

Dex sighed and shrugged. "I guess I'll stick to being the star of this summer's biggest movie."

Kade almost dropped his soda in shock. "Are you serious?"

His brother grinned. "We got a distribution deal today."

Pride and excitement filling his chest to beyond capacity, he yanked Dex up from the couch, and pulled him into a bear hug.

"It's just what you've always wanted," Kade said once they had some distance between them again and he could wipe off the Sprite that had spilled onto his hand.

"Cheers to having it all," Dex said, raising his Dr Pepper in a toast. "Or at least almost it all."

"You'll figure out what to do," Kade said, clinking his can against his brother's.

"We both will," Dex said, "because I'm not going to grow old with you. God, I can't think of a worse punishment."

Kade flipped off his brother, but he was laughing. So was Dex, until his phone buzzed and he read the text on the screen.

His face went white. "Fuck."

"What?" Was it their mom? Had the distribution deal

fallen through?

"Jackie can't find Thea," Dex said. "No one has seen her since she snuck out of her RV hours ago."

Kade was on his feet and out of the door before he'd even taken his next breath.

Chapter Twenty-Nine

Several hours—and almost an entire small bottle of vodka—later, Thea sat underneath a tree overlooking the beautiful if utterly foul-smelling river and contemplated the absolute shit she'd made of her life. This was what happened because she'd listened to her therapist and tried to find her true self.

Disaster. Heartbreak.

Public humiliation.

Well, fuck that shit.

She'd tried having a fight response and ended up asking Kade—in front of the entire live-stream-watching world—if he wanted to go have an anger bang, which (let's face it) was him throwing her a pity fuck so she could get back at her sister.

Her cheeks burned with humiliation at the memory.

She'd tried freezing when it had come to decorating that stupid giant foam heart for the wedding ceremony.

Kade had come to her rescue on that one, obviously feeling sorry for the dorky sister of the bride. Her own very human heart had melted into a useless puddle of goo in her chest with that one.

Then, of course, there was the motorcycle ride (AKA flight) when Kade had taken her to the museum and they'd hidden in the closet.

What did all of these things have in common? Kade fucking St. James. And what was the result? Her making an ass out of herself.

Well, breaking news alert, if she was going to be miserable and heartbroken, she could do that from her fawning comfort zone. She didn't *need* to try other options. So fuck it. Fuck flight. Fuck freezing. Fuck fighting. She was done.

D.

O.

N.

E.

DONE.

She rested her head back against the tree and watched the stars appear in the night sky as dusk gave way to night. Just like that first night with Kade, the sight filled her with awe, even if tonight it was a little blurrier thanks to the tears that kept falling...and the vodka. She really should get back to her RV. Justine and the camera crew had to be gone by now. As soon as she stood up, the stars went all wibbly-wobbly along with her stomach, and she eased back down so she was sitting on her butt in the grass instead of being planted face-first in it.

All she needed was a few minutes to catch her breath, and she'd go back to the RV. That was a solid plan. At least it was more solid than her on her feet right now.

She leaned back against the tree again to take in the stars, but the insistent buzzing of her phone vibrating against the vodka bottle yanked her attention downward. She grabbed her phone, scrolled past the messages from Jackie, her mom, the producer, and Kade—and tapped on the latest one from the group chat with Astrid and Nola.

ASTRID: *ARE YOU OKAY???????????*

Okay, the usual freak-out via extra punctuation and all caps from Astrid.

NOLA: *You're starting to scare us. Where are you?*

Do you need us to call 911? Are you hurt?

And the rapid-fire questions from Nola.

ASTRID: *And if you weren't trying to scare us, that Kade guy sure as fuck did. He said you disappeared upset and no one can find you.*

What? Kade called them? She stopped reading the incoming screen and shot back a question of her own.

THEA: *How did Kade get your number?*

ASTRID: *SHE LIVES!!!!!!!! And he said he made the production crew share your offsite emergency contacts from your release forms.*

NOLA: *Are you okay? Are you in a safe place? Do we need to get on a plane?*

THEA: *Sorta. Yes. No.*

That was probably about as close to the truth as possible at the moment. Plus typing out "fell in love with a guy who said he's going to forget me as soon as he gets on the airplane out of here" was too pathetic.

ASTRID: *Who do we need to harm? All I need is a name. I know people.*

NOLA: *You know the same people we do, and none of my uncles are actual Irish mobsters. They just talk a lot at the bar.*

ASTRID: *So you say.*

NOLA: *So I know, but that's not the point. Thea, what happened? Do you want to talk? Is a call easier?*

Thea smiled even though she ached like she'd gone down the rapids of the Stinkingwater River in a cardboard box. This was why she loved her friends. The promises of avenging her through questionable means from Astrid. The string of concerned questions from Nola. They took care of one another, told one another their secrets, and were always there for each other through the good times and bad. And this was definitely a bad time.

THEA: *He said he wouldn't even remember my name in a few weeks.*

NOLA: *Who said that? Who could ever forget you?*

THEA: *Kade.*

NOLA: *No!*

ASTRID: *That's it. We ride at dawn.*

Thea sniffled and wiped away the tears that were flowing again with the back of her hand.

NOLA: *But he seems to really like you on the live stream (sorry we've been watching, everyone has been watching). I thought it was real. What is going on? How can we help? Are you just acting about the relationship?*

THEA: *I'm not.*

The ache of that filled her up, taking over almost everything else. The little dots of an incoming text appeared and disappeared several times as her friends were no doubt workshopping what they could say to make her feel better when the reality was such a thing didn't exist.

NOLA: *Oh, Thea. I'm sorry.*

ASTRID: *We hate him.*

Thea wished she did, but it was all too fresh for that.

NOLA: *Okay so we might know people.*

ASTRID: *I knew it! I'm always right.*

That's what Thea had thought, too. That's why she'd been so sure with Kade. She been confident that she couldn't get hurt. She'd never been so wrong in her life.

THEA: *I should have known better. I kissed him. I swore I wouldn't. That it would all be for fun. Revenge plus orgasms. What could go wrong, right? And then I kissed him. And I couldn't stop. And I didn't want to stop. But he's not even going to remember my name in a few weeks.*

ASTRID: *I'm on the Southwest app right now. We can be there by four tomorrow afternoon.*

NOLA: *Will you be all right until we get there?*

Despite everything, she smiled at her phone screen, picturing Nola and Astrid pooling together the couch cushion money for a last-minute flight to Wyoming. They really were the best. But she couldn't do that to them. She'd make it through this. There were only twenty-four hours to go, and then it was all over.

THEA: *You don't have to come. The wedding is tomorrow, and then I'm at my dig for two weeks. I'll see you when I get back to Harbor City.*

NOLA: *Are you sure? We're here for you whatever you need and whenever you need it.*

THEA: *Yeah, I'm sure.*

ASTRID: *Does that mean we can't send the uncles either?*

THEA: *No Irish mobsters either.*

NOLA: *Good because they're in their seventies and Uncle Mick doesn't even have a driver's license anymore so he doesn't have ID to get through airport security.*

Thea chuckled softly and dried the last of her tears. Tomorrow was going to be awful, but she had her dig, she had her friends, and she had acting experience to fall back on so she could make it look like she wasn't dying inside.

THEA: *I love you two.*

ASTRID: *WE LOVE YOU TOO!!!!!!!!!*

NOLA: *Ditto. You'll call us tomorrow? Or do you want us to call you? Or is it text only because talking is too upsetting right now?*

THEA: *I'll call you tomorrow. Night.*

She put down her phone and yawned in the middle of drinking the last mouthful of the small-batch vodka that smelled of lilacs and tasted like she should probably be using it to strip paint. Seriously, after downing the small bottle over the course of the past few hours, she was surprised her eyebrows hadn't been singed.

She could probably head back to her RV now, but damn

her eyes were tired. And the ground was so smooth on this spot, and the grass wasn't itchy against her skin. Even the Stinkingwater River was less smelly, and the sound of the water moving over the rocks was actually kind of nice.

Laying back, she promised herself that she'd head back in a minute. She just needed to rest her eyes for a bit, and then she'd deal with the mess of her life—and she'd do it the usual way. She'd go along to get along. She'd fawn, just as she had for years.

Her life would go back to what it was, and she'd like it. Because honest to God, anything was better than this pain cinching her chest.

As her eyelids drifted closed of their own volition and her breathing grew deeper, she promised herself that she'd find a way to make herself like the old Thea again.

She had to.

Chapter Thirty

The first thing Thea noticed was the constant *thump-thump-thump* starting in her head and reverberating through her body to the soles of her feet that were—

She wiggled toes. Yep, still in her shoes.

A dry-mouthed, achy-feeling sense of self-preservation kept her from opening her eyes as she got her bearings. She hadn't made it to her bed last night. She must have fallen asleep in one of the chairs in her RV.

Giving her shoulders a tentative stretch, she realized that they rubbed not against the smooth leather of the RV seats but something hard, scratchy, and—she inhaled—piney-smelling.

Her eyes snapped open before she could finish the "what the fuck" going through her head.

At first, she was blasted with the bright morning light of the next day, but when she finally blinked out the overexposure, her gaze landed on a deer with her fawn eating grass by the river. They looked up and stared back at her, the doe with an amazing freeze that made her look like someone's very detailed lawn statue and the fawn doing a close replication, but its attention flicked from Thea to another spot off to the side and back to Thea again. She didn't blink; she wasn't even sure that she breathed as she watched the deer in the early morning light. This was the kind of thing no one ever saw in Harbor City, and she was lost in the moment. "THHHHHEEEEEEEEEEAAAAAAAAAAAAA!"

At the sound of someone yelling Thea's name, the doe burst into action, sprinting toward the line of pine trees. The fawn stayed a few seconds later, watching Thea before following its mom into the woods.

Getting up gingerly, because the sky and the ground kept switching spots, Thea braced her hand against the tree and looked around the trunk. Jackie was standing at the top of a hill in what could only be described as full-on-Princess-Di-on-her-wedding-day cosplay. Her white dress had a voluminous skirt, and her sleeves were so full and puffy they were nearly chin height. Then, in a moment that seemed scripted for reality TV, a warm breeze swooped down from the mountains and sent Jackie's skirt, long lace veil, and ginormous eighties-style hair flying gracefully in the wind. She would have looked like the picture-perfect (if dated) bride if it wasn't for one thing—the look of absolute terror on her face.

But why—

And it hit Thea. Her stomach dropped down to her knees right as her toe knocked into the empty vodka bottle. She'd only meant to rest her eyes for a minute. Now her sister was pulling a runaway bride, except instead of looking for her freedom, she was searching for Thea.

The second she spotted Thea, she lifted her skirt and started into a sprint, running full speed right at her.

"Oh my God, Thea," she said, wrapping her arms around her tight enough that her front ribs felt like they were going to touch her back ribs. "Everyone has been looking for you!" She pushed Thea back but held onto the tops of her shoulders and gave her a once-over. "Are you okay?"

Thea plucked the pine cone out of her rat's nest of hair and tried her best to give her sister a reassuring smile, but any use of her facial muscles was still wonky at this point.

"My head feels like it got hit with a line drive," Thea said, letting the prickly pine cone drop from her hand. "But other than that lovely little reminder not to try to drink an entire sample bottle of craft vodka in one night ever again, I'm fine."

"You scared the shit out of me." Jackie pulled her in for another hug. "When you went AWOL, we all dropped everything and started searching."

A twig snapped behind her, and Thea caught sight of a camera behind one of the pine trees dotting the landscape. Everything came into focus at once, and Jackie's full wedding getup made sense.

Take something real—like Thea dropping off the map for a few hours—and amp up the drama—she's missing!—and give it can't-look-away visual appeal—Jackie in all of her wedding glory. That was the reality TV formula for success. That little part of her that thought that maybe, just maybe, the concern she'd seen on her sister's face was real fizzled, leaving her feeling more empty than she had been before. Which was a statement all its own.

Thea stepped back from the hug. "That must be great for the ratings."

Jackie cocked her head to the side in confusion. "What do you mean?"

A huge part of Thea just wanted to slink back into her comfort zone, pretend she didn't see what was really going on here. It would be easier. She could just fawn her way through this moment. Damn, it was tempting and the quick clip of her pulse had her skittering toward fawning, but she yanked herself to a mental stop. What she wanted wasn't to just go along. She wanted everyone—but most especially her sister—to stop looking at her and seeing a doormat.

Her hands were shaky and her nerves were jittery enough to register on the Richter scale, but she had to do this.

"Don't act like it matters to you," Thea said, keeping her voice as steady as she could, considering she felt like she was balancing on a plastic storage bucket lid in the middle of the Atlantic Ocean—during a storm. "You never even wanted me here in the first place. I don't fit in with your friends. Hell, I don't even fit in with our family. I'm not exactly part of the aesthetic you and Mom are building for your brand."

Jackie rolled her eyes and huffed out a dramatic sigh. "Are you fucking serious?"

Steadying her nerves, Thea glared at her sister. "Yeah, I am."

"I swear, you are always like this." She threw her hands up in the air and said with a snarl, "For a scientist, you sure do go off half-cocked instead of getting all of the information. Gah! You always have. Do you remember when Mom and I threw you a surprise Sweet Sixteen?"

"You mean when you invited all of the most popular people from high school to our house and none of them would speak to me?" There were still nights when the memory of that pity party would keep her up staring at the ceiling and going over every humiliating moment until the sun came up.

"Because you stood in the corner and would barely even look at anyone—not even Kevin Mohr."

"Please," Thea scoffed, "he was only there for you."

Jackie's entire body tensed with coiled fury. "That. Is. Bullshit."

Nope. Not this time. Thea was not going to roll over and just agree with her sister's version of things. "Because you knew I liked him and yet you still spent the entire party talking to him."

"Only because I was trying to convince him that you didn't hate him," she yelled. "Let me tell you, it would have been a helluva lot easier to do that if you weren't ignoring him the whole time."

Ignore? She hadn't done that. She'd been protecting herself. Staying in her lane. It's what she did, had always done, and still did. It's why she didn't make a fuss about the promotion. It's why she always went with what her mom and sister decided. It's why— Thea startled, the hint of a realization almost coming into the light. The memory of Dr. Kowecki asking her if she was ready to change and grow popped into her head unbidden and unsettled her.

"Whatever." Thea shrugged as if none of this bothered her, as if she wouldn't be replaying this conversation at three a.m. in the near future. "It doesn't matter."

Glaring, Jackie shook her head in disgust. "It does when you are still jumping to conclusions without having all the facts—like about this wedding."

There was stoking the fire of someone's anger, and then there was throwing a tanker truck of fuel into the flames, which was exactly what Jackie had just done.

"So it's not a fact that you didn't want me here?" Thea hollered. "What? Are you saying you lied about that?"

"No." Jackie's shoulders slumped, and she dropped her gaze to the ground. "I didn't lie."

The acknowledgment shouldn't have hurt. It wasn't breaking news. But it did. It sliced through all the armor Thea thought she'd built up over the years and left a gaping hole in its wake.

Jackie's gaze jerked over to something behind Thea's shoulder. No doubt she was keeping aware of the camera. Then, she pulled her phone out of a pocket hidden in her massive skirt and swiped on the screen until a steady stream of screaming guitars, pounding drums, and the voice of a woman who sang like an angel as the music went at demon speed behind her came pouring out of its speakers.

Jackie turned her flinty-eyed attention back to Thea, her expression unflinching. "Do you want to know why I didn't want you here?"

Thea nodded, the first seeds of regret blooming in her now-shifty stomach.

"Because this whole wedding is a farce and I wanted to protect you from that," Jackie said, her chin trembling. "I am surrounded every day, all day, by people who fling bullshit and pretend it's the truth—except for you." She grabbed Thea's hands, holding them in her own like they were a lifeline. "You are the *one* person who doesn't do that. Mom does it. She does it because she wants to support me, but I know she still tells me all sorts of stuff that isn't quite the truth. But you don't. You give it to me straight. And how do I repay that? By acting—yes, acting—like the biggest bitch in the known universe in the wedding of my nightmares in front of the one person whose opinion I value the most. I didn't want you here because I was embarrassed." Her grip tightened until they were both white-knuckled and the intensity in her eyes went from a million on to a billion. "I don't want you to see me like this, and I sure as hell don't want to be married like this."

Thea blinked.

Then she blinked again and again as her brain buffered.

What in the hell was happening?

She couldn't breathe. Her heart was speeding. Her thoughts were bouncing around in her head like a pinball.

It was too much for her to process, so she grabbed onto the last thing her sister said as a sort of starting point to unwinding it all. "You don't *want* to get married?"

"That's the awful part," Jackie said, her shoulders slumping as she let go of Thea's hands and dropped her head so she was looking at the ground. "I *do* want to get married."

Now it was Thea's turn to give her sister a reassuring touch. She wrapped an arm around Jackie's shoulders but didn't lean in close because if she did she'd lose an eye to the puffed sleeves. "But to someone other than Dex?"

When her sister looked up, her eyes were filled with tears and the tip of her nose had gone cherry red. "No. To him. Only ever to him."

Yep. That cracking sound wasn't a cameraperson getting closer—it was the sound of Thea's brain breaking. "So this wedding is a *good* thing?"

"It's the biggest mistake of my life," Jackie wailed. She gathered up her billowing skirt and started marching back and forth in front of Thea. "I've loved Dex since we worked on *Laguna Beach High* together. We started dating, and my agent told me that if I didn't want to lose my role, I had to focus only on the show. She said the producers were concerned that I wasn't working out." She paused long enough to wipe her teary snot from the tip of her now very red nose with a lace handkerchief she'd pulled out of another pocket in the never-ending skirt, then went back to pacing.

She had the pinched and pained expression that was a mix of bittersweet agony and self-directed thunderous rage. "I lost the love of my life because of a show that didn't make it past the first season. So when the publicist suggested this wedding as a way to get ratings up for *Starship 3000*, and then Dex mentioned it might help get the indie movie he just wrapped a distribution deal, I jumped at the chance."

She stopped and turned to Thea. Her eyes were wide and red-rimmed, but there was a hope there, just a tiny little shadow hidden in her eyes, that maybe somehow everything could work out. "Sure, I told myself it was for the show and so Dex and I could keep our jobs, but really, it was because this was the only way I thought he'd ever look at me again like he used to, like he loved me—even if it was only for the cameras. And you? I never wanted you to have to deal with all of this again, but the second the producers found out I didn't want you to have to do it, they insisted. God, I'm such a selfish bitch."

Thea threw her arms around Jackie's shoulders and squeezed her tight, eye-jabbing sleeves be damned. "You're not."

Jackie scoffed. "Oh, I am. I know this." She pulled back and then sat down on the ground, pulling her knees up to her chest, which left only her eyes visible thanks to that obnoxiously large skirt. "What I hadn't known when I agreed to do this is that to make this wedding happen, I'd have to bring the big bridezilla drama. I couldn't just be the bride, I had to be the bitchiest bride to have ever emerged from bridezilla hell."

More tears spilled over as Jackie sucked in a breath as if to steady her nerves. "Yeah, everyone would talk shit about me, but they would watch. You'd have to give up your anonymity, but I told myself that it wouldn't be that bad. You'd avoid the cameras. No one you work with at your job would watch some trashy reality show, so it wouldn't negatively impact your career. Plus, I told myself that *Starship 3000* would gain an audience, the movie would get picked up, and I'd be married to Dex, so it was okay." She didn't say anything for a moment, but her shoulders shook as she cried silently.

Then, with the kind of willpower it took to keep going even when you were perfectly manicured eyebrows deep in a world of shit of your own making, she pulled it together. Looking up at Thea, she said with a heavy certainty in her tone, "Now I've fucked over you, because there's no way the people you work with haven't seen at least one post about you being here, and I've fucked over Dex by marrying him when he doesn't want to be married to me—not really. You see, I really *am* a selfish bitch."

Thea used her foot to nudge away a pile of pine cones and sat down beside her sister. "Jackie, you were put in an untenable position."

"No, I put myself there," she said, laying her head on her

sister's shoulder. "I've fucked it all up for myself, but it doesn't have to be that way for you. Promise me you won't follow my example. I've seen how happy you are with Kade. The whole world has seen it! But you're too worried about everything to make your move with him."

If only it were that simple. She'd made moves. He'd made moves. They'd made moves together. And that's what had fucked everything. If she'd just been her usual self and had fawned about her sister's now-understandable attitude, then she never would have gone over to him. She never would have asked him if he wanted to go have an anger bang. Then she wouldn't have started falling for him, and her heart wouldn't be a broken fucking mess.

"It's not that simple," she said, her voice barely loud enough to be heard over the din of the speed metal coming from Jackie's phone.

"You are so full of shit," her sister said with a snort. "It's totally obvious that you're head over heels for him, and yet you run for the hills?"

Thea collapsed back onto the grass with a defeated sigh. There was a pine cone sticking its little points into her left shoulder blade, but it wasn't anything compared to the pain coming from her chest whenever she thought of Kade.

The mental image of his crooked smile was a shiv to the aorta. Her right ventricle ripped a little more each time she remembered the shiver of anticipation that went through her whenever she spotted him. Her left ventricle cramped at the ghost feeling of his touch or the phantom sound of his voice when he whispered in her ear or the stupid belief she couldn't quite completely shake that there was something between them. She should know better. There was no fawn or fight or freeze or flight for this. There was only accepting the absolute jagged knife to the superior vena cava that was the reality that he didn't give two shits about her.

He'd said so himself.

"He told his mom that I was just something to fill the time while he was here," she said, her voice wavering as she did her best to hold her shit together when it felt like it was all crashing around her. "He said that he wouldn't even remember my name in a few months."

Jackie sighed and laid down in a wave of white satin and ivory lace next to Thea in the grass. She reached out and wrapped her pinkie finger around Thea's, giving it a quick squeeze as they both looked up at the clouds. Despite everything, Thea's pulse slowed and the weight pressing against her chest lifted a little, letting her fill her lungs with a deep breath. When was the last time they'd done this? Just sat together and allowed themselves to be there for each other? So long that Thea didn't remember.

She may have thought she was always fawning with her sister, giving in, letting her roll over her, but in truth, it had been all flight. She'd run away from her years ago, way before she'd left for college, by othering Jackie, giving her the role of the always-on diva to play and never letting that change no matter how much they grew and matured as people. Thea finally exhaled, letting go of that typecast view of her sister, and squeezed her sister's pinkie finger back.

On Jackie's phone, the band switched to a song about recycling, which was very much not what Thea had expected. They were halfway through the chorus when Jackie spoke up.

"I've been around Kade for years, ever since I met Dex," she said. "He's a giant pain in the ass, and he has the absolute worst taste in soda, but he's never looked at anyone the way he looks at you. He barely speaks to anyone besides Dex, but you? He can't talk to you enough. And going by the amount of time you two have spent together thinking that cameras weren't around, which they always are—*why does no one listen to me about that*—he doesn't want to do anything but spend as much time as possible with you. Kade St. James isn't a man having a fling. He's a man rushing headfirst into the brick wall of love."

Thea kept her gaze firmly on the cloud in the shape of a dick with three balls, because if she didn't, she would cry, and if she started she wasn't sure she could stop.

"I don't even know where he lives," she said after a minute of trying not to let the seed of hope in her chest grow into anything. "I don't know how he likes his eggs or if he is one of those monsters who puts the toilet paper on so it rolls under instead of over."

"Does any of that matter? Would it change how you feel about him?"

Thea didn't even have to think about it. "No."

"Then don't make the same mistake I did." Jackie sat up and dragged Thea into a sitting position, too, so they were eye to eye. "Be honest with Kade and tell him how you feel. Fight for what you want. You owe yourself that."

"And what do you owe yourself?" Thea asked, desperately looking for a way to divert this conversation from Kade so that her whole chest would stop feeling like it was being pried open.

Jackie narrowed her eyes at her sister. "We're talking about you here."

Thea knew they absolutely were not *only* talking about her, but sometimes fawning was the best option when it came to waiting until her sister was ready to talk about the really important stuff.

"So what's with the music?" Thea asked.

Jackie smiled and shook her head because of course her sister knew exactly what she was doing. "I know the lead singer, and Stankville Stink refuses to give permission for their music to be used in shows, so if I play this, production can't use any of the sound."

"So everything we say stays with us?" Thea asked, her panic edging upward into the stratosphere as she mentally reviewed all of the things they'd both just spilled.

"Well, they still have the recording, but they can't release it." Jackie tilted her head so her mouth was close to the mic hidden in all of the fluff of her right sleeve. "Hiya, Chuckie."

"Stankville Stink is my new favorite band." Thea took a hard look at her sister, who was still doing the post-crying sniffle thing. "You are full of advice for me, but the person who should be taking your advice is you."

Jackie got that look she always did when she was ready to go toe to toe—the one where her eyes narrowed, her nostrils flared, and she pressed her lips together hard enough that a white line appeared around them. She opened her mouth, and Thea braced for whatever was coming next. But then her sister closed mouth, then opened it again before throwing her arms up in the air and letting loose with a groan loud enough and melodramatic enough to have been written into the script for one of her shows. It was the kind of outpouring of frustration that was usually accompanied on-screen by moody lighting and rain as well as the character dropping to their knees and screaming at the sky.

"You're right," Jackie said with a harumph. "I hate it when you're right, but you always are."

Swallowing the urge to I-told-you-so her sister (some things never went away with age), Thea asked, "So what are you going to do about it?"

Jackie lifted a brow in challenge. "I'll tell you if you tell me what you're going to do about Kade."

Thea fell back into the grass with a groan of her own. "I have no idea."

Jackie laughed and stood up. "This is why real life should come with scriptwriters."

"Or at least more greasy hamburgers," Thea said after

her stomach growled.

Planting her hands on her hips, her sister shot her a look that always meant trouble. "I'm the bridezilla who is actually getting married in hell. I can demand that cheeseburger."

"Really?" Thea asked, practically jumping up from the grass in her excitement.

"If I can't use my bridezilla powers to help my sister, what good are they?"

Thea had nothing to say to that, so instead she hugged her sister. A big hug. The kind of hug someone gave when they needed to tell them all of the millions of ways they loved them but couldn't get the words out.

"Don't you dare make me cry again," Jackie said, sounding like it was already too late. "No matter what happens next, I'm going to have to go on camera, and now there will be pics of me after I've ugly cried going viral."

"A fate worse than death," Thea said into her sister's puffed sleeve.

Jackie laughed out loud. It was her real laugh, a big, booming sound that the directors of the kids' shows they were in always said was too over-the-top. "You're a pain in my ass."

"I love you, too," Thea said.

"Come on. Let's go cure that hangover of yours." Jackie stepped out of the hug and then hooked her arm through Thea's before marching them both back toward the resort. "I'm getting married today, remember?"

Thea was all in favor of that, but she couldn't get rid of the feeling that she already knew what she had to do next, and she was not going to enjoy it.

Chapter Thirty-One

Somewhere between Jackie in all of her badass-bride glory demanding a cheeseburger for Thea immediately and Thea's devouring of said cheeseburger (made with a poppyseed bun and the delicious, never-found-in-nature bright-yellow French's mustard), she'd lost her sister. Well, not just Thea. The entire crew had lost Jackie. She'd just gone *poof* and disappeared like she had her own VFX crew.

Her wedding dress was a giant pile of white silk and ivory lace on the floor of her RV.

Her mic pack was abandoned in the middle of the bed.

Her phone was sitting on the counter in the RV's mini kitchen next to a blueberry muffin missing its crumbly, sugary top.

"I swear you two are just peas in a pod," her mom said as she did a one-eighty in the middle of the RV's living room area, scanning the place as if Jackie was just hiding behind a couch cushion. "If one of you up and disappears in the middle of a reality TV wedding that took more work than you could ever imagine to put together, then the other one has to do it, too."

"Jackie wouldn't do that," Thea said. Her sister *always* honored her work obligations. She'd once gone to work with two broken fingers and filmed an action sequence.

"And yet, here we are." Mom let out a huff of frustration and shook her head. "I swear, even when you were kids, she just wanted to follow in your footsteps. Why, her first audition only happened because she tagged along with you on yours." Her mom started walking around the RV's tiny living room, straightening the couch pillows and refolding the blanket as she continued. "Do you remember the mac 'n' cheese commercial? Remember that one? I had you wear the gingham dress that matched the box the mac 'n' cheese came in?"

Thea winced as all of the anxiety from trying out for parts came flooding back. "You dragged me to a million commercial auditions, and I've done my best over the years to block out the vast majority of them."

Her mom waved a hand at her dismissively. "You say that like you never even wanted to act."

"I didn't." It had always been her mom's dream, never hers.

"That's not right. It was your idea." Her mom stopped straightening the fashion magazines on the coffee table, planted her hands on her hips, and cocked her head to the side as if she was really confused. "You came home with that flyer from the national casting call and said you would do extra chores if I just signed the permission form. You loved acting."

"No." Thea shook her head, her gut twisting as she pushed through the uncomfortableness of not just nodding along with her mom to end the discussion and instead telling her the truth. "I wanted to win the VIP behind-the-scenes all-access pass to the *Jurassic Park* set they were giving to one person picked at random."

Her mom blinked several times before her gaze dropped to the floor and her shoulders slumped.

"But you sang the song about the hot dog," she said, her tone so soft and sad that no one who'd ever tried to negotiate a contract with the momager from hell, as she was known, would have believed it. "You got the part. You danced all the way back to the car."

Thea gulped and pressed forward. "Only because I saw how excited you were and how happy it made you."

Her mom had been beyond thrilled. The way she'd looked at Thea? As if she was the rising sun? Nothing had ever felt like that before—or after.

"I don't believe it," her mom said as she sank down so she was sitting perched on the edge of the oval coffee table. "You would have said something. You would have told me—just like you did when you decided you were done with acting."

As if that was even close to the truth. All the old insecurities and anxiety zapped her like the burning zing of bacon grease popping up out of the pan and landing on her exposed skin.

"Mom, the offers stopped coming in," Thea said, holding on to that burning feeling, needing to let it blaze inside her so she could finally get all of this out. "You pushed me into audition rooms for years where I got rejected time and time and time again."

"They were fools. They just didn't see you like I did."

"As what?" Thea choked out. "The wimp you could push around?"

She gasped and looked at Thea wide-eyed. "I've never thought of you like that. You're amazing."

"But never enough." Thea didn't even try to hide the hurt in her voice as she wrapped her arms around her middle. "Definitely not star material like Jackie. That's why after I left for college we barely talked."

Her mom pursed her lips together and inhaled hard enough that her nostrils flared. "I left messages. You never returned them." She paused, looking up at the ceiling and blinking rapidly. "I texted. You sent back a *K*." Her chin trembled, and she let out a shaky breath. "And the time I showed up on campus for parents' weekend even though you hadn't told me about it? The look of horror on your face when I asked if an acanthopholis could fly was like a knife to the heart, but I understood. I wasn't smart in the ways you and your friends were. I'm sure that was very embarrassing." Tears spilled over and slid down her cheeks, which she brushed away with the back of her hand. "I still don't know the difference between a stegosaurus and a brachiosaurus. All I know about is how to get an actor paired with the part that will make their career. You didn't care about that, so you didn't care for me in your life. That hurt. But I'm your mom, and I love you no matter what, so I gave you what you wanted—space. Came to you only when you reached out first. Kept our conversations centered on what we had in common—Jackie. I did what I thought you wanted."

Thea stared at her mom, seeing her—perhaps for the first time—not as a mom but as a human being. A person who made mistakes. Someone who did the wrong thing because they thought it was right. A woman who kept trying despite it all. The realization knocked her sideways, reset some old memories in more detailed context, and eased the ache in her chest that she'd always thought would be there forever when it came to her mom.

"I thought you were disappointed in me because I wasn't made to be an actor," Thea said, her voice wobbly. "That I was a failure in your eyes."

"You could never be that. As long as you're happy, I'm happy. I thought I was doing what you wanted by leaving you alone." Her mom got up from the coffee table and came over to Thea, wrapping her arms around her and holding her tight. "You know it might be a good idea if instead of just assuming what the other one wants, we both actually asked."

Thea chuckled at the simplicity of the solution that had somehow eluded them for years.

"That sounds like the best plan." Heart hammering against her ribs, Thea asked the thing she never thought she would. "Maybe we could try it out after the wedding? You can come to Harbor City, and I can show you around the museum and we can go to the theater?"

Breaking the hug, her mom looked at Thea, tears—happy ones now—falling down her cheeks, and smiled. "I would love that."

They hugged again, a brief, hard squeeze that didn't change the past but went a long way to fixing their future. When they let go, her mom handed her a tissue from the box on the desk littered with Jackie's makeup and looked around at the otherwise empty RV.

"There's only one thing. There has to be a wedding first. Where could Jackie have gone?" her mom asked, frustration and fear clinging to each syllable.

Now it was Thea's turn to look around the RV.

Jackie's closet door was open, and her clothes were still inside. There was a script for *Starship 3000* laying on the bedside table, several of her character's lines highlighted in different colors. Her shoes—including her collection of never-left-behind designer high heels—were lined up along one wall.

Thea's gaze moved over to the open door of the bathroom but jerked back to the shoes. There was one pair missing right between the red-heeled stilettos and the bow-bedecked kitten heels. That's where Jackie had her tennis shoes—the ones she only wore when she was either working out or needed to be Jackie the real person that most people never got to see instead of Jackie the Hollywood D-lister.

And that's when Thea knew exactly where her sister was.

Well, not *exactly* location-wise, but she knew who she was with. Jackie was with Dex.

The question Thea had, though, was whether Jackie was

breaking it off because she knew she couldn't be married to a man who didn't love her or if she was telling Dex she loved him and always had. No matter which way the conversation was going, Jackie obviously wanted it to be as far away from the live-streaming cameras as possible.

She was about to share her revelation with her mom when a loud commotion outside yanked her attention over to the RV's window. Justine was marching toward the RV alongside Kade, his mom trailing a few steps behind. The producer was gesticulating wildly, her hands going everywhere, as she gave Kade a what-for that going by the volume and the grimace on her face was legendary. For his part, Kade didn't seem to be paying the producer any mind. His steely focus was solely on the RV. Thea took an unconscious step back, her heart jumping up into her throat as the rest of her body screamed in joyous anticipation.

He was coming.

Kade St. James was coming, and she was already gone—for him, at least.

There was half a second where the air practically sparked with expectations, and then Kade burst into the RV. His hair stood up as if he'd been shoving his fingers through it for the past century and a half, and his jaw was set in a grim line. He looked around, his attention bouncing from Thea's mom to Justine the producer and his own mom, who'd both entered right after him, to Thea, where it stopped.

Something nearly feral made his gaze darken as he looked her up and down as if he could barely control himself from storming over, throwing her over his shoulder, and taking her away—maybe to yell at her, maybe to fuck her senseless, possibly both at the same time.

Her pulse sped up, and every sensitive spot on her body that he'd ever touched zeroed in on him. Her gaze glided from the possessive look in his eyes to the fullness of his lips that had set her skin on fire to his broad shoulders, perfect for bracing herself when she was riding his hard dick, to the way his jeans fit his strong thighs to the absolutely undeniable aura of power and determination licking against her nerve endings. Fucking A. No one should have that much raw sex appeal.

"You're okay?" he asked, his voice heavy with the hoarseness of a man who'd stayed up all night in misery.

She nodded, not trusting herself to say anything.

"You're sure?"

"Yes," she said, the single word coming out breathy and hot and needy and oh-my-God exactly how she shouldn't be talking to anyone in front of her mom and the producer of a reality TV show.

He didn't take a step toward her, but it still felt like he was right beside her, wrapped around her, a force field of testosterone.

"If you ever do that again without leaving at least a heads-up to where you'll be," he said, his body nearly vibrating with barely repressed ferocity, "I will completely lose my shit. Do you understand? You want to leave or need space? Just say so. But I can't spend another night ever thinking that you're hurt or need help and I'm not there for you. Got it?"

She nodded, her ability to speak obliterated by his words.

"Good." He waited for a beat, staring at her like he could see all the way down to her soul, and then scanned the room. "Dex said he'd be here."

Thea gave an internal "I knew it."

"The groom's gone, too?" Thea's mom said, her eyes as round as an Oreo cookie. "Are they eloping, or are they breaking it off?"

"They better have been kidnapped by aliens, because I don't know another excuse that will keep them out of lawsuit hell for fucking up this reality TV wedding," Justine grumbled. "When I find the two of them, I'm going to post every single second of it, no matter how much I have to pay extra to pixelate non-sponsored products out."

The last thing Jackie probably wanted right now was for Justine and a camera crew to find wherever she and Dex were holed up.

She was scrambling for an idea about how she could help when a cameraman and boom operator came clomping up the three steps to the RV's door and entered the now-way-too-crowded living room.

Justine shot him a dirty look. "What are you doing here, Angus?"

"We've searched everywhere," the mullet-haired cameraman said with a shrug. "They're in the wind."

The producer let loose with a string of curses that would make a sailor blush as she checked the time on her phone. "The live stream starts in ninety seconds, Angus. If all I have to show is a few tumbleweeds by that stupid stinking river, I'm going to have your ass. Nepo baby or not, you're going down for this."

Angus rolled his eyes. "My dad will have your job."

"He's too busy fucking the nanny to come after me, Angus," Justine said, jabbing her finger in the air next to his face. "Where. In. The. Fuck. Are. Jackie. And. Dex."

Thea pressed a hand to her twisting stomach, her nervous gaze flicking from the stressed-out producer to the bored cameraman and back again. The air in the RV was spiked with tension sharp enough to make her skin prickle. Her sister had tried to protect her—it had been a ham-handed effort, yes, but Jackie's heart had been in the right place—and now it was Thea's turn.

"One minute until we're live, Angus!" Justine said, her voice cracking. "I'm gonna sue them for everything they're worth. By the time I'm done, they won't ever get another job in this town. They're done. Finished."

The boom mic operator stepped back as if he was trying to become one with the wall while Justine kept ranting, but Thea blocked her out.

There was only one way Thea could help her sister at that moment. Her gurgling gut flipped and flopped. Fuck. Anything would be better than this, but she was out of options. She not only had to shove herself into the center of attention, but she had to crack open her soft underbelly and tell Kade exactly how she felt while the entire world looked on. She had to give Justine enough drama to give Jackie enough time to do what she needed to do and to keep her from losing the career she'd sacrificed so much for.

Her belly rumbled in a very this-is-not-good way.

She was going to throw up.

She was going to make an absolute fool of herself in front of the entire world, and there was no way her colleagues would miss it.

She was... Well, it didn't matter because she was going to do it anyway.

Gathering her strength, she settled her shoulders, lifted her chin, and caught her gaze on Kade. The man was glowering at Justine, but he must have felt Thea looking at him, because his attention moved over to hers. The absolute unbending strength and dawning understanding in that look almost knocked her to her knees.

For half a heartbeat, she thought she might melt into a puddle of Oh-my-God-I-am-so-falling-for-you. Then, his expression changed. He lost the avenging-badass expression and gave her that crooked grin of his—the one that she never saw him give anyone else, not even Dex.

That's when she knew for sure it wasn't a case of *if* she'd melt but *when*—and if she'd ever be able to put herself back together again.

But she didn't care.

She didn't want to fawn or freeze or fight or run as far and fast as her feet would take her. She just wanted to help her sister—and tell Kade St. James everything.

Before she could open her mouth, though, he pivoted and turned his attention back to Justine.

"I'll talk to my mom," he said, glancing over to his mom, who gave a quick nod. "On camera. No restrictions."

Justine went bug-eyed.

"But it has to happen right now. Live."

The producer didn't say a word. She just pointed a finger at the boom operator, who got into place. When Angus didn't jump into position fast enough, she let out a low growl. The cameraman grumbled under his breath but got ready for the shot.

Justine morphed from on-the-edge to all business in a millisecond. It was impressive, actually. "In five, four, three—"

Thea looked over at Kade, and warmth bloomed in her chest, heating her down to her toes, because she knew exactly what he was doing. Just like that first night when she'd asked him if he wanted to go have an anger bang, he'd come to her rescue again.

The truth of it was, Thea didn't need to know how he ate his eggs or or what his go-to song was for singing in the shower. She knew his heart.

Chapter Thirty-Two

That look on Thea's face—the agony mixed with embarrassment and determination to do it anyway—it's what had gotten him that first night, and it was exactly why he was about to do the last thing anyone had expected. Including himself.

Turning away from Thea, he looked over at his mom. The woman should be terrified. She had no idea what he was going to say after he'd fought against talking to her on camera for so long. Then there was how they'd left things yesterday. He wouldn't blame her if she was mentally prepping for war.

But instead, she looked proud as she smiled and gave him an encouraging nod.

His gut cramped up and sweat popped out along his hairline as everyone in the RV watched him. The tug to look over at Thea, to reach out to her, was nearly overwhelming, but he held firm. He'd made this stupid move so she wouldn't have to do the thing she hated and be the center of attention. The last thing he wanted was to drag her into it.

Man the fuck up, St. James.

Bracing himself, he focused his attention on his mom and just started talking, all of the words he'd been holding back for years pouring out of him.

"You just left," he said, feeling as unsure as the teenage boy he'd been when he came home that day. "I went to my friend's house to go swim, and when I got back you were just gone. There wasn't a note. I didn't get a chance to say goodbye. I had no idea where you were." In an instant, he was back to that day, trying to unravel a knot while his hands were tied behind his back. "Dex stopped speaking. Dad couldn't stop yelling. And my life changed forever." It hadn't happened right away. He'd held on to the hope that his mom would come back, but finally, he'd accepted the truth—and as soon as he had, the world became smaller and darker and less trustworthy. "Ever since that day, I've done everything I could to make sure that no one would ever have the power to break me when they left again."

His mom lifted her hand to her pursed lips as she looked away, blinking rapidly. Then she walked over to him, stopping just outside of his personal bubble, as if she wasn't sure if it would do more harm to hug him or to stay back.

"Oh, Kade, I'm so sorry," she said, reaching out her hands and letting them hover in the air between them. "For the drinking I couldn't control. For the way I left. For the fact that I gave up on being in your life until it was too late. I have made so many mistakes, but the one thing I never did was stop loving you or your brother—even when I couldn't find it in my heart to love myself." She let her head drop as her shoulders shook with silent tears.

Kade knew he should say something to ease her pain, tell this woman in obvious agony that everything was going to be okay, but he couldn't yet. He still hurt too bad. Dragging each word past the gravel in his throat, he finally asked the one question the fourteen-year-old in him still needed to know. "How could you leave me, Mom? I was just a kid, and I still needed you."

When she looked up at him again, tears were flowing unchecked down her cheeks. "Addiction can be a vicious cycle, Kade. I hated myself for not being able to choose anything over my next drink, then drank to forget how much I hated myself for making the choice that I did. And I knew I couldn't stop the cycle alone. I needed help." She swiped a hand across her cheeks. "But I want you to know that I didn't leave you or your brother that day. What I left behind was a mother who chose her next drink over her son's soccer game—so I could become the mother you really deserved, who *could* stay when you needed her most. I know I have too much to make up to you, but I really hope you can give me another chance, son."

He flinched back as if she'd burned him with her plea even as he blinked the moisture from his eyes.

"Let's just take this one step at a time," he said, willing himself not to close up completely—not again. "I don't know that I'm ready for you to be in my life full-time. I'm not sure I can do that yet."

"That's fair, but as a sort of good faith contribution to this relationship, can I offer you a piece of advice from someone who learned this the hard way?"

He nodded, steeling himself for whatever was coming next.

"If you wall yourself off to the chance at happiness because you're afraid of being heartbroken, you're only hurting yourself," she said, letting her hands drop back to her sides. "There are no guarantees in this life. As one of your fellow true-crime writers said, life is chaos, be kind. I'd add to that, be kind to yourself even if it's scary, even if you're not sure how it's going to turn out, even if you might end up heartbroken. Love, family, and friends are all worth it."

She smiled at him as she wiped the tears away with the back of her hand again and then nailed him with the kind of soul-deep look only a parent could give a child. "You were and are always worth it."

Kade had spent his life looking at other people's motives to better understand why they committed the crimes that they did. The whole time, he'd only half admitted that he'd done it because he wanted to finally grasp why his mom had done what she'd done. Never in a million years had he considered that he was trying to figure out his own why.

Christ, he'd lost the plot completely.

He reached out and took his mom's hand, squeezing it as he opened his mouth to say something—he had no clue what—but before he could say anything, the door flew open, banging against the outside of the RV. Jackie and Dex stood in the open doorway—or at least versions of the bride and groom Kade had never seen before.

Jackie was wearing a blue dress that looked like an oversize men's shirt. It was misbuttoned—badly. Dex had lipstick smeared on the collar of his T-shirt and, unless Kade was mistaken, a hickey on the side of his throat. They both had pine needles in their tangled hair and absolutely besotted expressions on their faces as they looked at each other.

The boom mic could have picked up a pin drop, the shocked silence in the RV was so complete.

After what seemed like a year but could have been five seconds, Jackie tore her gaze away from Dex and addressed everyone standing in the RV with their mouths hanging open. "Who's ready for a wedding?"

Saying chaos ensued would have been an understatement. Everyone started talking at once, asking questions and offering to help get all of the pine needles out of the soon-to-be bride's and groom's hair. Kade hung back as the moms went to work like a pair of gorillas grooming their babies. He caught Thea's gaze, and all of the mayhem faded into the background.

"You okay?" she mouthed, obviously knowing that unless she shouted there was no way she would be heard over all the racket.

He smiled and gave her a thumbs-up. Was he all right? He had no fucking clue. He was unmoored and adrift in a whole new ocean. Part of him couldn't help but figure that there were dragons that way or that he'd drop off the edge of the map, but somehow it didn't matter because he realized two very important things at that moment.

One, his mom was right. He'd spent his entire adult life trying to force life into giving him concrete for-sures. That wasn't going to happen.

Two, whatever it took to make things up to Thea—he was going to do it. Love really was worth it, and he was manning up and admitting to himself he was deeply, irrevocably, never-gonna-be-the-same-again in love with that incredible woman.

"Thank you," Thea said silently.

He started to make his way over to her so he could explain that he was the one who should be grateful when the kind of loud, screeching feedback that could be heard from space filled the crowded RV.

Glaring at everyone, Justine turned the volume knob on some equipment the sound guy was carrying, and the noise cut off.

"Shut up, all of you!" the producer said before flattening her mouth into a grim line as she death-stared at them all, just daring anyone to open their traps. "Not until the bride and groom are mic'd up and the crew is in place. Our viewers are expecting a wedding, and they're going to get one, or I'm going to sue the ever-loving shit out of everyone here. Holy fuck, you people are enough to make me go on a silent retreat with Jared Leto again, and that was the worst fucking hell I've ever experienced—until now." She gave them the evil eye. "Bride's people and groom's mom, stay here. Groom's folks, to his RV. Now go!"

Kade dragged a blissed-out Dex halfway through the door before Kade stopped and looked back at Thea. Once he did, though, everything that had been clanging around in his chest settled.

"Talk later," he mouthed.

She nodded, the corners of her mouth tilting upward and giving him hope that he hadn't fucked things up completely, and he went back to leading Dex to his RV to get ready for his impending nuptials.

"Ain't love the fucking best?" Dex asked as they neared his trailer.

Kade could have said anything at that moment and his brother wouldn't have noticed—he was that out of it over Jackie. Still, the words came unbidden.

"Yeah," Kade said, already trying to plot out what he was going to say to Thea to convince her to give him a second chance. "It really is."

Chapter Thirty-Three

Eight hours and one reality TV wedding that turned out to be 100 percent real later, Dex stopped grinning only long enough to shout at Kade, "What in the fuck are you doing here with me instead of across the way talking to Thea?"

Kade glared at his brother as the door to the RV snicked closed, but Dex was grinning like a jackass after laying out that stupid-ass question.

"What am I doing?" Kade shot back. "Being the lookout for the cameras while you change into my shirt, since all of your buttons somehow flew off when you snuck into a supply closet with your new bride."

"Yeah, that makes sense." Dex smirked as he buttoned up what used to be Kade's powder-blue ruffled tuxedo shirt. "Guess I'm just a speed bump on the road to your eternal happiness."

Kade wasn't going to kill his brother—not on his wedding day—but still, the temptation to at least smack him upside the head was there. He'd been trying to sneak in a minute with Thea since he left the RV this morning. It was like the universe, his brother, and the production crew were enjoying the hell out of watching him lose his cool by a few more degrees with every missed opportunity.

First, there was the actual marriage ceremony, which—unlike just about everything else during this weeklong live-streamed reality TV wedding event from hell—went off without a hitch.

Kade had stood next to his brother and had produced the giant diamond ring at the appropriate time, even though he kept losing track of everything because he couldn't stop watching Thea. They were back into the outfits from when they'd first met outside Jackie's RV. He was in his baby-blue tux with the ruffled shirt, and she was in that giant pink fluffy dress with a skirt that was so wide she'd had to turn sideways to walk through the door for the ceremony.

The only good thing about the actual ceremony—besides the fact that Dex looked happier than he ever had in his life—had been that it was short.

Half an hour after they'd all done that weirdly paced walk down the aisle to stand in front of the obnoxious flower heart he and Thea had built together, they were walking back out—him with Lakin, the maid of honor, and Thea with Kyan, the groomsman who'd stood third.

That was fine, though, he'd decided, because he was going to see her at the reception, and then they'd find a nice closet to have a very private and—please, God—naked conversation.

He seemed to always be a few minutes behind her after the ceremony and when he had finally gotten to the barn where the reception would be held, he was chasing her shadow again.

Following Thea's giggle, he made it through the throngs of people who had flown in from L.A. to serve as guests to get to the private rooms at the back of the barn that used to be the bunk rooms. He was about to call out her name when Thea had disappeared into a room with the rest of the bridesmaids to help Jackie change into another dress for the reception.

Without any other choice, he had paced back and forth down the hallway, glaring at the closed door—from which a few high-pitched giggles escaped but no Thea. He was about to go bang on the door when Dex and Jackie had come running around the corner, looking like they'd been doing exactly what newlyweds did.

"I need your shirt," Dex had said as he'd grabbed Kade and strong-armed him into an alcove across from where Thea was.

He had just enough time while Jackie snuck into the room she was already supposed to be in to sneak a peek at Thea. She'd ditched her parasol and that ugly-ass hat. Her dark hair was starting to spill out of the low bun it had been in. Her cheeks were flushed, and she was giggling so hard she was having trouble catching her breath. Their eyes caught, and she stilled, staring at him with a look of pure hunger.

That's when Jackie closed the door behind her and his jackass of a brother demanded Kade start to strip.

"Tell me again why you needed the actual shirt off my back?" Kade asked as he scanned the hall for a cameraperson.

"My agent doesn't want any more bare-chest shots, so people start thinking of me more as an actor that's an indie-award contender and less as the hot guy on TV with the six-pack," Dex said with a groan. "The fans have expectations."

"You know, sometimes I think you have the worst job," Kade said as he put his tux jacket back on.

"But the best brother." Dex tucked the blue shirt ends into his pants. "There, good as new. You, however, look like a mess."

Kade didn't bother to look down at the white undershirt that was now all he was wearing under his tux jacket. Instead, he flipped his brother the bird and started back toward the door, determined to do whatever it took to get to Thea.

He hammered his fist on the wood, and the unlatched door swung inward. The room was deserted except for the bridesmaids' abandoned parasols, hats, and high heels that were in a great heap on the floor and looked a lot like the beginning of a bonfire.

Heart slamming against his ribs, he scanned the room, trying to figure out how in the hell they'd gotten out. That's when he spotted a second door that was half open. On the other side was the barn's reception area. The dance floor was already full by the time he walked through the door, and he nearly plowed into someone doing the running man in honor of the eighties theme.

What in the fuck did it take for a man to finally get to talk to the woman he loved? A lot, apparently, because he couldn't find her anywhere. She wasn't by the bar with the moms. She wasn't in the circle of people watching some guy break-dancing on a large piece of cardboard. She wasn't over by the DJ booth ready to request some eighties power ballads.

She'd disappeared. Again.

"Okay, all you single ladies," the DJ called out over the speakers. "It's time for the bouquet toss."

There was a rush of women hurrying over to where Jackie stood on a table, her humongous pink-and-teal bouquet in her hand. He only gave the bride half a glance, though. It was Thea he couldn't look away from, because he'd finally found her.

Her glasses were a bit cockeyed; she'd given up on the bun, so her hair was loose around her shoulders; and she was grinning so hard there was nothing Kade could do but smile with her. She had that effect on him. His shoulders relaxed, his pulse finally chilled the fuck out, and he took a deep breath because everything was finally going to go according to plan.

He took a few steps forward and, out of the corner of his eye, saw Jackie toss the bouquet. She must have played softball at some point, though, because the flowers left her grasp with the speed of a pitcher letting loose in fastpitch. It sailed upward in a long arc that sent it straight into the path of the huge ceiling fan above the dance floor. One of the blades caught it and sent it flying in a ninety-degree turn. Kade barely had time to turn his head before the cloyingly-scented bouquet caught him square in the head with a thump against his ear—and he caught it reflexively.

Still, he didn't miss a step—not when he was this close to Thea.

People parted like the sea as he marched across the dance floor while grasping the slightly mutilated bouquet. All of the bridesmaids and the other single ladies scattered. But Thea stayed. Her hands clasped together, she stood her ground.

Mindful of the handful of remote-controlled cameras placed throughout the barn, he stopped himself just short of carrying Thea off and making just the kind of scene she'd hate. They weren't mic'd anymore (thank fuck) but there were still watchers somewhere catching the last few minutes of the live stream. Instead of scooping her up, though, he just stood there, his arms crossed behind his back with the annoying bouquet, and tried to figure out what in the fuck he was supposed to say now that he was finally with her.

Thea smiled up at him. "You okay?"

"I'll live," he said as he picked pink petals out of his hair, his voice coming out more gruffly than he meant. "I have been trying to get to you since this morning. We need to talk."

Her eyes rounded, and she swallowed as her gaze shot around nervously. "Yes. I have something I want to ask you."

"I have a question for you, too." Nervous and unsure all of a sudden, his words were just flying out of his mouth, faster than Jackie's bouquet jetted through the air. "Do you want to go happy bang?" The question exploded out of his mouth before he could stop it, a firehose of stupidity set to full blast. *Holy shit, St. James. What were you thinking? Are you even thinking?*

"That was bad," he said before grinding his teeth

together in an effort not to screw this up even more. He let out a quick huff of breath and started over. "I'm sorry. Can I have another try?"

Thea had her lips pursed together as if she was trying to stop a giggle from squeaking out. She nodded.

Thank God.

"I know all of this started as a way to get back at your sister, and we agreed on no sharing of personal information."

"Yeah," she said with a chuckle, "we kinda messed that up."

"Exactly," he said, every part of him focused only on her. "And then there was the no-kissing part."

She pressed her fingertips to her lips. "Another miss."

"Right. And we promised each other that nothing would happen after the wedding. That whatever happened in hell stayed in hell," he said, relieved that this was finally it—this was what he'd been waiting all day to tell her. "Well, I think we should fail at that, too."

He waited, sucking air into his lungs like a man who'd been underwater for a year, hoping Thea would say yes or anything close to that.

But she didn't.

She didn't say a single thing.

Chapter Thirty-Four

Every nerve in Thea's body was raging an epic battle that had her somehow fighting for breath, frozen to the spot, ready to run a million miles away, and arguing to just go with the flow to minimize the conflict.

All around her, people were dancing or laughing at the joke someone else said or downing another drink as they covertly scrolled their phones under the table. Jackie and Dex were leading the rest of the bridal party in the Cupid Shuffle while the moms were behind the bar mixing nonalcoholic mocktails for everyone.

No one was watching.

The camera crew had put down their cameras once their part of the live stream ended. There were the remote cameras, but Jackie's mission before she ended up in a supply closet with Dex was to strategically place laser pointers around the room to disable the camera's optics. All of the camerapeople were relaxing at what had become a crew table by the bar. They were barely even eyeing the dance floor as they sipped their virgin cranberry sangrias, listening to Justine tell what was no doubt a war story from the foxholes of reality TV.

Still, Thea had that buzz of electricity making her jittery as she stood there in the spotlight of Kade's attention. Her heart was threatening to burst out of her chest, and her lungs had ceased to function without her mentally yelling at herself to inhale and then exhale.

Kade closed the last few inches of distance between them, blocking the rest of the world from her view. There was only the two of them. Her pulse started to slow, and her body remembered how to breathe on its own.

He tucked a strand of hair behind her ear, his fingertips brushing her skin and sending waves of yes-please shivers down her spine. "You look like you aren't sure if you should implode in on yourself or kiss me."

"Oh, good," she said, finding it hard to form words when she was finally so close to him after a day of everyone and a TV producer keeping them apart. "I look exactly how I feel."

The lights changed above them, glowing softer as the DJ swapped from "Rapper's Delight" by The Sugarhill Gang to Madonna's "Crazy for You."

"Well," he said, his touch trailing down the side of her neck. "I have a little secret for you."

"What's that?" she asked, her voice breathy with anticipation.

His touch, the slow steady rhythm of the song, and just being close to him scattered her in the best way possible. Oh, her heart was still hammering, but it wasn't from anxiety. It was from hope and desire.

"You don't have to decide right now what happens after we leave the wedding." Kade slipped the hand still holding the bouquet around her and laid his palm against the small of her back before taking her other hand in his and bringing them into perfect dance position. "We can simply dance."

"Right now?" She looked around suddenly, remembering there were other people in the room besides her and Kade.

"It *is* a wedding reception," he said as he eased her out onto the dance floor. "It's kinda what people do."

They started moving to the beat, and no one paid them any mind. Everyone was lost in their own worlds at the end of a week of being constantly on, everyone looking so damn glad to finally get to be totally themselves again. Even Lakin and Piper were arm in arm and swaying to the beat.

Tomorrow, they'd all leave for home, and the sulfur-scented fantasy—or nightmare—of it all would fade away. Kade wanted to give it a try, to see what could happen after Wyoming. It was exactly what she wanted, and yet all of her anxiety responses were duking it out in an epic battle of I-want-to-but-I'm-scared.

She dropped her gaze so she was staring at their feet—his in dress shoes, hers in blinged-out flip-flops that said *bridesmaid*—as they danced. "There are a million reasons why this is never going to work out."

He hooked a finger under her chin and tilted her face so she had to look him in the eye. "And one that outweighs them all."

"What's that?" she asked, the butterflies in her stomach doing the conga now.

One side of his mouth curled up in his crooked grin. "We're in the middle of falling in love with each other."

She stopped dancing. She stopped breathing. She stopped *everything*.

"That's presumptuous of you," she spluttered, her pulse rate skyrocketing because oh my God it had only been a week. And yes she wanted to scream, "Yes, we are!" but she was too overwhelmed.

"Probably." He lifted a brow and grinned down at her, every bit the cocky guy who'd given her Sprite in a flask that first day. "But am I wrong?"

She started to sway in his arms again, moving with the beat, her cheek resting against his chest as she unwound it all.

All of the emotions she'd always tried to keep folded up and in a pocket.

All of the hopes and dreams that went with taking a leap like falling in love.

All of the ways their future could turn out.

Before this wedding, before Kade, she would have given in to her fear of uncertainty of her feelings and just agreed to keep from having to deal with her emotions. The urge was there still, but it wasn't an overwhelming wave of anxiety that threatened to drown her. It was just being nervous and scared and hopeful and thrilled and—yes—in love.

That's when it hit her.

What Dr. Kowecki had been trying to show her with her exercise about trying out different reactions was really to just be mindful about what she was actually feeling and to know that whatever it was, it was okay. Thea had been so focused on how she was reacting that she hadn't realized she'd really been learning to unfold her emotions and deal with them instead of ignoring them and letting them fester.

Damn. Nola had been onto something when she'd insisted everyone could use some therapy to work through all of the shit life had thrown at them. Life had been rough for everyone over the past few years, and working through that was important.

Filled with a new certainty about herself, about Kade, and about them that settled into her soul, warming her from the inside out, she lifted her head and looked the man she loved straight in the eye.

"No, you're not wrong, but all of this is a lot, even though I want it really bad."

"Relationships are a risk," Kade said, his deep, growly voice cracking with intensity. "They're chaotic. They're the absolute fucking nightmare of ripping open your chest, exposing your heart, and saying, 'Go ahead. I trust you.'"

"What makes you so sure?" she asked, her heart fluttering in her chest.

Kade laughed, a soft chuckle, as if the answer was so damn obvious. "Because *you*, Thea Pope, are worth the risk.

Even if you left tomorrow and I never got to see you again, it would have been worth it. You are worth it."

Now was when she was supposed to say something amazing, to put into words all of the thoughts in her head to explain how much she felt the same, but her brain was on strike. And all that came out was the very wrong thing.

"Do you want to come to the dinosaur dig with me?" she blurted out. "You don't have to stay for the two weeks I'll be there. I'm sure it'll be boring, and it will definitely be hot and dirty, and I'm sure you have things to do and—"

He cut her off with a solid-nine-point-six-on-a-five-point-scale kiss that may have been brief but still calmed her nerves. She needed to tell her therapist that she'd found a fifth *F* for how she could react when nervous—French kiss, specifically French kissing Kade. That, obviously, could have its drawbacks and probably shouldn't be a go-to unless she wanted to make the people around her and Kade uncomfortable, but still, it was an option that she couldn't wait to utilize again.

"Thea," Kade said, pulling her back to the here and now. "I want to be wher*ever* you are."

Flummoxed and flustered, Thea did the only thing she could think of: She went for her new favorite *F* reaction and kissed Kade with everything she had.

It wasn't until she came up for air that she realized they were in the middle of the dance floor alone because the DJ had taken a break. Laughing, she grabbed Kade's hand, and this time it was her turn to lead the way out of the barn and into the garden area behind it.

Turning so her back was against the wall of the barn, she looked up at Kade. "So, if we're gonna give this long-distance relationship thing a try, you should probably tell me where you live so we can figure out the logistics."

He closed the distance between them so they were thigh

to thigh and not even a sliver of moonlight could get between them.

"In Waterbury, a subway ride across the water from Harbor City," he said as his hungry gaze dropped to her mouth. "I'm on Galveston Street and Thirtieth."

Delighted shock making her giddy, Thea grabbed him by the lapels of his tux and pulled him in close to check his face for a fib. He had to be kidding. There was absolutely no way. He shot her a questioning look, but there were no lies detected.

"I live at Galveston and Twenty-Fifth," she said.

Kade threw back his head and laughed. "Less than five blocks apart, and I had to go halfway across the country to find you."

"Hope it was worth the flight and the fact that the whole world has seen you in that baby-blue tux," she teased.

All the humor drained from his face, and he said, "Without a single solitary doubt."

Then he dipped his head down and kissed her. It wasn't soft and sweet. It was hard and demanding and promised a million orgasms and a forever's worth of tomorrows. By the time he pulled back, she was breathless, blissed-out, and beyond ready to get him back to his RV. The tux looked good on him, even with just the undershirt, but it would look great on his floor.

There was one thing she still had to figure out, though.

"I've gotta ask one more question."

He took her hand in his and brushed a kiss across her knuckles. "Whatever you want to know."

"How do you like your eggs?"

Kade went statue still and then scooped her up in his arms and started toward his RV at a fast speed, considering he was still in slick dress shoes and carrying her.

"I like my eggs sunny-side up with extra toast at a diner,

but scrambled with extra pepper at home." He made the turn on the path leading to his RV and was all but sprinting toward it with her in his arms. "How about I make you some later?"

"Much later," Thea said as he started up the steps to his RV. "I *am* falling in love with you, Kade St. James."

He flung the door open and looked down at her with a crooked smile that stole her breath. "The feeling is mutual, Thea Pope."

Then he carried her over the threshold, still gripping the bouquet in his hand, and their tomorrows started right then and there.

Epilogue

Three Years Later...

Nervous?

Worried?

Anxious to the max?

Thea Pope sucked in a deep, calming breath because OH. MY. GOD. YES!

Leading her first dinosaur dig was a huge deal, but when the folks at the Stinkingwater River Dinosaur Museum had reached out about a possible find nearby, her boss at the Harbor City Natural History Museum gave her the go-ahead.

Yeah, that's right. She had emotions, and she didn't fold them up and stuff them in a pair of too-tight pants. Instead, she now worked through the layers of her reactions to all things good, bad, and panic-inducing. That didn't eliminate the uncomfortable feelings—which to be honest kinda sucked—but she also wasn't beating herself up about it anymore, and that was its own kind of relief.

Giving the tiny tent one last scan to make sure she wasn't missing anything she'd need out on the site, Thea grabbed her vented floppy hiking hat and went to go kiss her partner goodbye.

As she approached, Kade stood up from the camp table his laptop sat on. He was working on the follow-up to his best-selling narrative nonfiction about a Jack Russell that had beaten the odds by finding its way back home to its family after a hurricane and had inspired a nation.

"Man, it's hot here in the summer," he said as he reached behind his head and yanked his T-shirt off.

Then he had the audacity to stretch, showing off all the extra details he'd added to his owl chest tattoo. In addition to a fierce and powerful Athena, he'd added a T. rex in the middle of a terrifying growl—the tough-guy effect blunted by the baby rattle it was holding.

He flexed and gave her a wolfish leer. "Caught you looking."

"We're in a tent," she said as she took her time moving her heated gaze from his crooked smile to the scruff on his jaw that had gotten a little gray over the past few years, and then to his bare chest, which still made her think very dirty thoughts. "It's not like there are a lot of places for me to look."

Kade snorted in disbelief and scooped up the baby giggling in the playpen next to his desk. He looked down at their son, his whole face softening.

"And that, Rex, was what she said to me right before we made you." He sniffed the baby and scrunched up his face before reaching for one of the diapers on the corner of his desk. "If your mom keeps this up, Rex, it's going to become a tradition." He laid the baby on the pop-up table and went to work changing his diaper. "We'll have to shorten the name Baryonyx to Onyx or Stegosaurus to Steg. Maybe we go with another Tyrannosaurus-inspired name with Tyra."

"Your mom will be thrilled with that," Thea said, already planning backup names as she rubbed the belly bump just beginning to protrude.

Kade laughed and blew raspberries on the baby's tummy. "Your mom will, no doubt, push her classic Hollywood choices."

It was true. Her mom had lobbied *hard* for Marilyn, Monroe, Cary, or Grant. She'd been less than thrilled with

Rex but had eventually relented when she remembered Rex Harrison.

"Meanwhile," she said, "Dex and Jackie will sit back and let the two moms offer all of their unsolicited naming advice for our next baby in hopes that it gets their attention off the fact that they went with the name Hawkeye for theirs. Very duplicitous of them."

He shrugged and started the job of getting a new onesie on a squirming baby. "So remind me, why did we all decide to move to the same building in Harbor City when Dex and Jackie got parts in the same theater production?"

"Because we love them." And now there were weekly family brunches, casual shopping trips, and just hanging out together as the kids napped. "Even though they're a lot."

"You know," he said as he snapped the buttons on Rex's onesie closed. "I think there's only one way to get everyone to stop offering up their opinions on baby Raptor."

Thea giggled and walked over to the playpen, grabbing Rex's favorite triceratops-shaped rattle. "We are not naming our child Raptor."

"Good thing I have another plan to distract our moms from their insistence on helping us name the baby." He picked up Rex and turned him around. "How about a dinosaur-themed wedding?"

Thea was still trying to process the question when she glanced at Rex's onesie. Then she really looked. It read: *Mommy, will you marry Daddy?*

Her heart sped up, emotion clogged her throat, and she gasped. Then, a rush of love and excitement and joy crashed over her, so strong that there was no way she'd ever be able to stuff those feelings away even if she wanted to—which she most definitely did not.

"I thought you never wanted to get married?" she finally managed to get out.

Hugging Rex close to his chest, Kade crossed over to her and dropped a quick kiss on her forehead. "That was before I met you."

"Kade, you don't have to." She looked up at him, her heart filling at the offer but not so much that she'd plow over him like people used to do to her. "I'm happy how we are. I love you, and this works for us. You don't have to marry me to make me happy, and I promise I'll never leave."

"I know, but I love you, Thea, and I can't imagine a day when you aren't the first person I kiss when I wake up and the last one I hold at night. You are the best thing to have ever happened to me." He swiped the rattle out of her grasp and gave it to Rex before putting the baby down in the playpen and turning back to her. "Say yes."

That three-letter answer was on the tip of her tongue, but she hesitated. Was this really what she wanted? To spend the rest of her life with Kade, traveling from dinosaur digs to book signings before going home—together—to Harbor City, where they were surrounded by the families they were born into and the one they were making? A certainty settled in her belly, an undeniable knowledge that she'd never wanted anything more.

"Yes," she said, then immediately held up her hand to stop whatever he was going to say or do next. "But only on one condition."

He stilled. "What's that?"

"We make all the bridesmaids wear inflatable T. rex costumes."

"That's only fair," he said before sweeping her up into his arms and kissing her, sealing the deal and their forever.

Acknowledgments

Writing books is the best job somedays, and others it has me questioning all of my life choices. What I never wonder about is the fabulous folks I get to work with at Entangled. Y'all have been putting up with me for years now, and I am so incredibly grateful for it, even if some days I do question your judgment when it comes to letting me come back for another book. Liz: We've been doing this for a while now and haven't killed each other, which, looking at both of us, is kind of a miracle. Thank you for always pushing for a better book and for all you do to make the book the best it can be. Hannah: Thank you for pretending that my misuse of commas and misplaced modifiers aren't the absolute worst and that I shouldn't go directly to grammar jail. Elizabeth: I love your covers so hard, and I am THRILLED every time I find out we get to work together. Jessica, Meredith, Riki, and Debbie: Marketing and publicity in Romancelandia is a tough calling, and y'all have proven again and again what badasses you are. Thank you for helping readers find my books. Of course, without the production team this book wouldn't be in any readers' hands. That's where the good people in the production department come in. A huge thank-you to y'all, especially Curtis (I'm sorry my Junk Folder has such a crush on your email), for working the magic that you do.

Thanks have to go out to the good folks at Valentine PR (special shout-out to Nina and Kim) for everything you do to connect readers with all of the good romance books out there. I love working with you.

And for Andrea and the entire Recorded Books team, thank you for being a part of the journey on this one. May it be the first of many!

I wouldn't be writing at all if it wasn't for the readers. Romance readers are the absolute best, even if my TBR is never-ending thanks to all the great recommendations I get. But really, is there such a thing as too many books? (No. The answer is obviously no.) Whether this is your first book of mine or you've binged my entire backlist or you're somewhere in between, thank you for giving up some of your limited free time to read *Anger Bang*. I hope you've had a blast!

Xoxo,
Avery

About the Author

USA Today and *Wall Street Journal* bestselling romance author Avery Flynn has three slightly wild children, loves a hockey-addicted husband, and is desperately hoping someone invents the coffee IV drip. She lives with her family (including the dogs Gravy, Pepper, Tater Tot, and Eggnog, who are either sleeping or guarding the house from squirrels as well as the cat, Dwight, who is totally plotting world domination) outside of Washington, D.C. She loves to chat with readers. You can email her at avery@averyflynn.com and join her reader group, The Flynnbots, on Facebook!

averyflynn.com

Discover more romance from Entangled...

BREAKING ALL THE RULES
a novel by Amy Andrews

Beatrice Archer is taking her life back, starting with moving to Nowhere, Colorado, to live life on her own terms. But then, a much younger and delightfully attractive cop is called to deal with her flagrant disregard for appropriate clothing outside the local diner (some folks just don't appreciate bunny slippers) and Bea realizes there's something missing from her little decathlon of decadence. When it comes to breaking rules, Officer Austin Cooper is surprisingly eager to assist. He's a little bit cowboy, and a whole lot sexy. But Bea's about to discover that breaking the rules has consequences. And all of the cherry pies in Colorado can't save her from what's coming...

THE BEST KEPT SECRET
a Where There's Smoke novel by Tawna Fenske

When nurse Nyla Franklin's best friend spills his biggest secret ever, Nyla knows she's not just holding a secret. She's holding a ticking time bomb. Mr. Always Does the Right Thing Leo Sayre's post-surgery confession has everything flipped upside down and turned inside out...including his relationship with Nyla. Secrets have a way of piling up, and it's just a matter of time before someone lights a match. Because while the truth can set you free, it can also burn completely out of control...

It's Raining Men
a novel by Julie Hammerle

After my single best friend got engaged, I decided to drown my loneliness in booze. Several Old Fashioneds later, I woke up to thirty-nine text messages. I had apparently offered myself up in marriage to every guy in my phone... Thirty-seven rejections later, two guys have actually said yes, and I'm left to choose between Rob, my old high school crush, and Darius, a flashy news reporter. Let's see if happily ever after is meant for me...

A Sweet Spot For Love
a novel by Aliyah Burke

Former pro baseball player Linc Conner knows exactly where his head's at. But when it comes to single mom Emma Henricksen, Linc can't see straight. Emma's too busy raising her gifted little girl to have a sex life that's not battery-operated. Still, how could she resist being engaged to a guy who's the sexual equivalent of her favorite dessert, even if it's just pretend? Now it's a game with a whole lot of chemistry between the guy who's used to playing the field—and the woman who opted out of the game long ago. All that's missing is one helluva curveball...

Printed in Great Britain
by Amazon